W9-CBD-686

Black Orchid

Maggie felt her stomach knot with tension as Judd slowly, deliberately began to unbuckle his belt. It was of a thick, heavy leather, the strap flat and wide. The buckle was large and weighty looking. He took his time drawing it through the stiff loops of his jeans before cracking it loudly against his thigh.

Tina was trembling openly now and Maggie shifted in her seat, pressing closer to Anthony. She gasped as Judd coiled the buckle end of the belt around his fist and brought the other end, without warning, across the back of Tina's stocking-clad thighs. Tina whimpered but kept her legs pressed tightly together.

By the same author:

A Bouquet Of Black Orchids
Avenging Angels
Black Orchid Hotel
Jewel Of Xanadu
Western Star

Black Orchid
Roxanne Carr

Black Lace books contain sexual fantasies.
In real life, always practise safe sex.

This edition published in 2008 by
Black Lace
Thames Wharf Studios
Rainville Rd
London W6 9HA

Originally published 1993

Copyright © Roxanne Carr 1993

The right of Roxanne Carr to be identified as the Author of the Work has been
asserted in accordance with the Copyright, Designs and Patents Act 1988.

A catalogue record for this book is available from the British Library.

www.black-lace-books.com

Typeset by Palimpsest Book Production Limited, Grangemouth, Stirlingshire
Printed and bound in Great Britain by CPI Bookmarque, Croydon, CR0 4TD

Distributed in the USA by Macmillan, 175 Fifth Avenue,
New York, NY 10010, USA

ISBN 978 0 352 34188 4

*All characters in this publication are fictitious and any resemblance
to real persons, living or dead, is purely coincidental.*

This book is sold subject to the condition that it shall not, by way of trade or
otherwise, be lent, resold, hired out or otherwise circulated without the publisher's
prior written consent in any form of binding or cover other than that in which it is
published and without a similar condition including this condition being imposed
on the subsequent purchaser.

The Random House Group Limited supports The Forest Stewardship Council [FSC],
the leading international forest certification organisation. All our titles that are
printed on Greenpeace approved FSC certified paper carry the FSC logo.
Our paper procurement policy can be found at www.rbooks.co.uk/environment

1 3 5 7 9 10 8 6 4 2

1

Maggie felt the familiar irritation as Richard's voice, growing plaintive now, came across the line.

'This is the third time this week you've had to work late, Mags. I thought we'd go to the cinema, spend some time together ...'

'We spent time together last night, Richard,' she interrupted him firmly, 'tonight I have to work.'

She listened for a few more minutes to his petulant complaints before saying calmly, 'If that's the way you feel then I think it's time we called it a day, don't you? Goodbye, Richard.'

She put down the telephone, quashing the pang of regret as she remembered the feel of his strong, lean body covering hers as it had last night, his slender white prick moving urgently inside her.

She caught Janine's eye as her colleague walked into the office and made a face. 'Men!'

Janine, who had just caught the tail end of the conversation, perched her neat behind on the corner of the desk and grinned.

'Given up on him?'

'Had to. Why can't I find a man who can accept that the job I do is important to me? I just can't handle it when they sulk and pout every time I have to work late. I neither have the time, nor the patience, if I'm honest, to tiptoe round some man's ego.'

'I know what you mean,' Janine shrugged sympathetically.

'Still – they do have their uses!' Maggie said wistfully.

'Hmm. What we need, though, is the male equivalent of a bimbo – always ready for sex but otherwise undemanding!'

Maggie laughed ruefully and opened a file she should have read already.

'For myself, I'd stick to one night stands if it wasn't for the risks nowadays.'

'You know, years ago the best brothels used to have all the girls checked regularly by a doctor for disease. That's what we working women need now. Gigolos, guaranteed safe, hired with an American Express Card.'

'A brothel for women? If only!' Rolling her eyes, Maggie turned her attention to work.

Later, when most of the office had left for home, Janine stopped by Maggie's desk again.

'Nearly finished?'

Looking up, Maggie was distracted.

'Hmm?'

'I was wondering – you seemed like you needed a fillip earlier. I'm off to my health club in half an hour. There's a good gym there which Members' Guests can use. Care to join me?'

Maggie's first thought was to refuse. She barely knew Janine and it had been a long day. Then she thought of the relief from stress that hard physical exercise would bring and thought, what the hell?

'In half an hour, you say?'

Janine's smile was positively cat-like as she nodded and left.

Maggie was surprised by the health club. She had never noticed it before, it was slightly out of town, on Lady's Lane and although it was tucked behind a mess of other buildings, the converted warehouse was too big to be completely hidden.

They entered by what seemed to be an elaborate screening procedure.

'This must be some Health Club!' she quipped as Janine's membership card was electronically scanned.

'Membership is by invitation only. See what you think and I'll put you up for acceptance if you like.'

Once through the outer entrance and past the ferociously well groomed receptionist in the lobby, they stepped through heavy oak double doors.

'Wow!'

Maggie whistled softly through her teeth as she took in the gleaming reproduction antique furniture in the hallway, the wall to wall, ceiling-high mirrors which reflected the highly polished marbled floor.

'This way.'

Maggie's heels clicked loudly on the floor as she followed Janine into the changing rooms. Janine quickly shed her work-aday clothes and poured her lean, lithe body into close fitting yellow lycra. Brushing her thick blonde hair into a smooth curtain, she plaited it into a single braid which hung over one shoulder. Her heavy, blunt-cut fringe fell in a line along her eyebrows, forming a frame for her clear violet eyes.

Maggie dressed more slowly, looking about her with interest as she did so. As in the hallway, the walls were mirrored and she could see herself and Janine reflected from every angle. Vivaldi was playing softly in the background. The vanity basins which swept along one mirrored wall were dotted with fine porcelain bowls overflowing with fragrant pot-pourri.

'What do you think?'

Maggie was aware that Janine was watching her closely for a reaction and was momentarily disconcerted by the intensity of the other girl's gaze.

'It seems very . . . luxurious,' she replied cautiously.

'It is. Your every desire catered for.'

Maggie looked up in surprise as she caught the innuendo in her colleague's voice, but Janine merely smiled innocently back at her and beckoned her out of the room.

At the end of the corridor, to their right, Maggie could see another set of double oak doors, firmly closed. She could hear loud, throbbing music, muffled by the thickness of the doors, but unmistakable.

'What's through there?' she asked Janine, but Janine shook her head.

'Members only. Come this way.'

She crossed the corridor to the doors opposite, waiting for Maggie to follow her. Maggie cast a thoughtful look along the corridor before catching up with her.

The gym was vast, the best equipped Maggie had ever seen. There was the latest electronic equipment, plentiful, soft-piled towels hanging in readiness on the brass bar which ran around the walls. And the ever present mirrors.

'You can't get away from your own reflection!' she said, wondering at the inexplicable *frisson* of tension which ran through her.

Janine laughed.

'You get used to it.'

'Janine! How lovely to see you!'

Maggie stared as a golden haired Adonis strode over to them and took Janine into his arms. He was tall, at least six foot three and his body, shown to advantage in the pristine white shorts and singlet, was muscular, exquisitely defined and gleaming with good health.

'Antony! Darling, I've brought a friend with me,' Janine stood on her tiptoes to whisper something in his ear, then they both turned to Maggie. 'Maggie, meet Antony, owner of the Black Orchid Club.'

'The Black Orchid?'

'That's right. Delighted to meet you.'

Antony moved Janine to one side so that she was held by one arm while he encircled Maggie with the other. She felt its strength around her shoulders and caught the faint, erotic odour of fresh male sweat.

Unaccustomed to such familiarity, her eyes flew upwards – and collided with Antony's frank grey gaze. His eyes narrowed assessingly and she frowned, squirming under the intense scrutiny. His arm tightened round her shoulders, making her still. At last he released her and Maggie sighed as she realised she had been holding her breath.

'Come,' he said briskly, 'warm up on the exercise bikes then Tristan here will discuss a programme for you. Tris!'

An athletically built, fresh-faced young man appeared at his side.

'Look after these lovely ladies, Tristan. An hour's workout I think, followed by a soothing massage and a session in the steam room.'

With a little push, Antony left them with the smiling trainer.

'Is he always so domineering?' Maggie puffed as she pedalled, bemused by Antony's high-handed arrangement of her evening. 'I mean, supposing I don't *want* a massage, or a trip in his blasted steam room?'

Janine laughed.

'Relax. You don't have to make any decisions here. You pays your money and somebody else tells you what to do. You'll love the massage, I promise. You're lucky – normally guests are restricted to the gym and showers. And after that, you'll definitely be ready for the steam room! Go with the flow.'

Maggie said nothing, contenting herself with looking around her. The gym was deceptive, the mirrored walls making it look far larger than it actually was. Some half dozen women were working diligently at their exercises, watched closely by the trainers. Unusually for a ladies' gym, this appeared to be an exclusively male role. Each was dressed in black shorts and singlet. Those who weren't actively supervising a client were using the machines themselves.

One in particular caught Maggie's eye. He was working on the leg press at the far side of the room and, like all the men present, was young and well developed. As he pushed against the weights the muscles in his thighs bulged, then retracted as he brought them back up to his chest. His back was to Maggie, but she could see his face reflected in the mirror.

It was an extraordinarily beautiful face, tanned, square jawed, the features symmetrical. Even from this distance, Maggie could see that his eyes were a startling shade of blue. Perspiration glistened on the sculpted shoulders revealed by the cutaway back of his black singlet and his blond hair was slick with sweat as he strained single-mindedly against the weights.

Maggie found herself pedalling harder as she watched him, enjoying the sensation of the supple leather of the saddle rubbing against her lycra covered pubis. The music piped into the gym washed around her so that she was conscious only of the rhythm of her pedalling and the graceful spectacle across the room of the lengthening and contracting of the young man's muscles.

Raising her eyes back to the reflected image of his face, she suddenly became aware that he was looking back at her in the mirror. As she caught his eye, he winked.

Maggie jumped guiltily as a sharp 'ping' signified she had pedalled enough and Tristan materialised at her side as if from nowhere. He was smiling.

'I see you've noticed our Alexander,' he said approvingly.

Maggie was embarrassed and changed the subject. From then on she concentrated on pushing herself to her physical limit, revelling in her own strength and suppleness. It felt good to challenge her body, to be made aware of every muscle, every sinew as she moved.

Slowly she was beginning to relax, to unwind. No one bothered her. Janine was concentrating on her own routine. Tristan was on hand to offer encouragement by way of a gesture or a smile, but he did not try to engage Maggie in conversation again. The music lulled her, the lack of chatter refreshing. She was able to think of nothing but her own body and the demands it was making of her.

She was almost sorry when the hour was up, though her limbs ached from her efforts and she was drenched in perspiration. Tristan offered her two warm towels to take into the shower.

Crossing the corridor to the changing room, her eyes were drawn again to the door at the end. Janine noticed her interest and smiled.

'Another time, maybe! Right now we're expected elsewhere.'

Maggie allowed herself to be steered into the changing room. The hot flow of water cascaded over her skin, making it tingle and turn pink. When she emerged and shook her long, dark hair out of the complimentary shower cap, Maggie followed Janine's example and wrapped the dry towel, sarong style, around her naked body before making for the massage room.

The room, which led off from the opposite side of the changing rooms, was small with only enough room for two tables, reflected in the ever present mirrors. Janine discarded her towel and lay face down on one and Maggie followed suit, closing her eyes as she waited for the masseuse to arrive. She opened them as the door clicked softly shut and found herself caught, not by the professional eye of the expected female attendant, but in the smiling blue gaze of Alexander.

Maggie half rose, then, remembering she was completely naked, sank back down again. Her heart hammered erractically against the padded table as she watched Alexander cross to the vanity unit in the corner of the room and take out a large bottle of massage oil. As he unscrewed the cap the strong, heady smell of jasmine filled the room. He too had showered and she could see the damp hair curling in the tender dip at the back of his neck.

Janine's masseur was black-haired and muscular, his shoulders sprinkled with a covering of dark hair. Maggie noticed him catch Janine's eye in the mirror and sucked in her breath at the look that passed between them. Yet, no one uttered a word as the two men approached.

Maggie gasped involuntarily at the first contact of Alexander's hands with her skin. His fingers were long and clever as he kneaded the tense muscles in her neck and shoulders, coaxing her to let them go. Slowly, under the insistent persuasion of his hands, she began to relax, to unclench her arms and buttocks and give herself up to sensation.

There was no music in the massage room, only the rhythm of her own breathing which sounded unnaturally loud in her ears, and the occasional slosh of oil against bare skin.

Closing her eyes, Maggie bit down on a groan of pure pleasure as Alexander's palms ran the length of her arms and back up again in long, firm strokes. After a few moments he turned his attention to her hands, one at a time, stroking each finger and gently manipulating each joint.

He was endlessly patient, intent only on her satisfaction as he eventually moved further down her body to the long sweep of her slender back and the sharp indentation of her waist. As his palms travelled across her shoulder-blades and moulded the sides of her body, Maggie felt her breasts swell against the table, anticipating his touch. She was almost disappointed when the brush of his fingers missed them repeatedly and he moved instead to her legs.

Her calves and thighs quivered under his tender ministrations as he methodically massaged away the tension in them. Maggie felt that if she should attempt to stand at that moment, her legs would be too weak to bear her weight, they seemed as if liquefied.

She gasped as suddenly, unexpectedly, he turned his attention to her naked buttocks. Instinctively clenching the muscles there, she felt herself grow pink with mortification as her resisting cheeks were gathered up, one in each of Alexander's large hands, and squeezed gently until she felt herself reluctantly beginning to let go, the final vestige of resistance rippling away.

She was breathing in short little gasps, as she felt the familiar, sexual warmth spreading through her body, radiating from her centre. The indirect stimulation of her most intimate places made her feel moist, the delicate folds swelling, anticipating the touch that never came.

Alexander was scrupulous in his attention, not missing a square inch of her bottom, kneading and squeezing until Maggie felt the dampness between her thighs seeping into the soft towel beneath her hips, mingling with the warm, slippery oil which had been liberally applied over her tingling rear.

She half opened her eyes and watched Alexander's face surreptitiously in the mirror as he rhythmically parted and closed her buttocks. He was watching the movement created by his hands, his eyes heavy lidded. So she wasn't the only one enjoying the massage!

Closing her eyes again, Maggie tried to put herself in Alexander's place, imagining what he could see. Without conceit, she knew her body was good, the skin smooth and blemish free. From the back she knew she had a harmonious shape, her shoulders were straight, her waist small, her hips flaring gently outwards.

The way Alexander was handling her now, she knew he would be exposing the dark, secret crevice between her buttocks with its small, puckered opening and probably, too, the soft, moist curls at the apex of her thighs. If it hadn't been for Janine lying on the next table . . .

She glanced across at her colleague. The other girl was lying supine, her face twisted towards Maggie. Her eyes were closed and a small, blissful smile played around her soft lips. Maggie knew the expression on Janine's face was reflected on her own and she sighed.

Closing her eyes she revelled in the delicious languor that had invaded her limbs. The silence enfolded her, soothing her mind so that she was conscious of nothing but Alexander's strong, knowing hands kneading her body.

Only when she had totally let go of the tension in her muscles did Alexander begin to work his way back up her back to her shoulders. This time as he kneaded, Maggie knew that his fingers encountered none of the resistance they had before. Now his touch felt more like a caress and she felt a tingling running down her spine.

He was leaning over her now, close enough for her to be able to feel the heat of his body. She wanted to roll over on the bed and reach up her arms to draw him down.

She gasped as she felt his lips brush the tender place behind her left ear. The kiss was feather-light, fleeting so that she wondered if in her aroused condition she had imagined it.

While she was still trying to decide, Alexander ran the palms of his hands down the sides of her body, smoothing the skin one last time. Maggie watched through hooded eyes as he walked past her to wash the oil from his hands at the tiny sink in the corner. She smiled as she caught sight of the distinct bulge in his shorts – she had always admired a man who enjoyed his work!

Nevertheless, she was left with a definite sense of disappointment as she and Janine silently gathered up their towels around them and slipped off the tables. Her legs felt wobbly as she followed Janine into the steam room and she was glad to sink down on the hard wooden bench.

The steam was fragrant and thick. So thick that Maggie could barely make out Janine's features as she sat down beside her, their bare shoulders almost touching.

The massage had made her feel sleepy so Maggie leaned her head against the cold tiles and closed her eyes. She imagined she could still feel the brush of Alexander's lips against her skin and she reached up to touch the place where he had kissed her with her fingertips. Strange that such a small kiss had sent such a powerful erotic charge through her and she found she could not forget it. Images of Alexander, working out in the gym, entering the massage room, manipulating her body, filled her mind to the exclusion of all else.

What if she had given in to the urge to reach for him . . . What would he have done then? In her mind's eye Maggie saw herself pushing him back on the table while she explored that strong body herself as he had hers. She shifted a little on the bench as she imagined fastening her mouth on his, tasting him, drawing his tongue into her mouth while she wrapped herself around him.

It was some moments before she realised that someone else had entered the steam room. Caught up in the harmless fantasy, she was only vaguely aware of the soft swish of the door opening and closing.

Her eyes flew open as she felt the firm, sure touch of

masculine fingers trailing up her calf from her ankle. The steam was so thick now her eyes couldn't penetrate it, even though she could feel the kiss of warm breath against her shoulder.

A small sigh from the girl beside her told Maggie that Janine was receiving the same treatment and she cooperated when the girl twisted slightly on the bench so that they were sitting back to back, supporting each other.

Her initial alarm began to recede as the hand smoothed the hair away from her neck and arranged it across her shoulder. The fingers felt familiar, almost friendly and Maggie smiled as she recognised Alexander's sensitive touch.

She held her breath as for one long, exquisite moment he left her alone. Allowing her heavy lids to fall closed, she was unprepared for the sudden, shocking press of his thumbs against her erect nipples.

It was as if an electric charge had flashed through her. Touching her nowhere else but on the very tip of her hard nipples, it felt like Alexander had flicked the 'on' switch to her desire. Her mouth felt dry, her throat constricted, the tender places between her legs swelling and moistening in direct contrast.

The bare skin of Janine's narrow back was damp against hers as Maggie leaned her head to one side, using the tiled wall as a support, and thrust her breasts forwards, yearning for more than that brief, shocking contact.

Alexander's breath was hot in her ear as he moved his hands to the soft skin of her inner thighs. She was unresisting as he parted them, bending her knee so that her left foot was flat against the bench, the other just touching the floor with the toe.

Maggie braced herself with her hands against the wall and bench as he began to describe small circles on the tender flesh of her inner thighs, slowly inching closer to her swollen labia. The wait was unbearable, her clitoris straining towards his teasing fingers, quivering in anticipation of his touch.

Her entire body, awakened by the long, sensuous massage and her ensuing fantasies was burning with the need for release. Nothing mattered but the satisfaction of the desire that gripped her. In a voice which she didn't recognise as her own. Maggie heard herself whisper, 'Please . . . Oh please!'

The backs of his fingers brushed almost fondly against her damp curls and a hoarse groan escaped her lips. It was hard to breathe in the steamy atmosphere and she let her mouth fall open slightly as she found herself struggling for air. He made her wait a few seconds more until, at last, with unerring accuracy, he took her burgeoning pleasure-bud between forefinger and thumb and tugged gently.

Maggie felt the warm flush race through her body, spreading more slowly right to the tips of her fingers as he gently rolled the engorged flesh between finger and thumb. His breath was hot in her ear as he whispered,

'Wider.'

Maggie obeyed automatically, spreading her legs as wide as she could. She gasped as he used his free hand to push her right knee even further away from the left, still bent on the bench. When he was sure she could hold the position, he caught her left leg by the ankle and straightened it so that her foot was braced against the wall.

Feeling as if she would be split apart by the pressure, Maggie cried out as he suddenly plunged three fingers into her hungry sex, curling them upward whilst at the same time pressing her quivering bud with his thumb. Maggie could hold back no longer. As spasm after spasm passed through her, she held her legs up in the air, opening herself as wide as physically possible.

Just as she thought it had to stop, Alexander removed his

hands and she felt his hot, wet lips close over her clitoris, sucking every last quiver of sensation from her.

When at last the orgasm ebbed away she collapsed, exhausted, against Janine, her legs flopping down, her body bathed in perspiration. Janine's skin was slippery against hers and Maggie clung onto her as the girl turned and put her arms around her. Opening her eyes Maggie saw the ecstasy glowing on Janine's face and smiled.

The steam was beginning to evaporate now and she realised that Alexander and the man who had been with Janine had melted away. She felt a sharp stab of disappointment that she had not been given the chance to pay Alexander the same compliment he had paid her. She would have taken great pleasure in bringing him to the same feverish pitch of mindless ecstasy as she had experienced.

Gradually she became aware that Janine's small breasts were pressing insistently against her own, the erect tips rubbing hers back to hardness. Janine's fingers were tracing a path around her hairline and for a moment Maggie did not know what to do.

The other girl's face was so close to hers she could smell the sweetness of her breath. Her parted lips were so near, Maggie could see the moist, pink tip of her tongue as it snaked out and licked at the beads of perspiration on the soft down of her upper lip.

She had never been kissed by another woman before and she held her breath as Janine moved her soft lips across hers, backwards and forwards, coaxing her to open her mouth. Maggie's eyes fluttered to a close as the other girl's tongue probed her own, her sweet, warm mouth closing over Maggie's. Shifting her weight, Janine straddled Maggie on the bench so that she was sitting astride her lap, her knees either side of Maggie's legs.

Maggie could feel the wet, open mouth of her vagina against her own primly closed thighs, and she tensed. It wasn't an unpleasant sensation, but Janine's softness was very different to the feel of a masculine body which she craved. Right now Maggie wanted the hard, musky strength of a man and, though she did not want to offend Janine, she gently pulled away.

Janine's violet eyes stared back at her reproachfully and acting on impulse, Maggie kissed the end of her nose. Janine smiled and climbed off her lap with a little shrug.

'Ready to go?' she asked ruefully and Maggie nodded.

They dressed in silence and by the time they emerged in the now pitch black street, Janine was her usual self again.

'So – what did you think?' she asked Maggie as they reached the car-park

'It was . . . different!'

'And would you like to join?'

Maggie thought of Alexander's enigmatic smile and did not hesitate.

'What do I have to do?'

'You have to convince Antony to let you in.'

Antony. Maggie recalled the way he had looked at her and felt a small *frisson* of excitement race up her spine. She caught Janine's eye across the roof of the car.

'Antony? How do I apply?'

Janine smiled her confident, cat-like smile.

'You don't. I'll set up an interview.'

Maggie nodded before slipping into her car and firing the engine. She had a feeling Janine would consider she was owed a favour if she got Maggie into the Black Orchid Club. She thought of her unfinished business with Alexander and smiled to herself. That was another debt she owed.

As she drove home Maggie wondered how long it would take Janine to organise her interview. A vision of Antony's glowing, muscled body pushed its way into her mind and she shivered deliciously.

2

For two long, frustrating weeks, Janine answered Maggie's enquiry with a shrug of her shoulders and the same reply.

'It all depends on when – and if – Antony can fit you in.'

The memory of Alexander's clever hands haunted her and Maggie found herself daydreaming in the middle of a working day, imagining their next encounter. Yet, now she came to think of it, she realised that not a word had passed between them. She was both intrigued and vaguely ashamed that she could have become so excited by such an impersonal encounter.

Just as she was beginning to despair that Antony would ever deign to 'fit her in', Janine stopped by her desk one lunch-time and mentioned, quite casually, that an appointment had been made for seven that evening.

'This evening?' Maggie's mouth fell open and Janine laughed.

'Yes – aren't you free?'

Maggie thought of the long, lonely, frustrating nights she had spent waiting for this appointment and almost laughed aloud.

'I'll be there,' she promised and, before she realised her intention, Janine leaned across the desk and kissed her, smack on the mouth.

Maggie was so stunned that she watched her walk away without a word. She could feel Bob at the next desk looking at her in total disbelief, but when she finally plucked up courage to meet his eye, he looked away hurriedly and began to fiddle with something on his desk.

'What a sense of humour!' Maggie said shakily and Bob laughed politely, without looking up.

The incident so unsettled Maggie that she found she could not concentrate any longer, so she left work early and hurried home. Making time for a long, hot soak in the bath, she wallowed in the scented water. Closing her eyes, she ran her palms along her slippery skin and imagined they were Alexander's. Or Antony's.

How could it not matter which? She frowned as she realised she wanted to be accepted as a member of the Black Orchid Club more than she could ever remember having wanted anything. She wanted to have the right to see what went on behind the heavy oak doors at the end of the corridor.

She had the feeling that Antony's selection procedure would be nothing if not inventive and that the forthcoming interview would be a rigorous one. She couldn't remember feeling this nervous about anything, not even when she had applied for her current job.

After her bath she moisturised and powdered her skin before easing herself into a pure silk basque which had been a Christmas present from an old boyfriend. Until now it had languished, unworn, in the back of a drawer. There had never seemed to be an appropriate time to wear it and as she adjusted the straps, Maggie was glad she had saved it.

Over the top she wore a plain navy shift so that, from the outside, at least, she looked her usual efficient self. Inside, though, she was quaking as she approached the club. Taking a few deep, calming breaths, she parked the car in the private car-park and checked her make-up in the driving mirror before going inside.

* * *

Antony watched through the window of his third floor apartment as Maggie strode across the car-park. She looked cool, self-possessed, her elegant features calm. He imagined those same features screwed up with passion and felt a stirring in his groin.

'Is she here?'

He turned away from the window as Alexander, bleary eyed and dressed in black shorts, meandered across the room, drink in hand. Antony frowned.

'Champagne for breakfast?' he asked, raising an eyebrow.

Alexander smiled, unoffended.

'But of course. Breakfast, dinner and tea. I'm on duty in half an hour so I'll have to sleep during the day tomorrow, too. See you later – have fun!'

Antony watched him as he pulled on his singlet and bounded across the room and out the rear entrance. He shook his head ruefully. No one could ever stay mad at Alex for long, least of all him. Alexander was simply one of those rare people who loved to give. He had no concept of exclusivity when it came to his sexual habits and he gave equally willingly to anyone who wanted his company. Which is why he was so popular, Antony reminded himself, turning his attention back to the matter in hand.

He smiled as the door opened and Maggie was shown in.

'Hello!' he said, going forward immediately to take her hand in both of his.

It trembled slightly in his grasp, betraying her inner agitation. So she wasn't quite as self-possessed as she appeared. Alexander had been right – he was going to enjoy introducing this one to the club. He smiled.

'Glad you could make it. Drink?'

'Yes, thank you. A dry Martini please.'

He poured her a Martini and champagne for himself, using

the glass Alexander had abandoned on the coffee table. Maggie sat warily on the white leather sofa. As she sank down on it, her skirt rode up over her thighs, offering Antony a tantalising glimpse of firm, white flesh above her stocking tops. He allowed his eyes to linger, enjoying the spectacle until she self-consciously smoothed the skirt down to mid thigh.

'So – you'd like to become a member of the Black Orchid Club?'

He watched her moisten her throat with the Martini before she spoke.

'I don't know for certain yet,' she told him, her tone businesslike. 'Janine recommended you and, since I enjoyed my first visit two weeks ago, I thought I'd find out more.'

Antony watched her, spinning out the silence between them. He remembered the visit that she mentioned and wondered what she would say if he told her he had heard about everything that happened in the steam room. She was trying to sound so cool, so nonchalant, yet Antony could see her desire to join the club burning in the depths of her bright hazel eyes.

Very slowly, he reached along the back of the sofa and trailed his fingertips along her naked collar-bone. Her skin was cool, smooth to the touch. He felt her shiver and knew that, if he made a move now, he would not be rebuffed.

It took an effort to hold back. He wanted her, but he had learned to wait until he could be certain that a potential client knew exactly what kind of a service the Black Orchid Club provided. Besides, with what he had in mind for Maggie, it wouldn't pay to rush things.

Removing his hand, he put down his glass.

'Right. I'll tell you more about the club while we're walking round.'

* * *

Maggie followed Antony along the hallway into the lift at the end. She had been sure he had been about to make a pass at her a few minutes ago and she was puzzled that he hadn't followed it through. She wanted to reach out and touch him, but wasn't sure of the etiquette involved in this strange place.

He was wearing casual taupe trousers and a short-sleeved shirt this evening, so his sexuality was more muted than the first time she had seen him in singlet and shorts. Nonetheless, in the cramped confines of the lift she could feel the heat of his skin through the thin cotton of his shirt.

She had never considered herself to be a small woman, yet Antony seemed to tower above her, making her feel tiny, vulnerable. The long period of anticipation which had preceded this interview had made her edgy, a two-week hiatus in her sex life making her impatient. Perhaps she had been wrong – perhaps the vibes she had picked up from Janine, and Alexander's outrageous behaviour, had not been a taster of what the Black Orchid Club had to offer?

As if feeling her bemused eyes on him, Antony turned and looked at her, his expression enigmatic. As the lift came to a smooth halt, he ran his eyes very slowly down the length of her body and back up again in a frank, unsmiling appraisal which made Maggie's breath catch in her chest.

His eyes narrowed slightly as he noted the sudden colour which flooded her cheeks, yet his tone, when he spoke, was quite conversational.

'You've already seen the changing rooms and the gym,' he said as they stepped out of the lift.

Maggie nodded as he opened the double doors of the mirrored gym and she glanced around. Alexander was helping a client master the bench press. He looked up as the doors opened and smiled at her briefly before turning his attention back to the woman on the bench. She was younger than Maggie, but hard-faced, her efforts on the bench press perfunctory as she leaned into Alexander's solid body beside her. Would she be treated to a massage afterwards? Maggie wondered. She turned back towards Antony and saw that he was smiling knowingly at her.

It was at that moment that she knew for sure that she had not made a mistake. A peculiar tension gripped her stomach as, without warning, Antony suddenly reached out and ran the pad of his thumb across her slightly parted lips. The contact was brief, yet it sent an erotic charge racing through Maggie's body. She bit down on her lower lip where he had touched it as he turned away and they left the gym.

'What made you start this place?' she asked him in a bid to recover her equilibrium.

'I saw the need. An old girlfriend of mine complained that men never had to play games when they wanted sex – there was always somewhere they could go to be satisfied with no strings attached. But women are naturally more cautious than men.'

'We have to be,' she replied sharply.

'Of course. That's why I had the idea of providing a controlled environment with carefully selected staff – and equally carefully selected clients. This way.'

He opened the double doors at the end of the corridor which had so intrigued Maggie on her previous visit. She looked around her eagerly and saw that they had entered a large lounge area with a semi-circular bar at the end and a small raised stage in the centre. It was dimly lit, but not excessively so and the decor and soft furnishings were nothing short of opulent. Large, comfortable sofas were covered in the same fabric which curtained the floor to ceiling windows along one wall. The curtain fabric itself was generously gathered and fell in extravagant, expensive folds to pool on the floor with contrived carelessness.

On the sofas and around the numerous tables some two dozen women sat, alone or in small groups, drinking, playing cards, chatting, generally relaxing. From their dress and attitude, it appeared that most had come straight from the office and were unwinding after a hard day. One or two were talking with one or other of the young men who were in attendance, waiting, presumably, until they were required.

The atmosphere was relaxed and friendly. The predominance of women put Maggie in mind of one of the better aspects of the few remaining gentleman's clubs. As in those, everyone here gave the impression that they felt as if they belonged and could use the club as a home from home.

Antony was greeted by all the women there and he kissed each one on the cheek, in turn, like a benevolent night-club owner, passing a few words here and there. Maggie found herself returning smiles, refusing the offer of a drink from one woman when Antony urged her on.

'Is there anyone in the Exhibition Hall, Liz,' he asked the woman.

'I think Tina booked it – she disappeared in that direction with Judd.'

Maggie raised her eyebrows at Antony and he took her by the hand.

'There's a lot more to see yet,' he murmured close to her ear, 'but I think you'll find this entertaining. I know I will.'

Intrigued, Maggie followed him into the next corridor. There were several doors leading off it, some of which had 'Engaged' signs hanging from the handles. Antony opened the first vacant door and closed it behind them.

Maggie looked around her with interest. The room was small, no more than a cubicle, really, with just enough room for a large, cushion-strewn couch against the opposite wall to the door and two easy chairs with a coffee table between them. On the coffee table was a silver champagne cooler with a bottle and two glasses at the ready.

The chairs were facing the far wall which consisted entirely of glass, through which could be seen a larger room, surrounded by mirrors.

'Each mirror represents a cubicle such as this,' Antony told her as they sat down.

'Two-way mirrors?'

He nodded. Opening the champagne bottle with a discreet 'pop', he handed her a full glass.

'Watch.'

The room before them was empty apart from a huge unmade bed. The unsheeted mattress was covered in a grubby, striped ticking and there were several mismatched pillows piled up against the peeling bedhead. A single light hung from the ceiling, the red bulb casting a ruddy glow over the scene so that it looked almost surreal, like a stage set of a seedy hotel room.

The corners of the room were in shadow. As Maggie watched, a door at the far side opened and a man and a woman entered.

The man was big, at least six feet five, and solidly built. His dark hair was cut aggressively round his ears and shaved at the nape. Dark stubble patterned the lower half of his face and crept over his jawline to his neck. Maggie could see the muscles of his thighs bunching under his oil-smeared jeans as he strode into the room and took off his leather jacket which he flung on the bed. Underneath he was wearing a heavy denim shirt, the top button undone so that a few coarse, dark hairs showed between his collar-bones.

'Get in here!'

Maggie gasped as he snarled at the small, well-dressed woman who she now realised was hesitating in the doorway. She turned to Antony in some alarm and he smiled at her.

'It's all right. This is Tina's fantasy. Judd knows exactly what to do.'

Maggie watched as Tina walked slowly into the room, swaying slightly in her neat, high-heeled court shoes. She was dressed in a well-cut grey wool suit, a dark pink blouse buttoned demurely to her throat and fastened with a silver brooch.

As she reached the bed, she quietly put down her handbag and stood just outside the circle of light surrounding the bed, waiting. She gave a good impression of fear as Judd threw himself on the bed and leaned back on the pillows, folding his hands behind his head and crossing one booted foot over the other. The metal toe caps glinted menacingly in the reddish light, incongruous against the bare mattress.

For a few seconds there was complete silence as Judd made Tina wait. The tension between the two participants was palpable, even through the two-way mirror, and Maggie felt her throat tighten. She gulped at her champagne as Judd flicked his wrist at Tina and, moving forward slightly so that she was in the light, she began to undress.

He watched through hooded eyes as she slowly unclipped the brooch at her throat and put it carefully in her pocket before removing her jacket and her blouse, allowing them to fall in a disregarded heap at her feet. Her movements were graceful, seductive even, as she slowly slipped the button at the side of her waistband out of the buttonhole and opened the zip.

Maggie watched, mesmerised, as the other woman eased the skirt down over her narrow hips. She was wearing a full-length white slip underneath and she stood quietly, submissively, before the cynical gaze of the man on the bed, as if waiting for his command.

Maggie judged her to be in her early forties, though her body was still taut and firm, well cared for. She was small boned and delicate, her short, stylishly cut brown hair leaving her neck exposed. Her skin was lent a pale pink, pearlised sheen by the glow of the red light bulb so that it looked fragile, almost translucent.

'Pretty, isn't she?' Antony breathed in her ear.

Maggie nodded, transfixed. She felt uncomfortably voyeuristic, watching the tableau below, yet she could not tear her eyes away. She gasped as Judd suddenly swore, graphically, making the woman flinch.

'What are you waiting for?'

He jabbed a cigarette between his teeth and struck a match. The flickering flame seemed to mesmerise Tina so that she jumped when he shook the match and extinguished it.

'Get it off,' he snarled, blowing a thick stream of smoke at her.

Very slowly, Tina pushed the straps off each shoulder in turn and let the slip fall in a silky pool around her feet. Maggie sucked in her breath. Underneath the smart, ordinary clothes, Tina was wearing a garish red, push-up bra which gathered up her small breasts and thrust them forward. Her ripe, red-tipped nipples peeped obscenely over the top as if she was offering them to the man on the bed.

A cheap black lace suspender belt encircled her slim waist and held up her sheer black stockings. She was still wearing her high-heeled black court shoes and Maggie's eyes were drawn to the slender length of her legs from her ankles up to her stocking tops and beyond to where the gently rounded globes of her buttocks were displayed in shiny red satin panties, edged with scratchy black lace.

'Whore!' Judd hissed and Tina hung her head.

'Turn around.'

Tina jumped to obey and, although Maggie knew she couldn't be seen watching through the two-way mirrors, she drew back in her seat. She could see Tina's face now and understood at once the intent expression in her eyes. Her lips parted slightly as she turned away from Maggie again and bent over from the waist. Maggie was unexpectedly shocked to see that the red panties were crotchless.

From the position that Tina had automatically adopted, legs straight, thighs together, her breasts spilling out of their inadequate restraint, Maggie could clearly see the shadow between her buttocks and the tender, pink-lipped triangle of flesh beneath. The dark pubic hair shielded her secret places coyly, curling delicately round her outer lips.

Judd opened a can of beer. The sharp crack followed by a gassy hiss sounded unnaturally loud. He took a swig before jumping off the bed and sauntering round her, looking her up and down with exaggerated menace.

'Legs apart,' he shouted, his scowl deepening as Tina shook her head slightly and pressed her face into her shoulder. 'Do we have to go through this every time?' he asked with exaggerated patience.

He sat down on the bed in front of Tina so that she could see him, though she did not move. As the silence continued, Maggie could see the barely imperceptible shaking of Tina's shoulders. Judd waited for a few minutes more before swearing under his breath and suddenly leaping to his feet.

'Very well. Though I don't see why you don't do as you're told immediately since you know you'll do it anyway – in the end. What do you think you're here for?'

Maggie felt her stomach knot with tension as Judd slowly, deliberately began to unbuckle his belt. It was of a thick, heavy leather, the strap flat and wide. The buckle was large and weighty looking. He took his time drawing it through the stiff loops of his jeans before cracking it loudly against his thigh.

Tina was trembling openly now and Maggie shifted in her seat, pressing closer to Antony. She gasped as Judd coiled the buckle end of the belt around his fist and brought the other end, without warning, across the back of Tina's stocking-clad thighs. Tina whimpered, but kept her legs pressed tightly together.

Judd waited for a few seconds before carefully aiming another blow parallel to the first. This time Tina cried out and slowly, reluctantly it seemed to Maggie, she shifted position so that her feet were shoulder width apart. Her naked labia were now exposed. The pink flesh, framed by the cheap red and black crotchless knickers, glistened moistly and Maggie felt an answering wetness gather between her own thighs.

Judd reached forward and caressed Tina's bottom approvingly, almost lovingly.

'On your knees,' he commanded and Tina obeyed at once, pressing her lips fervently against his boots, bottom high in the air.

Maggie felt Antony's warm breath against her as he explained, 'Tina is in banking – about as high as you can go. All day long she has to be in control, make decisions, be strong. She comes here to let go.'

Judd was pouring scorn and abuse on her head now, abusing her in the crudest possible terms, some of which made Maggie flinch. Yet Tina seemed to be lapping it up.

At his command, Tina began to crawl around the room, her small breasts hanging down, swinging so that their reddened crests brushed the rough carpeted floor, her glistening sex exposed to all the watchers. The fragile fabric of her stockings had ripped and torn, the ladders running up her legs.

In spite of herself, Maggie felt herself grow warm and she pressed her own thighs together tightly. Judd was following Tina around the room, beer can in hand, cigarette between his teeth, laughing at her, calling her names.

'If the men under you at work could see you now! The big Boss Lady! You love it, don't you?' he laughed harshly and cracked the belt across her swaying bottom.

Suddenly he reached down and tore the panties off her, throwing them to one side with a display of disgust. With her naked white bottom exposed, Tina looked even more vulnerable. Maggie watched, her fascination overcoming her initial horror as Judd hit Tina several times across the buttocks with the leather belt and the tender skin became striped with pink.

Tina was panting now, crawling frantically around the room as if trying to escape from the sting of the belt. In vain she changed direction, darting this way and that, writhing as he caught her with it. Judd derided her efforts, bringing the belt down between her legs so that the tender skin of her perineum was stung by the merciless tip, the flat leather tormenting the tight, exposed anal opening.

The crack of the belt echoed around the room, each one sending a shiver through Maggie as she imagined herself in Tina's place. Finally, Judd stopped and, gripping Tina by the elbows, he hauled her up onto her knees. Tina whimpered audibly as he thrust his face close to hers and snarled, 'What do you want, whore?'

In response, Tina merely tossed her head from side to side and Judd shook her, hard.

'What do you want? Tell me!'

Maggie held her breath as in a small, breathy voice, Tina replied, 'I want you to fuck me.'

Maggie's hand flew to her mouth as Judd shook her again. 'Say please,' he sneered.

'Please,' she whimpered, 'Oh please!'

Judd hauled her to her feet and carried her over to the bed with one arm as if she were weightless. Stubbing his cigarette out on top of the beer can before throwing it aside, he sat down heavily on the bed and flung Tina across his knee. She lay there face down, limp and helpless as a rag doll with her head and legs dangling either side of his lap.

She cried out as he began to spank her, his large, calloused hand paddling her already tender behind, mercilessly. Her face was pressed into the grimy mattress and Maggie could imagine the stale, sweaty smell of it, mixing with the pungent odour of Judd's oily jeans. Under the red stripes caused by the belt, Tina's white skin grew pink from the slaps as the spanking went on and on.

Her voice muffled by the mattress, Tina begged him to stop, but Judd merely laughed, bringing his hand down harder and faster in response. Maggie felt her own bottom tingling in sympathy and she wriggled in her seat.

She welcomed the touch of Antony's cool hand as he massaged the back of her neck, held rigid with tension. She swallowed as she felt his hot, wet tongue begin to explore the outer whorls of her ear. She wanted to turn and seek his mouth with her own, but the scene which continued before her eyes held her transfixed.

Surely Tina could not bear much more? Just as Maggie thought he had gone too far, Judd suddenly tipped her off his lap, letting her fall in an undignified heap. He nudged her with his toe so that she rolled onto her back and stared up at him as he stood, towering menacingly over her. The look in Tina's eyes was one of adoration mixed with fear.

Maggie's eyes skidded from Tina's face to Judd. She could not take her eyes off the movement of his fingers as he unzipped his jeans and released his swelling penis.

'My God!' Maggie whispered. 'Will you look at *that*!'

Like the rest of him it was larger than life, soaring up proudly from his parted zip. Maggie could see the purple veins standing out in the smooth white skin. A bead of moisture glistened at the tip and she unconsciously ran her tongue across her lips. Antony followed the movement with one finger and she drew the tip of his finger into her mouth without thinking and circled it with her tongue. She felt suffused with liquid heat, her senses caught up in the drama being enacted before her.

Meanwhile, Judd had taken a condom out of his back pocket and was slowly unrolling it over his rock-hard cock. Without bothering to remove his clothes, he scooped Tina up off the floor and threw her carelessly face down on the bed. Pushing several pillows under her hips so that her glowing bottom was high in the air, he held her cheeks apart and entered her from behind.

Maggie could see Tina's face, eyes glazed with what looked like a mixture of pain and ecstasy as he thrust in and out of her and she twisted in her seat to find Antony was watching her, his eyes hot.

Without a word, Maggie rose and, standing in front of him, pulled her shift over her head.

3

Antony smiled slowly as she stood before him in her grape silk basque. Without taking his eyes from her, he pulled the couch closer to the mirror so that Maggie could still see Judd and Tina when he beckoned her forward.

Maggie held her breath as Antony sank onto one knee in front of her and carefully unclipped each of her suspenders. With tantalising slowness, he rolled down one stocking, pressing small, dry kisses all the way down the inside of her leg to her ankle. He kissed each of her toes in turn as he peeled away the delicate nylon, tickling the sensitive spaces between them with his tongue. He took his time before repeating the procedure with her other leg.

Standing absolutely still, she watched him as he rolled down her damp panties, bringing them briefly to his lips before discarding them. His face was on a level with the moist curls between her thighs and Maggie felt her legs turn to water as he gently rubbed his nose against her quivering mound, breathing in the scent of her.

His strong hands came up to cup her buttocks, pressing her to him as his tongue snaked along the glistening crevice between her legs. She was ready for him, her tender flesh swollen with passion, bathed in her feminine juices. She shifted position slightly to give him easier access and moaned softly as his questing tongue found the small bud of desire burgeoning hopefully between her nether lips.

Maggie's eyelids felt heavy as she opened them and looked

through the window to the hall below. Judd had denied Tina the relief of orgasm and had tied her by the wrists and ankles. She lay, spread-eagled on the bed, face up, while he knelt astride her waist, his great cock, naked now, looming menacingly over her.

Maggie's legs began to tremble as Antony's tongue flicked firmly backwards and forwards across her straining clitoris. Judd was masturbating himself now, milking that incredible organ so that, when he came, the thick, creamy fluid spurted across Tina's rapturous face and breasts.

As a copious amount of fluid hit Tina's cringing skin, Maggie lost control. She cried out as her own orgasm broke from her, throwing back her head and sinking slowly to her knees.

She found Antony's mouth with her own. She could taste herself on his lips, a sweet, sticky warmth and she welcomed the invasion of his tongue into her mouth, sucking it in. As he kissed her, he pushed the straps of her basque over her shoulders and released one aching breast.

Still kissing her deeply, he rolled her swollen nipple in the warm palm of his hand until it had hardened to a bursting peak. She ached for the hard nub to be enclosed by his hot mouth, but Antony had ideas of his own. Breaking away from her for long enough to lift her and lay her gently on the couch, he looked down on her with heavy eyes as he quickly dispensed with his own clothes.

His body was smooth skinned and powerful, the shoulders broad and well defined. Maggie ran the palms of her hands over them and across his lightly hair-roughened chest. He lowered himself onto her, letting her feel his weight along the length of her body as he kissed her. He nipped the sensitive skin inside her lower lip with his teeth before soothing it with his tongue and Maggie groaned.

Any other time she knew she would have welcomed this

long, slow build up to release, but the scenes in the Exhibition Room she had just watched made her need more urgent. She had *been* there in the room with Judd and Tina. She had been Tina.

Already her recent climax had ebbed away and she was eager for more, her over sensitised flesh quivering in anticipation. She could feel the hardness between Antony's thighs nuzzling her navel and she murmured restlessly. The memory of Judd spilling his seed over Tina pushed itself to the forefront of Maggie's mind and she was suffused with heat.

As if reading her mind, Antony took his weight on his hands placed either side of her head and levered himself away from her. His cock bounced off her breasts and hovered above her chin. It was long and thick, the circumcised purplish tip already beaded with a small drop of moisture.

Maggie craned her neck so that she could reach up to dab at it with her tongue, savouring the salty taste as she licked around the velvet-skinned helmet. Antony rolled onto his back beside her, watching, narrow-eyed as she slowly took the entire length of his shaft in her mouth. Inch by inch she eased it to the back of her throat. Releasing her muscles there, she flicked her tongue back and forth against the underside as it slipped in. At last her lower lip kissed the weight of his balls.

His engorged flesh, slippery with her saliva, filled her mouth, nudging at the back of her throat. She frowned in protest as he unexpectedly withdrew.

'No,' he whispered urgently, pulling her up the couch into his arms, 'not yet. First I want to come inside you – here.'

Maggie gasped as suddenly, without warning, he hooked two fingers inside her and found unerringly that secret, sensitive place which had the power to drive all reasonable thought from her mind. Her entire being seemed centred on those few folds of flesh and her muscles clenched.

Clinging onto his shoulders, Maggie squirmed, impaled on his probing fingers. A kaleidoscope of colours danced on her closed eyelids as he rubbed her, her entire body exploding into sensation as his thumb pressed against her exposed clitoris.

Quickly, he rolled her over onto her back and plunged into her so that those sensations radiated throughout her body in a series of never-ending waves, over and over until he joined with her, giving a triumphant cry as his sperm burst from him.

They lay, sweat slicked and exhausted, entwined in each other's arms for several minutes. When Antony raised his head and smiled down at her, it took all her strength to muster a few words.

'Did I pass the test?'

'Hmm?' he nuzzled her neck, sending little shivers through her.

'The interview – can I join the Black Orchid Club?'

He laughed, his now flaccid penis slipping out of her as she joined in.

'Maggie, I think you'll be an asset to the club.'

Maggie smiled and reached for him, satisfied to feel him growing hard again under her hand.

'You can bet on it,' she murmured as she slithered down the bed.

Antony felt the last vestige of the day's tensions float away as Maggie took him into her skilful mouth again. Most women he had known paid lip service to this kind of 'lip service', but Maggie had turned it into an art form. Better still, she genuinely seemed to be enjoying herself, her eyes were closed, her long, dark hair enclosing him in a fragrant, ticklish curtain.

He lay back on the cushions and sighed as she cupped his

balls in her cool, elegant fingers. Her tongue swept delicately along the length of his shaft, flicking expertly round the tip before travelling back down to his testicles.

She had twisted so that her body was at right angles to his on the couch, her long, slender legs curled beneath her. As she worked her tongue leisurely round his cock, Antony coiled his fingers round one of her ankles and pulled her gently towards him. She shifted slightly so that her body was soon resting lengthwise on top of his, her warm, pale pink sex inches from his face.

Gently parting her lips he could see the remnants of their combined juices and he lapped at the sticky concoction with his tongue, breathing in deeply the musky odour. Slowly running his fingertips around the moist flesh leaves, he wetted them thoroughly before running them along the line of her perineum and up to where the skin puckered around the tight little orifice of her anus.

He felt her lapping tongue falter momentarily as he began to trace ever deepening circles around it. As soon as she had regained her rhythm, he dipped back down to her sex and used the moisture there to lubricate the reluctant mouth, dipping and wetting, dipping and wetting until at last he was able to slip the tip of one finger inside. Her muscles tightened around it, pushing against the intrusion and he waited until they had relaxed before working it in further.

Lightly flicking her clitoris with his tongue, he saw with satisfaction that her juices had begun to flow faster. His finger was in up to the second knuckle now. Using the fingers of his other hand, he spread her inner lips, lapping at the pulsing opening with his tongue before delving into that hot, melting passage with three fingers.

He could feel his finger in her bottom through the thin membrane separating the two places and he rubbed the fingers of his two hands together slowly. Finding her hard bud again with his tongue, he flicked it quickly back and forth.

A fluttering sensation in his balls warned him that he could not hold back much longer. Maggie was sucking him hard as her own body went out of control. He felt her clitoris buck against his tongue and he nibbled at it, very gently.

As she came, Maggie ground herself onto his face, almost enveloping him with her heated flesh as he lapped the fluids flooding along his fingers and worked his finger faster in her bottom. When the last wave of her orgasm ebbed away, Antony quickly withdrew his member from her mouth and flipped her onto her back.

She looked up at him with wide, heavy eyes as he held her mouth open and slipped back inside. He placed his palms against the wall for balance as he thrust into her willing mouth. He wanted to watch her face as she swallowed his sperm. His eyes felt glazed as he felt it begin. Every muscle in his body clenched as his orgasm surged into Maggie's hot mouth, spilling over her cheeks and down her neck as he withdrew before the end.

Maggie swallowed and tried to catch the droplets on her chin with her tongue. Antony stared down at her, his breath coming in short, sharp gasps. The beautiful, intelligent face, smeared with semen, her dark hair splayed in wild disarray across the cushions, her body opened to him in total abandon. It was one of the most moving, erotic sights he had ever seen.

Dipping his head, he kissed her, tasting the salty emission on her tongue. Then very slowly, he began to suck at the sticky fluid now drying on her face and neck. He felt her shiver, her soft skin raising up in goosebumps as he trailed his tongue along the mid-line of her body, lingering over her navel.

Her thighs tensed in half-hearted protest as he parted them

again. He smiled to himself as he saw the swollen, satisfied flesh resting in the folds. Slowly, with the tip of his tongue, he licked the grooves either side of her tender clitoris, coaxing it out from under its protective hood so that it stood proud, inviting his kiss.

Maggie moaned softly as he laved it with his tongue, curling it round and round the bud until it began to quiver with life again. Ignoring her muffled protests, he licked it with long, slow, merciless strokes until her thighs tensed and wrapped themselves around his neck. Pressing his face against her he felt the strong, throbbing pulse of her orgasm. It was gentler this time, less intense, but longer lasting.

Maggie's fingers curled in his hair and she pulled him up, away from her.

'No more!' she begged, half laughing. 'Please – that's enough!'

Antony considered ignoring her. He had the urge to take her through the barrier of pain to that other level of pleasure, but something told him that would be going too far. This time.

He kissed her eyelids as she closed them and lay his head on the cushions, watching her as she fell into a light doze.

Maggie stood under the stream of water and let it simply cascade over her tender skin for a long time before taking up the soap and washing herself. She felt tired and heavy limbed, yet exhilarated.

The tender skin of her labia was still sore and engorged, the inner lips protruding so that they rubbed against her panties. As she dressed she felt as if she were turning back into herself, as if that lascivious, insatiable creature she had been with Antony did not really exist. And yet, with every step she took, she was reminded of that other Maggie by the gentle pleasure/ pain of the friction between fabric and tender skin.

He smiled at her as she joined him in the bar. A glass of mineral water was waiting for her and she picked it up gratefully, glad to quench her thirst. Looking around her she was unsurprised to see that the lounge was half empty. It was late, past midnight, and most of the women would be working the next morning. As would she, she had to remind herself. Somehow that other, every-day world seemed very far away.

Antony introduced her to Judd in the bar some time later.

'How do you do,' Maggie felt herself blush as she recalled the scene she had witnessed earlier in the Exhibition Hall and realised that Judd would guess what it had led to.

He merely smiled warmly back at her, however, and shook her hand. He had changed out of his menacing leather jacket and was dressed in the black trousers and white shirt which appeared to be the uniform for all staff whilst not in the gym. Away from the stage set of the Exhibition Room he appeared quite normal, wholesome even, and Maggie couldn't help but chuckle as they took their drinks to a table in the corner.

'What is it?' Antony grinned back at her.

'This place is so bizarre. Your men. Do you pay them well for all this?'

Antony's expression was serious as he answered what had been a very flippant question.

'Very well. And they earn every penny, believe me. They sign a three-month contract during which they must live here, on the premises. They aren't allowed any sexual contact outside the club during their three-month shift, nor are they allowed to take any kind of drugs, or indulge in any kind of sexual practice between themselves. Anyone who breaks the rules is out.'

Maggie was stunned.

'Presumably they are allowed to enjoy what they do here?'

'Sure. Some of them sign one contract after another. And they all have the option to refuse to take part in anything they don't personally feel comfortable with. We do get some pretty weird requests at times.'

'I bet you do! Why so strict though?'

'My first responsibility is to my clients. All my staff are screened for disease and for attitude – I won't have any misogynists here. They all have to be young, fit, committed and, most importantly, love women.'

'And Judd,' Maggie glanced over to where he was leaning on the counter, chatting to the barman, 'does he love women?'

'Why don't you book him and find out?'

Maggie glanced at Antony in surprise, unused to such a suggestion from a man with whom she had just made love. He was smiling at her and she was sure he could read her mind. Looking back at Judd she remembered the sight of his long, hard cock springing from his jeans and, despite her recent exertions, felt a stirring in her womb.

'Maybe I will,' she murmured.

'Good.' Antony was suddenly businesslike. 'Once your application has been processed, he's all yours.'

Maggie felt bemused.

'How long will that take?'

Antony chuckled and cupped her chin with one hand.

'Patience is a virtue, darling. Chastity will be good for you for a few weeks.'

'A few weeks?'

Antony laughed at her dismay.

'You'll be just in time for next month's party night. I'll book Judd as your escort, if you like.'

'Party night?'

'That's right. Next month we have The Body Beautiful to entertain us.'

'The Australian glamour act? I thought they were gigging all over the country?'

'Sure they are – and the shows are a sell out at every venue. No one else will be seeing the version they're doing for us though. Excuse me, Judd's about to go off for the night. I'll catch him before he goes.'

Maggie concentrated on her drink, watching through her lashes as Antony went up and spoke to Judd at the bar. She felt the heat creeping into her cheeks as both men looked in her direction and she saw the spark of interest on Judd's face.

He nodded several times as he listened to Antony, and Maggie was glad she could not overhear what was being said about her. She wasn't sure if she liked the way Antony was smiling as he came back to her.

'Well?'

'It's all fixed. Judd's your man on the twelfth.'

'Oh. You know, it just occurred to me – Judd and Tina – I wouldn't want that sort of thing.'

Antony's eyes gleamed as he regarded her.

'No? Well, you'll find that Judd will very quickly work out what it is you do want.'

He raised an eyebrow at her and raised his glass in a silent toast before putting it to his lips. Maggie's mouth felt inexplicably dry and she gulped at her drink.

'I'd better be going. Will I see you on the twelfth at this party?'

'You might.'

'And Alexander? I . . . I'd rather like to spend some time with him.'

Antony was suddenly remote.

'And you shall, my dear. Count on it.'

His lips twisted slightly into a smile which seemed to

Maggie to be bitter. She watched as he drained his glass before saying, 'Well, as I said, I'd better go. It's very late.'

Antony suddenly reached out and cupped one demurely covered breast in his hand. He took its weight and seemed to study it intently, brushing his thumb over its tip and watching the nipple spring to attention beneath the fabric of her dress with satisfaction. Squeezing gently, he raised his eyes to hers.

Maggie felt unable to move as she was pinned by his curiously inquisitive gaze. Her lips parted in a silent gasp as, without taking his eyes from hers, he intensified the pressure of the squeeze until it was painful. He watched her reaction expressionlessly until, suddenly, he let her go.

'Good night, Maggie,' he said softly.

She rose and gathered up her things before turning away, her legs unsteady.

4

She was in a small, intimate, square room lit by candles, their flickering light dancing on the deep red velvet of the walls. The sweet, heavy smell of incense clogged the air. Soft music played continuously on a music system which couldn't be seen and a couple danced close together in the middle of the room. Alexander and Janine.

Janine's short, white dress clung lovingly to every curve of her slender body which was pressed against the length of Alexander's as if they were melded together. Her blonde head rested lightly on the muscular cushion of his shoulder and they were swaying slowly, languorously, in time with the music, their movements unhurried and in complete harmony.

Maggie watched them jealously from the shadows in the corner of the room. She turned as she felt a light tap on her shoulder and found herself caught by amused hazel eyes.

'Poor Maggie!' Judd murmured. 'Here – I've brought you another drink.'

He was so close she could smell the heavy musk of his skin, feel his warm breath caress her cheek. She reached out her hand to touch him and he seemed to melt away, laughing softly. Frustrated, Maggie turned her eyes back to the dance floor and the couple who, oblivious to their surroundings, were now kissing deeply.

Janine's skirt had ridden up her thighs to reveal lacy white stocking tops and suspenders which framed her naked bottom. Alexander's large hand looked shockingly tanned against

Janine's white skin as he cupped the buttocks and squeezed the malleable flesh.

The entire room was carpeted in luxurious, red plush pile, so long that the couple in the middle of the room were ankle deep in it. Glancing round the room, Maggie saw that there were several other small tables arranged in a semi-circle. All were occupied, but she was the only lone female..

Each of the couples seated at the tables appeared to be engaged in varying acts of seduction. To her left, a beautiful young man with ebony skin was feeding strawberries and cream to a tousle haired redhead. The woman's eyes were closed, a small frown of concentration etched between her eyebrows as she took another mouthful of the sweet concoction. Maggie watched enviously as the muscles in her throat contracted, imagining she could feel the sensation of the cream slipping down her throat.

She tore her eyes away and blinked as she realised that, directly opposite her, a couple were copulating frenziedly on the soft carpet under their table.

'Feeling lonely, Maggie?'

She jumped as Antony materialised at her side.

'Oh! Anthony please don't leave me . . .'

He shook his head sadly.

'Members only, Maggie. You know the rules.'

'But . . .'

He disappeared and she sipped angrily at her martini. She felt strangely disconnected from the scenes taking place around her, as if she were watching through a film of water. She could look, but she could not touch, could not speak to anyone.

Alexander dropped to his knees in front of Janine who was still undulating softly in time with the music. His large hands met round the tender span of her waist as he burrowed his head under her skirt and pushed it up, over her hips. The skin on the perfect, white globes of Janine's behind looked translucent in the candlelight and Maggie's fingers itched to reach out and run her fingertips over the gently rolling landscape of those twin mounds.

Janine threw back her head, her soft lips forming a silent ecstatic 'O' as Alexander's long tongue darted into her labia and began to lick back and forth in slow, delicious strokes. Maggie felt the moisture gather between her own thighs and pressed them together tightly.

She closed her eyes as strong fingers began to knead the tense muscles in her neck and shoulders. Whoever it was knew exactly how much pressure to apply to liquefy her limbs, leaving her feeling heavy and relaxed. She dared not turn to see the owner of the magic fingers for fear that he might disappear, just as Judd and Anthony had.

Opening her eyes, she saw that Alexander had laid Janine on her back on the carpet. She was naked now, but for her white lacy stockings and suspender belt and her high-heeled white stilettoes which had been hidden by the thick carpeting. Alexander was playing with the feathery blonde curls between her legs, teasing and tickling, making her moan softly. His other hand cupped her breast, tweaking at the pale pink nipple until it stood proud.

Maggie was suddenly overcome with the irresistible urge to join them, to enclose that hard, tempting nub with her lips. Shrugging off the massaging fingers, she stood up and began to walk towards them. They couldn't have been more than six or seven paces away, yet she felt as though she was wading through treacle. Her heels caught in the thick pile carpet, dragging her down. As she sank, defeatedly, to her knees, strong hands caught her and pulled her back towards her table.

She shook her head, struggling in protest, straining towards the centre of the room. Her mouth dropped open in surprise as she realised that Janine and Alexander were no longer there. The other tables were now empty – she was alone in the candlelit room and strong, unseen hands were pressing her, gently, but insistently, onto her back.

Sinking into the soft, deep carpet with a small whimper of defeat, Maggie made no protest as her clothes were gently stripped from her. Many of the candles were guttering, their gentle light flickering erratically. No matter how hard she tried to penetrate the velvety darkness, she could not see to whom these knowing, roaming hands belonged.

There were three pairs, that much she knew, two definitely male and the other pair . . . She moaned, partly in protest, mostly in encouragement. Soft, small, feminine hands were fluttering over her thighs, coaxing them apart. Maggie closed her eyes and allowed herself to be opened, her legs pulled slowly apart and her arms held above her head. It was a curiously comfortable imprisonment and she welcomed the soft, wet touch of unmistakably female lips on her breasts. Small teeth nibbled, a hot tongue darted out and circled the engorged nipple.

Maggie had never been so intimate with another woman and she was surprised by how pleasurable it felt. She murmured, wanting to encourage the unknown woman to continue, but her words emerged as an indistinct moan. A tongue insinuated itself between her lips and coaxed her mouth to open. Definitely male, this pleasure-giver plunged into her hot mouth and sucked at her tongue, drawing it into his own, slightly minty tasting, mouth.

Her legs, confined at the ankles by strong fingers, quivered with anticipation as the third person burned a trail of kisses up the insides of her thighs, alternating caresses between each one. The lips paused as they reached the apex, placing small, teasing kisses around the edge of her moist pubic hair.

The mouths were driving her crazy, her entire body, from her head to her captured feet, tingled with her impending orgasm. She knew that the moment someone kissed the swollen button of desire which throbbed violently between her legs, she would burst.

It had to be soon, she couldn't wait much longer . . . She gasped as the three anonymous mouths were withdrawn simultaneously.

'No! Oh no!' she cried out in anguish.

There was the sound of soft laughter, and she heard Antony's voice, close to her ear.

'Patience, Maggie, just a little longer . . .'

The sudden, silent coldness of the room told her before she opened her eyes that she was alone. The candles had all burned out and she blinked as a harsh electric light suddenly filled the place. Her clitoris throbbed in vain and she tried to touch herself, to relieve the agonising pressure, but she could not move her arms.

'No!'

Maggie sat up in bed, knocking the alarm clock off the bedside table as she flailed her arms. Her duvet was on the floor, her sheets awry, yet she was hot, burning as if with a fever. That dream again! Night after night the same long, tortuously slow seduction, followed by the cruel rejection at the very point when she was about to reach release.

She sank back on the pillows, wiping the sweaty damp hair out of her eyes. Running her fingers delicately over her unfulfilled clitoris, she shivered in response to the sensations radiating out from it. Slowly, she began to run her middle finger back and forth, her passage made slick by the warm juices which bathed her hand.

With a *frisson* of shame she remembered her lust for Janine in the dream and saw again the girl's temptingly sweet body, glowing like silk in the light of the fragrant candles. Felt again the wet, sucking, female lips which had travelled over her body.

She drew up her knees as she came, squeezing her thighs together as the throbbing went on and on until at last, she flopped, exhausted, onto the pillows. Dragging the duvet up off the floor, she wrapped it around her and fell at once into a deep, dreamless sleep.

God, she looked a wreck! Maggie peered at herself in the illuminated bathroom mirror the next morning and pulled a face. Damn Antony and his Black Orchid Club! She'd never noticed those tired brown smudges under her eyes or the faint lines showing at the corners of her mouth before. It was the strain of waiting to hear whether or not she was to be admitted to the club, coupled with the unwelcome, enforced chastity of the past six weeks. And the dreams, of course.

Relentlessly, night after night, they disturbed her sleep, leaving her haunted by image after erotic image all day. She couldn't concentrate on anything for more than a few moments at a time. She was jumpy, irritable. Every time the telephone on her desk rang, her heart almost arrested. And all because bloody Antony was taking his time to let her know if she was in.

What more did she have to do, she grumbled to herself as she poured boiling water over instant coffee. She'd subjected herself to the medical he insisted upon, kept clear of sex for longer than at any time since she was about sixteen. Hell, she felt like a born again virgin! And she had a suspicion that all this masturbation wasn't good for her soul.

She pulled herself up short. What *was* she doing? Here she was, a mature, sophisticated woman with a little black book which fairly bulged with addresses, and she was waiting around obediently chaste, like a lovesick teenager. And all at the direction of some domineering male.

Enough was enough. If Antony didn't contact her today, tonight she was going out. The self-imposed curfew would be over and Antony could stuff his bloody club right up his self-righteous arse.

Decision made, Maggie showered and dressed for work feeling happier than she had for a long time.

Janine was waiting for her as she stepped into the office.

'Maggie – I have a message for you. It's from—'

'Just a minute,' Maggie noticed Bob's avid gaze from the next desk and pulled the sliding glass privacy door across which separated them. Ever since Janine's enthusiastic kiss weeks ago, Bob had watched her like a hawk, studying Maggie when he thought she wouldn't notice as if trying to work out an intriguing puzzle.

Maggie had no wish to fuel his suspicions about her any further. He could still see them, of course, and since she didn't trust Janine's mischievous sense of humour, she walked round her desk and sat down, putting it between them.

'Have a seat,' she invited coolly, hoping her excitement did not show.

Janine took her time, sinking slowly into the moulded plastic chair and crossing one well-turned leg over the other. Maggie's mouth went dry as she noticed that she was wearing white lace stockings. An image of Janine sprawled in total abandonment beneath Alexander on a thick, red carpet superimposed itself on the self-contained young woman in her neat business suit who sat across from Maggie now.

She could feel the heat creeping into her cheeks as she remembered the sharp desire she had felt in her dream to possess the firm, soft body and she was appalled to feel the wetness gathering between her thighs at the memory.

'Is there something wrong?' Janine asked innocently.

Maggie's head shot up and met Janine's clear, violet eyes. There was a smug, knowing expression in them which made her bristle. She pulled herself together with difficulty and shifted into a more comfortable position in her seat.

'Of course not.'

'Only, you look tired.'

'Do I? I . . . I haven't been sleeping too well lately,' she admitted reluctantly.

Janine merely smiled and Maggie gained the distinct impression that she knew the cause of her sleepless nights. Her wearing of the white lace stockings today almost had Maggie convinced that Janine knew the content of her dreams, had dreamt them too. Telling herself to stop being so ridiculous, she continued.

'Anyway, what was it you wanted to tell me?'

Janine reached into her black leather document wallet and pulled out a purple envelope. Maggie's heart quickened as she took it and saw the large black orchid printed in the bottom lefthand corner.

'Your tickets,' Janine told her when she didn't immediately open the envelope. 'Tomorrow night is party night.'

'Does this mean I'm in?'

Janine grinned as she stood up.

'Sure does. See you there.'

Maggie waited until Janine had sashayed out of her office and had turned the corner before ripping open the envelope and pulling out the gilt-edged invitation. Judd was to be her escort for the evening, just as Antony had promised her, and The Body Beautiful would be performing a special, private show.

Bringing the invitation up to her lips, she placed a kiss of delight on its edge. Then, feeling Bob's curious eyes on her through the glass partition, she slid it into her desk drawer and took out the first file of the day.

Maggie had dressed to impress in a black chiffon blouse and matching skirt which swirled seductively round her calves. Underneath the semi-transparent blouse, she wore a red, underwired basque which gathered up her generously proportioned breasts and thrust them forward. She had taken the time to paint her finger and toenails scarlet and her wide mouth wore lipstick to match. She felt like a million dollars as she parked outside the club.

Antony, gloriously handsome in evening dress, greeted her in Reception.

'Lovely to see you, darling – welcome to The Black Orchid Club.'

'At long last,' Maggie muttered acidly, but he only laughed, slinging a casual arm around her shoulders as he led her inside.

'Everything comes to she who waits,' he murmured against her hair as they walked and Maggie felt a shiver travel down her spine.

She was still mad at him, though, for making her wait so long and her voice sounded petulant even to her as she said, 'I thought that Judd was my date for the evening?'

Antony laughed again, with genuine amusement. It seemed that nothing could offend him and Maggie felt her bad temper ebb away in spite of herself. As they went into the lounge, Judd appeared at her side, as if he had been looking out for her.

'Enjoy yourself,' Antony whispered in her ear before leaving them alone.

Maggie looked Judd up and down approvingly. Like Antony,

he was wearing a black tuxedo and pristine white shirt. His bow-tie and cummerbund were in a matching red and blue Liberty print and his black dress shoes gleamed dully as only the lovingly polished can. His hair was clean and slicked back and he smelled faintly of patchouli oil. There was no trace of the rough, unshaven biker who had abused Tina in the Exhibition Room on Maggie's last visit.

'Quite the chameleon, aren't we?' she said smiling as he offered her his arm.

She ordered white wine at the bar, raising an eyebrow as Judd bought mineral water for himself.

'I like to keep a clear head,' he explained and Maggie laughed.

'I don't!'

She liked the way his hazel eyes crinkled at the corners when he smiled. Feeling comfortable with him, she leaned against the bar and looked around the room as she sipped her drink.

The lighting was turned down low and a large space had been cleared in the centre of the floor for dancing. The raised stage at the end had been extended so that it protruded like a catwalk onto the dance floor. There were balloons pinned up in bunches round the edge of the ceiling, matt black and satiny white and the Australian flag had been hung above the stage. The whole look reminded Maggie of a slightly decadent version of the 1950s American high school dances she had seen in films.

The people, however, certainly did not look as if they belonged at any school. All the men were dressed similarly to Judd. Maggie caught a glimpse of Alexander, striking as ever in his tux, bending his blond head attentively to a hard-faced brunette in the corner. All the women had dressed with a sense of occasion and there was an air of subdued excitement as they drank and danced and waited for the show to begin.

Maggie wasn't sure what to expect. She'd been to a male striptease act with a group of women from her last job and it had all seemed pretty tame. The Body Beautiful had appeared on various chat shows on British TV to promote their act and as far as she could tell they were simply an antipodean copy of the more famous American Chippendales.

As the recorded music which had been playing faded away, Judd led Maggie closer to the stage, so that they were standing against one of the side walls. He slipped his arms loosely around her waist from behind so that her back was against him as he leaned against the wall. The lights went down and a hush descended.

Glancing round her, Maggie saw that all eyes were fixed on the darkened stage. The air was filled with anticipatory tension, conversation had dropped to a low murmur until, finally, that too faded away.

As if waiting for that moment of absolute silence, the stage was suddenly flooded with light. Music with a hard, driving beat blasted out of the sound system and, in a sudden flurry of movement, six young men catapulted onto the stage and began to dance.

They were all wearing close fitting jeans and crisp white shirts, open at the neck. All were young, but not too young, in their twenties, Maggie judged. Their movements were fast and furious, full of energy, yet all were in perfect time with the others.

Maggie ran her eyes over them and smiled cynically. They looked like refugees from an Australian soap opera, all sun-bleached hair and perfect white teeth, shown to advantage by their semi-permanent smiles. The women in the audience, caught up by the pounding music and the spectacle of six strong young bodies dancing with such enviable energy, were going wild, clapping and dancing. The escorts appeared to be keeping a low profile, melting into the background until they were needed to fetch drinks or partner the dancing women.

Judd nuzzled the back of Maggie's neck with warm lips.

'Not your scene?'

'Oh, I don't know. Maybe after a martini or two,' she replied.

He took the hint and disappeared in the direction of the bar. Maggie noticed Antony standing on the other side of the room. *He* seemed to be enjoying the act, though his face was impassive as he watched. The first number came to an end and the audience erupted into applause as five men left the stage, leaving the sixth to perform a slow, teasing striptease to the strains of Carly Simon's old standby: 'You're So Vain'.

As she watched, Maggie saw Alexander approach Antony and bend to whisper something in his ear. The two made a striking pair, standing so close together. Both blond, of similar height and at the peak of physical fitness. She already knew Antony's body well enough to know she liked it, and Alexander knew her body almost as well . . . Maggie felt a jolt of desire, in equal measure for both of them. Antony smiled as Alexander spoke and she had the irresistible urge to go over to join them.

She took a step in their direction just as Judd arrived back with the drinks. Smiling her thanks, she glanced over again toward Antony and Alexander, just in time to see them disappearing through the door.

Alexander had Antony's trousers undone before the lift to the private quarters had begun to move.

'Steady!' Antony laughed, his laughter turning into a groan as his eager shaft sprang free from his boxer shorts and was enclosed by Alexander's cool, knowing hand.

As the lift stopped on the top floor and the automatic doors opened, Alex led Antony to the white leather sofa by it, without saying a word. Pushing him down gently so that he was sitting with the small of his back pressed against the soft hide cushions, Alex knelt between his outstretched thighs and took him into his mouth.

Antony lay back his head and closed his eyes, giving himself up to the familiar, pleasurable sensations caused by Alexander's clever mouth. God, he loved it when he initiated sex like this, coming up to him when he least expected it and enticing him away from whatever he might be doing with his dirty words, so lovingly phrased.

He knew exactly how much pressure to apply, when to suck and when to lick and . . . Antony groaned as he began to come, thick, short spurts into the back of Alexander's throat. Alexander milked him dry, swallowing every drop until he had grown soft in his mouth. Then he withdrew his head and, looking up at Antony through his lashes, he grinned.

'In a bit of a hurry, weren't we?'

'You little bastard,' Antony replied affectionately, his voice hoarse, 'you know exactly how to get what you want out of me, don't you?'

Alexander cocked his head to one side and regarded him quizzically. 'Does this mean you're going to lean over the arm of this sofa and let me fuck your delectable little arsehole?' he asked lightly, in the same tone of voice anyone would have asked for a refill of their drink.

Antony said nothing, merely standing up and dropping his trousers and shorts to his ankles. The bulge in Alexander's trousers was satisfaction enough as Antony wandered round to the edge of the sofa and positioned himself over the arm, presenting his buttocks to the beautiful youth who watched him, in an act of supplication that had him growing hard again at the mere thought of it.

He pressed his face into the soft, pungent leather as Alex

lubricated the tip of his member and eased it into position. There was a brief, exquisite resistance as he pressed on, then he was filling him, screwing him onto his hot pulsating shaft. Gripping Alexander round the waist, he plunged in and out steadily, pulling slowly part way out of him, then driving the length of his hardness back in before slowly withdrawing again.

Antony felt hot, his own penis rubbing rhythmically against the soft leather of the sofa arm almost painfully. He felt he could not stand much more, yet Alexander went on and on, faster and faster until Antony's back passage burned and throbbed.

Alexander was ruthless, ignoring Antony's increasingly pained gasps as he neared his own climax. And when, at last, he came, it was with a shout of triumph. Seconds later, Anthony exploded over the sofa, allowing Alex to pull him onto the soft pile carpet as his sperm pooled on the soft leather.

Alex's mouth was hot as it sought his and he put his arms around him, holding him close as they kissed.

'God! I love you!' he whispered fervently.

Alexander stroked his hands soothingly down his face.

'I know,' he replied, repeating, almost sympathetically, 'I know.'

5

Maggie watched as the women surged forward to shove money down the miniscule gold posing pouch flaunted by the stripper. She felt curiously removed from the scene, as if it didn't quite have anything to do with her.

One thing she was sure about, though, was that after six weeks of enforced celibacy, her close proximity to Judd's virile, healthy body was slowly driving her wild. Since fetching her another drink, he had resumed his position behind her and was cradling her comfortably against the hard length of his body. Wriggling her bottom slightly, Maggie smiled as she felt the tell-tale tumescence in his trousers.

She could take or leave the act on stage, the real, warm, willing man behind her was just what she needed. She was just about to twist her head and suggest to Judd that they find somewhere a little more private, when the youth with the gold pouch, bulging now with booty, hobbled into the wings and the stage was filled with swirling blue smoke.

In spite of herself, Maggie was intrigued, watching with mounting excitement as from the smoke there emerged the most gorgeous hunk she had ever seen. Maggie held herself still as her eyes assimilated the vision before her.

He was very tall, well over six foot in his bare feet, and the breadth of his shoulders was in keeping with his height. They were strong, powerful, the muscles well defined, stopping just short of the extremes of the serious weight lifter. Even from where she was standing, Maggie could see the hard, carefully developed planes of his pectorals through his waistcoat as he flexed them and struck and held a body builder's pose, his biceps bulging impossibly large as he bent his arms at the elbow. He was naked from the waist up except for the buttonless, electric-blue leather waistcoat which was held together by two leather loops.

The hush which had descended across the room as he appeared gave way to tumultuous applause as he turned his back on the audience and began to gyrate his hips in time to the music. All eyes fastened on the firm, neat behind in the electric-blue leather trousers, so tight that they clung lovingly to every masculine curve and crevice.

Maggie felt a wave of pure lust roll over her and she unconsciously pressed herself against Judd's accommodating body. She couldn't take her eyes off the man on the stage. His long, staight black hair was fastened loosely at the nape of his neck by a strip of blue leather. Her fingers itched to untie it so that she could see that coal black hair flowing loose over his tanned back.

He looked over his shoulder at that moment and she held her breath as he looked directly at her, as if feeling her hot gaze above all the others. His profile was as strong as the rest of him, the bones of his nose and jaw sharply defined, almost hawk-like from this angle. As he turned slowly round and the light caught his face fully for the first time, Maggie saw that his cheekbones were high and prominent. With his glossy long, black hair, they gave him an almost North American Indian look which she had always found powerfully erotic.

For a moment, she thought she had imagined he had looked straight at her, then he sought her out again and she was pinned by eyes which were startling blue in his dark face. As he began to dance, he seemed to be performing for her and her alone and Maggie couldn't take her eyes off him.

As he moved sinuously along the catwalk towards her, Maggie felt her legs begin to shake, her sex, already slick with moisture, swelling uncomfortably in her tight briefs. The man stopped at the end of the catwalk, a mere few feet away from where she and Judd were standing, so close that she could see the faint sheen of perspiration on his naked shoulders.

Suddenly, he dropped to one knee and, leaning forward so that the top of his head was almost touching the ground, he undid the thin strip of leather which bound his hair and threw it aside. His hair cascaded around him, brushing the floor. Maggie had never seen such black, glossy hair on a man. Momentarily, she wondered what it would feel like spread across her naked body . . . She gasped as the man threw back his head and jumped up, speeding up the tempo of the dance, making his hair fly wildly about his face and shoulders.

Maggie ground her hips against Judd in a frantic attempt to ease the ache which was building between her legs. She sighed and fell weakly against him as he insinuated his hand between their two bodies and up the back of her skirt and began to rub her rhythmically through her knickers. It wasn't enough.

Sensing her need, Judd unfastened the ties at the sides of her briefs and pulled them tormentingly through her legs from front to back. He kissed her neck and massaged the rounded globes of her buttocks, tantalising her, making her wait for the cool touch of his fingers against her sex. Maggie moaned softly, past caring that they were in a room full of clapping, laughing women. The intimate, smoky blue darkness of the room was enough to shield them from prying eyes should anyone take their attention off the stage.

No one did, for the man performing on it had them all enthralled. The tempo had slowed again now and, once again, he caught Maggie's eye and held it, unsmiling, as he danced.

Maggie felt her cheeks grow warm and struggled not to react as Judd's fingers at last played over her hot, moist nether lips. She was sure that the man on the stage could not see what was going on behind her back, yet she had the stangest feeling that he knew, none the less.

With uncanny timing, he snaked out his tongue and touched the tip slowly along the inside of his upper lip just as Judd dipped two fingers into her hungry sex. The music soared in her ears as she watched, mesmerised, as the dancer circled his hips slowly before pumping them sinuously back and forth in a blatantly sexual gesture which mimicked the movements of Judd's thrusting fingers.

As Judd worked his forefinger over her clitoris, the dancer's movements became more and more feverish until, suddenly, he threw back his head and shuddered, his face screwed up in simulated ecstasy as if he had climaxed, before stretching his body like a sleek, satisfied cat. Maggie came at once, leaning her entire weight against Judd as she spasmed, to stop herself from falling.

As she came to herself again, she looked up at the man on the stage and he smiled at her wolfishly. He knew! Maggie didn't know whether to feel embarrassed, ashamed, or aroused by what she had just experienced. She chose the last.

Forgetting Judd now that he had so efficiently dealt with her first, insistent need, Maggie walked to the edge of the stage, her eyes never leaving the man dancing on it. She leaned against the edge of the catwalk so that her face was level with his strong, brown feet and gazed up at him, oblivious to everyone else. She half expected him to back away to a safe distance, but he stood his ground as he began his slow strip-tease.

The bright blue eyes stared straight at Maggie as he began to undo the loop on his waistcoat and she caught a flash of gold as the sides momentarily flapped open. She frowned slightly and he danced away from her, performing a perfect back flip before dropping to his knees at the end of the catwalk.

His bulging, leather-covered crotch was level with Maggie's face and she pulled her eyes away with difficulty so that she could watch him peel away the miniscule blue waistcoat. Her eyes opened wide in surprise as she saw that both his nipples were pierced by identical, narrow gold hoops between which was clipped a fine gold chain. In the middle of the chain, which glinted against his smooth brown, hair free chest, was one larger link, connected to which was a second chain. This hung loosely, following the mid line of his body and disappeared into the tight leather trousers.

Maggie tore her eyes away with difficulty and found he was looking straight at her again, as if gauging her reaction. Only vaguely aware of the wolf whistles and clapping which mingled with the heavy, pounding music swelling around her, Maggie wondered what he would do if she reached forward and tugged on the centre link of that fine gold chain . . .

He offered her hardly any resistance as she pulled him slowly down towards her. Maggie could not take her eyes off the way the skin of his hard brown nipples pulled and hardened under the slight pressure. She moistened her lips with the tip of her tongue as she imagined the sensation of encountering cold metal against her lips in counterpoint to the warmth of one perfect, tumescent nub.

The throb between her legs intensified as he suddenly gripped her wrist with one hand and stopped her insistent tugging. She looked up at him ruefully, holding her breath as he brought his lips within inches of her own. Softly, so no one else could have heard, he breathed,

'Later.'

Maggie had never heard such an exciting, promising word. Later. She let him go, reluctantly and he turned to the rest of the audience who, she now realised, had begun to grow restless. They went wild as he grabbed at his crotch and swivelled his hips crudely.

He knew exactly what they wanted, Maggie thought ad– miringly as she stood back and watched him dance. As the crowd whipped themselves up into a good-natured frenzy, the man dispensed with his leather trousers and posed again, giving them time to absorb the impact of his golden, heavily muscled body, covered only by an inadequate G-string made of some kind of black netting.

Maggie's eyes fastened on his barely restrained penis which was squashed into the straining G-string. The gold chain disappeared inside it and she caught a glimpse of a third gold ring. The heat rose within her as she realised that the foreskin of his penis was pierced in the same way as his nipples and that the three centres of arousal were linked by that simple arrangement of fine gold chains.

The music surged into several ever increasing peaks as he danced and whirled towards the back of the stage, adroitly avoiding the hands which grasped at him all along the catwalk. The crowd went wild as, half way down it, he dropped onto his stomach and performed several, effortless press ups in a blatant simulation of the copulatory act.

Maggie felt weak as she imagined herself under that firm, thrusting body, the thick black hair falling over her face as he drove into her. She could not have dragged her eyes away from him even had she wanted to as he rolled and jumped lightly to his feet, retreating to the back of the stage.

As he reached the back curtain, the blue smoke began to gather around his feet and slowly rise. The music built to a crescendo as, with perfect timing, he peeled the tight G-string down his legs and his leashed cock sprang up, held in tension by the chain which attached it to his nipples.

A collective gasp rose up from the audience as it swelled and grew, a magnificent animal which was all too soon concealed by the swirling blue smoke which rose up and obscured him. By the time it had cleared, he had gone.

Maggie did not hang about to watch the energetic young himboes who exploded onto the stage the moment the soloist's music had died away. The image of that huge, hard cock was indelibly printed on her memory. 'Later' would be too long – she wanted the man in blue, and she wanted him *now*!

It was easy to find him. Along the corridor which ran behind the stage there were three doors. Two were standing open and a glance inside told her that their occupants were even now strutting their stuff front of house. Costumes hung neatly on hangers in order of wear, everyday clothes lay haphazardly in heaps over chairs and on the floor. A large crate of beer stood half empty and, in one room a heavy fug of stale cigarette smoke hung in the air.

The third door was firmly closed. A hand written plaque was hanging from the doorknob with a cartoon star and 'Electric Blue' written in a bold, sloping hand in black ink. Maggie hesitated for a second before turning the handle, without knocking.

He was standing in front of a mirror, towelling his sweat streaked face and neck with a thick, white towel. He did not turn as she slipped through the door and locked eyes with him in the mirror. Without a word, he slowly towelled his chest and under his arms. Maggie could smell the heavy musk of his body. She licked her lips nervously.

On the stage, under the spotlights, he had looked approachable, harmless. Here, in this confined space where only the muffled beat of the music could be heard, he seemed to fill the room, taking over the space with his nervous energy so that he seemed like a wild animal, a panther waiting for a chance to spring.

While she was seeking him out, the vague notion in Maggie's mind was that he would be easy, that she would be in charge of their encounter. Now, though, as he slowly laid the towel on the table and turned to face her, she knew she had been mistaken.

Electric Blue was no sex toy. He was fully in control and something told her he could be dangerous to know.

Maggie moved round him towards the couch. His eyes followed her, unblinking, unsmiling, so that they both circled, like two wary boxers before a fight, each waiting for the other to be the first to speak. In the end it was he who broke the tense, sexually charged tension.

'How are you paying?'

Maggie felt her mouth drop open at the unexpected question and she quickly closed it again.

'Paying?' she frowned, unable to quite believe her ears.

Electric Blue flicked a derisive glance over her which somehow inflamed her desire even more.

'I don't give private shows for free.'

His voice was deep, throaty and, for a few seconds, Maggie enjoyed the sound of it, rather than hearing the words. When they did sink in, the anger finally began to push its way through the haze of lust which had enveloped her from the moment she first saw him.

'You want me to pay?' she said incredulously. 'You're not serious?'

'Deadly. It'll be worth it.'

She laughed, thinking for a moment that he was joking, though his face was deadpan. His next words left her in no doubt that he was indeed deadly serious.

'I take cash, Visa and American Express. No cheques.'

'I have a Gold Card – will that be acceptable?' she said, her voice dripping sarcasm.

'Very,' he replied and held out his hand.

Maggie stared back at him, unable to believe her ears. This . . . person, actually expected her to pay for sex with him? He was hot, but then, so was she, on a good day. She certainly wasn't so desperate that she had to resort to paying for it!

She was about to stalk out of the dressing room when she remembered the conversation she had had with Janine all those weeks ago. *'That's what we working girls need now,'* the other girl had said, *'Gigolos, guaranteed safe, hired with an American Express Card.'*

Electric Blue was still waiting patiently, hand outstretched for her sought after piece of plastic. It occurred to her that if she paid for his services, he would do anything she wanted him to – anything her heart or, more specifically, her body, desired. And he was very beautiful. If he was as dynamite in the sack as he was on the stage it might well be worth it. She smiled slowly.

'How much?'

He named a price which made her heart skip a beat. She narrowed her eyes at him.

'I'll expect a refund if I don't get value for money,' she snapped.

'Any complaints will be dealt with by the management,' he replied, straight faced.

Maggie reached into her bag and took out her purse. She watched as he passed the plastic card through the machine he produced from a drawer in the table and handed the slip to her to sign.

'Would you like a receipt?'

'A receipt?'

'Set it against expenses. I could be a hotel room, or a meal for a client?'

Maggie shook her head.

'No one would ever believe I could eat that much guacamole.'

He shrugged and put the credit card machine away. Then he strode to the door and locked it.

Maggie wondered why she didn't feel nervous. Paying for his time made her feel strong, powerful. I wonder if this is why some men use prostitutes? she thought. The person who's paying is the person who calls the shots?

Electric Blue glanced at her quizzically.

'I'll just go take a shower.'

'No!'

She stopped him with one well manicured hand on his hot bicep. He needed a shower, she realised, wrinkling her nose slightly as the strong smell of drying male sweat assaulted her nostrils.

'I want you now. Like this.'

She felt a thrill of power rush through her as he turned obediently, without protest and unzipped his jeans. Glancing quickly around the spartanly furnished, eight by ten foot, windowless room, Maggie saw the couch by the back wall and went over to sit down on it. He waited until she had settled onto the hard, mean cushions and nodded slightly at him to continue.

He no longer looked glamorous, stripping off his clothes under harsh electric light on a cold linoleum floor. His surroundings, though, did nothing to diminish his beauty. Maggie felt the moisture seeping through her dress as his enormous penis, shackled as it was to his nipples, came into view. He was hard, the state of his arousal belying his cool, sardonic air.

'Untie your hair,' she whispered hoarsely.

She watched as the magnificent black tresses cut a swathe

across his shoulders. She rose slowly to her feet and stood before him.

'Undress me.'

Maggie stood, absolutely still as he undid the buttons of her blouse and pushed it off her shoulders. He held her eyes with his as he reached down and eased the waistband of her skirt over her thighs, letting it pool in a gossamer heap around her feet. Something in the depths of his vibrant blue eyes told her that he only pretended to be submissive, that he would only be so while it amused him. After which, he wouldn't give a toss who was paying whom. She shivered.

Expertly unclipping the hooks and eyes of the tight red basque, he threw it away and watched as her breasts sprang free. Glancing down at herself, Maggie saw that her small, dark nipples had already swollen in anticipation of his touch. She was naked now apart from her lacy top hold-ups and shoes, her knickers having been removed by Judd some time before.

She toyed with the idea of keeping these on. But no, this was for her benefit, not his and she wanted to be naked. Gently, but insistently, she entwined her fingers in his nipple chain and coaxed him downwards.

'And the stockings,' she whispered.

He sank obligingly to his knees and rolled them down slowly, one by one. His warm breath played over her pubic mound, fanning the throbbing ache which was growing there minute by minute. Maggie looked down at his dark head, bent in a kind of supplication before her and felt a thrill of power.

Shifting her weight slightly, she brought her legs apart and presented her gleaming valley to his proud face. She did not need to tell him what she wanted. His long tongue snaked out and ran delicately along the needy cleft, circling her erect clitoris before plunging into the hot, wet cavern below.

There was something deliciously lewd that his first kiss was to this, most intimate of places. To not have shared a face to face kiss, or even the most impersonal caress made this act shocking to her, deliciously dangerous.

Maggie arched her back and thrust her pelvis towards him, resting her knees on his strong shoulders. Tangling her fingers in his hair, she held his face closer to her, unable to stop herself from grinding her clitoris against his thrusting tongue as he flicked it back and forth agonisingly slowly, making the sensations build, layer upon layer until the heat began to suffuse her and she knew that, if she allowed it, her orgasm would burst from her before she had time to catch her breath.

In the back of her mind, she wanted to call a halt, to remain in control until the very last moment. With a tremendous act of will, she sank down onto her knees so that they were on a level, leaning heavily against him as her legs began to tremble. She remained still, eyes closed in concentration as she continued to teeter on the brink of orgasm.

As, at last, the feeling drained slowly away, she allowed him to lay her down on the hard linoleum. She went limp as he sucked at her breasts, laving each nipple in turn with his rasping tongue. His long hair lay across her chest like a warm, ticklish blanket and the clean, fragrant smell of it tantalised her.

Strength restored, she pushed him onto his back and gazed down at him.

'Lie still,' she commanded, her confidence growing.

She wanted to examine all of him, run her questing fingers over every square inch of his strong, healthy body. First, she picked up his left wrist and placed it above his head. He allowed her to manipulate him, lying quiet and compliant, his eyes ever watchful. She brought the other arm up over his head and ran her fingers along the inside of it from his wrist to his armpit.

His glorious hair splayed out around his head and Maggie gave in to the urge to stroke it. It felt as soft and thick as she had imagined it would, like a skein of silken rope. Rope. Picking up a tress, she smoothed it upward to see if it was long enough to reach his wrists. It was several inches longer than it needed to be and she smiled wickedly.

She watched his face as she gathered up his hair and wound sections of it round her fingers until they resembled cord. Then she wrapped it loosely round his wrists, tying them together above his head. If he wanted to, he could easily extricate himself, but he made no move to do so.

Maggie sat up to admire her handiwork. He presented one of the most erotic sights she had ever seen. His helplessness curiously did not undermine his masculinity. His was a strength confined by softness, hard muscle constrained by soft hair.

Maggie ran her long fingernails lightly down one side of his body, bringing them over to one pierced nipple. Fascinated, she examined the ring. It was screwed through a perfect hole, as if it belonged there. She teased his aureole with her fingernail, pressing lightly on the tip as it hardened under her touch before following the line of the chain to the other nipple, to which she gave the same treatment.

She wanted to ask him why, what purpose did it serve to mutilate himself in such a way? But she did not want to break the spell of silence enclosing them. Picking up the chain which ran down his mid-line, she tweaked it gently, causing tension in both his nipples and penis. She watched his face closely for any signs of discomfort, but he remained inscrutable, watching her through sardonic eyes as she continued her exploration.

The end of the chain was attached to a slightly larger gold

hoop than those through his nipples. It pierced his foreskin, where a rosy glow showed the pink glans which peeked temptingly through to advantage. Despite the complete relaxation of the rest of his body, Maggie noted with satisfaction that he was semi-hard, the long, thick shaft growing upward towards his belly.

Glancing at his shuttered face, she had a sudden urge to see his expression alter from indifference to need. It was no longer enough to simply have him do what she wanted to her, she wanted to bring him to the brink of madness too, break down his reserve until that impassive face was screwed up in passion as he had mimed it on the stage.

Turning her attention back to the slumberous animal between his legs, she ran her finger delicately from its root to the tip, enjoying the rippling of the loose skin againt her finger pad. Very slowly, she circled the bulb at the end and hooked her finger into the gold hoop. His penis twitched in response. She glanced up at him and smiled slyly.

'You like that, do you?' she asked conversationally and watched his face closely as she tweaked it again.

A faint blush had risen in his cheeks and as she increased the pressure on the ring, a spasm passed across his smoothly expressionless face. It was gone in an instant as he regained control of his features. Maggie smiled to herself. She was going to enjoy breaking that control.

Moving into a more comfortable position, she cupped his hair roughened balls with her other hand, testing their weight and squeezing gently. The stem was growing before her very eyes, the chain that held it central growing slack as the ringed tip rose further up his body. The hard, sculpted muscles of his thighs clenched as she bent her head and nibbled gently at the delicate area of skin which joined cock and balls.

Gathering the moisture in her mouth, she licked a well lubricated trail along the underside of his penis to where the ring glinted, dull gold against the now angry purple of his glans. She licked around it, tasting the salty heat of him before hooking her tongue through the ring and using it to roll back the foreskin.

The bulbous tip glistened, the small orifice in its centre pouting as it gently oozed a bead of thick, creamy fluid. Holding the foreskin back with the circled fingers of one hand, Maggie licked around it, as if it were a particularly delectable ice-cream, Häagen Dazs on a stick. She left the centre until last, pushing the tip of her tongue gently inside him as she sucked up the secretion.

He was breathing heavily now and Maggie felt her own sex pulse with excitement at his unwilling gasp as she enclosed his shaft head with her lips. The ring felt cold, alien, coming between the hot flesh of his glans and her mouth. It rubbed along her tongue as she sank down on him, taking half his length into her mouth before withdrawing to the tip again.

There was no question of his not being aroused now, his member was hard, unyielding to the pressure of her lips and tongue. His hips strained upwards by instinct, inviting her to take more of him inside. The silky skin rubbed back and forth, causing a ticklish friction on the sensitive skin of her lips and at the sides of her mouth.

Maggie sensed that his iron control was gradually slipping away. He groaned as she squeezed his balls in the palm of her hand. It was at that moment that she decided to withdraw.

Taking the chain between her teeth, she inched her way up his body so that she could see his face. He stared back at her almost sullenly, only the slightly glazed expression in his eyes betraying the fact that he had just drawn back from the edge of orgasm. His arms were still loosely bound by his hair, though his hands, she saw, had been balled into fists as he fought to control himself.

Smiling wickedly down at him, she straddled him and began to crawl along his body, one knee either side of him. She paused as her sex drew level with his face and began to untie his bonds. His warm breath tickled the hot crevices of her inner skin and she felt the sudden rush of moisture as his tongue suddenly snaked out and lapped delicately along the petal soft folds.

She sagged slightly and her unsheathed clitoris touched against his hawk-like nose. The effect was electrifying, sending a jolt of lust through her entire body, so powerful that she moved purely by instinct. Linking her fingers with his as they lay, upstretched, over his head, she began to move her hips, rubbing her pleasure bud along his nose as his hot tongue delved ever deeper into her honeyed depths.

Closing her eyes against the bare, grey linoleum, she splayed herself wider, spreading her knees so that he had full access to her pulsating sheath. Suddenly, he penetrated her with his tongue. She bore down on it, grinding her clitoris against the tip of his nose. His tongue was long and stiff, a miniature cock working in and out of her.

It began, wave after wave of hot, weakening sensation beginning deep in her womb and radiating out until it consumed her.

'Oh God! Oh GOD!' she cried as his lips fastened on her quivering bud and he ground them against her, prolonging the climax until she collapsed, exhausted, his face still buried in her soaking sex.

6

Electric Blue hardly gave Maggie time to recover her breath before he suddenly reared up, flipping her over onto her back and pushing her knees up so that they touched either side of her waist.

He held her like that, completely open to him. She could feel the cool air on her exposed skin. Opening her eyes, she looked up into his intense face. There was nothing submissive about him now, nothing remotely compliant.

'Playtime's over,' he told her and there was a cruel twist to his smile that made her panic and struggle against him.

He laughed and opened her wider, dipping his head between her legs and running his tongue roughly from her perineum up to where her spent clitoris still throbbed. Bringing up his head, he licked his lips crudely, as if he had just enjoyed the finest wine.

Maggie no longer felt threatened for she sensed the violence in him was controlled, impersonal. She watched, meekly holding her legs apart as he let go one of them and reached for his swollen shaft. Grasping it lightly with one large hand, he manouvered the foreskin back and forth until a small tear of fluid oozed from the single eye of his glans.

Almost ceremoniously, he paused to release the chain from the ring in his foreskin. Unleashed, it seemed to grow even bigger and Maggie swallowed convulsively.

His movements were tormentingly slow as he positioned himself at the gate of her open sex. Pushing her knees back still further so that she thought she might split apart under pressure, he watched her face intently. His long, black hair formed a thick, fragrant curtain around them, brushing erotically against her cheeks as he lowered his head to run the tip of his tongue lightly across her trembling lips.

Their eyes locked, hers opening wide with shock as he suddenly pushed himself into her, plunging in up to the hilt with the first powerful thrust. He stayed there, letting her feel the cold metal of the ring against the neck of her womb before withdrawing and plunging in again.

Maggie wrapped her legs around his shoulders and clung to him as he rode her. His face was taut, unsmiling as he increased his rhythm and Maggie remembered her earlier determination to break through the cool façade behind which he had hidden all along.

Reaching down between them, she felt for the join of their two bodies, feeling the wet hardness of him as he alternately withdrew and thrust into her. Her own juices were overflowing onto the hard linoleum beneath her and she rubbed her forefinger around her bulging perineum until it dripped with honey.

Biding her time, she waited until he was near to orgasm before reaching round him and working her oiled finger into his tight little anus. The sphincter of muscle resisted momentarily, but she persisted, stirring her finger gently round the rim until the forbidden orifice opened just enough to admit her fingertip. Once she was in, she thrust at him with her finger, matching the rhythm of his thrusting pelvis and ignoring his attempts to expel her finger with his anal musles.

His eyes opened wide. A look of rage chased aross his face as he realised she had bested him. Then he threw back his head and roared as a flood of hot, gushing come poured from him into her convulsing sex. Squeezing his shaft tightly with her pelvic floor muscles, she milked him dry, bringing herself to orgasm by rubbing her over sensitive bud against him.

They collapsed, exhausted, in a tangled mess of limbs and lay, sweat slicked and panting for several minutes. It was the hammering on the door that brought them to their senses.

'Hey, why's the door locked?' an irritable male voice shouted. 'Stop messin' around, mate – you're on in five minutes.'

'OK.'

His voice scraped across Maggie's raw nerves. He sounded like she felt – totally drained. He avoided her eye as he hauled himself off her and disappeared into the bathroom. Hearing the shower running she wished she could take advantage of it herself. She felt hot and sweaty, decidedly smelly with the imprint of his hot, masculine body still on hers.

As she stood up, their combined fluids oozed out of her and ran down the insides of her thighs. She grabbed the towel he had used earlier and cleaned herself up as best she could before pulling on her clothes.

He emerged from the shower, still naked, as she was heading for the door. Fully back in control now, he looked her up and down as she stood at the door. Unexpectedly, he grinned.

'Still keen on a refund?'

Maggie smiled back and shook her head. The slightly dirty feeling which had been creeping over her receded rapidly and she felt good about what she had done again. Her eyes settled on his talented penis. It lay, quiescent now, between his legs, the gold chain firmly reattached.

'You give good value,' she admitted.

He reached into the drawer and took out a card. She ran her thumb absently along the edge, noticing it was engraved, not printed. Classy. Glancing at it, she saw it had his stage name, *Electric Blue* and an outer London telephone number on it.

'You're not Australian, then,' she commented, surprised.

'Only on Wednesday and Saturday nights. I can be whatever you want me to be. Call me sometime.'

He turned his back on her and began to dress ready for his next act. Arrogant little bugger! He hadn't been so cool a few minutes ago! Maggie smiled to herself. She knew she wouldn't call him, but she put his card in her bag all the same. She didn't bother to say goodbye as she left.

Janine found her in the lounge bar half an hour later.

'Hey! Where did you get to? Did you miss the second set from that guy in blue leather?'

She rolled her eyes heavenward to let her know what she thought of it and climbed onto the barstool next to Maggie. Maggie took a swig of her martini and regarded Janine through the mellow, alcohol induced haze which had enveloped her.

'I've seen all I want to see of *him*,' she pronounced definitely. 'He's just cost me the whole of last month's bonus.'

Janine's fine eyebrows arched upwards.

'Really? And was he worth it?'

An image of him lying, bound by his own hair as she explored his erotic, pierced body made Maggie smile.

'I thought so at the time,' she admitted ruefully.

Janine regarded her quizzically for a few moments, frowning slightly as Maggie knocked back her drink.

'Come on – we've both got work tomorrow. I'll drive you home.'

'My car's here—'

'You're in no fit state to drive. I'll pick you up in the morning and bring you over here at lunchtime, after the meeting with the Jefferson Corporation. You've remembered that, have you?'

'Of course,' Maggie lied, frowning at the mention of their

most important client. How could she have forgotten such a crucial meeting?

She allowed Janine to chivvy her to the door and drive her back to the flat, all thought of Electric Blue and his undisputed attractions consigned to the back of her mind.

The next afternoon, Janine seemed quiet as they drove to pick up the car. Maggie was relieved. She had one hell of a headache and the Jefferson meeting had not been the success it should have been. As they drew into the car-park, Janine said, 'By the way, Anthony asked me last night if I'd organise your badging. I've made an appointment for Saturday morning – will that suit you?'

Maggie had been fumbling in her bag for her keys and hadn't registered what Janine had said.

'Sorry?' she asked absently.

'I'll pick you up on Saturday at ten-thirty. That's a.m. All right?'

Maggie nodded. 'Sure, whenever. Thanks for the lift.'

'No problem.'

Janine fired the engine and drew away with a squeal of tyres. Maggie found her car and unlocked it. Badging? No one had said anything to her about wearing a badge. She glanced over at the club and considered going to see Antony for herself. Maybe grab Alexander for a massage. But no, she had a lot of work to get done if she was to salvage her reputation after her dozy performance this morning. Saturday would come soon enough and she would find out what was what then.

'I am *not* going in there! No way!'

Maggie stopped outside the blank windowed shop and regarded Janine in horror. The girl had been tight-lipped all the way here and now Maggie knew why.

'Why would I want to go to a tattooist?'

'Come in off the street,' Janine said patiently, 'and I'll show you.'

'You have to be joking!'

'Come on, Maggie – we're attracting attention.'

Maggie glanced over her shoulder and saw that a small group of youths were regarding them curiously from across the street. She thought how incongruous they must look, drawing up outside a backstreet tattoo artist's shop in Janine's ice-white Ferrari.

'All right,' she muttered ungraciously and followed Janine inside.

She had expected the interior to be dark and dingy and was surprised to step into what looked like the reception of a beauty parlour. Janine noticed her surprise, whispering, 'What did you expect? To be knee deep in sailors and a floor full of sawdust?'

She rang the bell on the bleached wood counter and a slim, attractive woman came out, dressed in a white overall.

'Hello. You must be Maggie – I'm Phoebe,' she introduced herself.

Maggie shook the exquisitely manicured hand she was offered and followed her through to the back of the shop. Phoebe took her coat and hung it, with Janine's, on a coatstand in the passageway. With a cool, professional smile, she showed them into a small, scrupulously clean room, well lit, and tastefully appointed. In the middle of the room was a padded couch, exactly like those used by beauticians and it was this to which Maggie was directed.

'You want the usual?' Phoebe asked.

'That's right,' Janine answered before Maggie could say she hadn't a clue what was going on.

Phoebe smiled.

'Have you ever been tattooed before? No?' she laughed at Maggie's apprehensive expression. 'Don't worry, there's really nothing to it. No worse than a trip to the dentist. Perhaps you'd like your friend to stay?'

Maggie nodded, biting her lip on the retort that she avoided dentists like the plague. Janine gave her one of her cat-like smiles and she had the uncomfortable feeling that she had read her mind. Phoebe had scrubbed her hands and was pulling on thin surgical gloves.

'Er . . . will it hurt?' she asked feebly.

'Only a little bit. You do know though, don't you, that a tattoo is permanent?'

'Um, yes. Of course.'

'Good. So long as you've considered that. Not that anyone but your closest friends will see yours!'

She flashed Janine a mischievous smile and Maggie felt a second's panic. What on earth were they about to do to her?'

It wasn't long before she found out. Having stripped naked she was asked to lie down on the couch. She gasped as her bottom cheeks were gently coaxed apart and a cold antiseptic swab was applied to the tender skin. Surely they weren't going to tattoo her *there*?

She was about to protest, but Janine had dropped down on her haunches at the end of the couch so that they were at eye level.

'It won't take long,' she said, soothingly. 'Once you've been badged you'll be able to be identified as a member of the club by anyone who knows about us. Ssh! Hold onto me,' she crooned as Maggie cried out.

The first touch of a needle to her skin was shockingly painful and Maggie was grateful to grasp hold of Janine's slender hands. The other girl's eyes were unusually bright as she monitored Maggie's every response.

Maggie could feel Phoebe's rubber covered fingers pressing lightly against her anus as she held her open with one hand whilst working with the other. The rubber felt alien against her skin, yet not clammy and unpleasant as she had expected. She could feel the warmth of Phoebe's fingers through it, the tenderness of her touch an almost erotic counterpoint to the merciless stainless steel instruments she was wielding with apparent skill.

'The skin breaks,' Janine intoned softly, 'a little blood is spilled and mingles with the ink. Would you like to see, Maggie? Would you like to know what the end result will be?'

Maggie merely stared at her, clenching her teeth against the stinging sensation between her buttocks. She couldn't trust herself to speak in case a shaming sob should escape her lips as Janine stood in front of her and, hitching up her dress, slowly rolled down her pantyhose. She was wearing white lace knickers which accentuated rather than hid her downy pubic mound.

Phoebe seemed oblivious to the striptease being performed in her consulting room, labouring over her task as Maggie's eyes widened in disbelief. Janine was slowly pulling down her knickers, letting them drop to her ankles before stepping out of them. She smiled at Maggie, a knowing, intimate smile.

Maggie could not take her eyes off Janine as she slowly turned around and bent over from the waist, presenting her with an unobstructed view of the perfectly symmetrical globes of her bottom. The discomfort in the cleft of her buttocks caused by Phoebe's diligently working fingers, receded as she watched the vision in front of her. In a gesture which would have been vulgar if it weren't so powerfully erotic, Janine arched her back, pushing her hips back, almost into Maggie's face. Then she reached behind and opened herself up.

Maggie drew in her breath. On the lefthand side of Janine's

inner cheek, there was tattooed the likeness of a perfectly formed black orchid. It was about an inch long by half an inch wide and was defined by a red border. Yellow ink had been used to form its delicately freckled throat and fragile double stamen.

Her own bottom cleft was one mass of stinging soreness now, but Maggie barely cared as she studied the tattoo displayed before her. She was so close to Janine's spread cheeks, she could smell the faint, sweet odour of feminine perspiration, could see the puckered pink gateway to her forbidden orifice.

With Janine's head turned away from her, Maggie felt free to examine her more slowly than she had ever dared to look at any other woman's secret folds. Between her demurely closed thighs, she could see her plump, pink sex peeking coyly through the dark blonde curls. She was wet, a sheen of female juices shimmering invitingly on the tender skin.

Janine pressed slightly closer and, without thinking, Maggie acted on impulse, straining her lips forward to place a kiss against the black orchid tattooed on the other girl's inner cheek. Janine shuddered and Maggie quickly drew away, appalled at herself.

'There – all done.' Phoebe's brisk voice, so cool, so clinical, saved her.

Maggie smiled slightly shakily at her as she helped her off the couch. She kept her eyes averted from Janine as she dressed hurriedly, wincing as the soft cotton of her briefs touched the plaster covered site of her new tattoo.

'I'll give you a supply of plasters. Salt baths are the best thing while it scabs over. Plenty of air – keep your briefs off as often as possible.'

Maggie winced as she left. It felt as though she had an inflated balloon in her cleft and the sticking plaster pulled the undamaged skin uncomfortably with every movement. She was grateful to Janine when she took care of the bill, holding her by the arm as they left as she suddenly felt quite faint. She could not sit down properly in the car and was forced to lean against Janine's slim shoulder as the other girl drove her home.

'Now I know why you insisted on driving me!' she broke the silence between them with a slightly nervous laugh.

Janine smiled, keeping her eyes on the road ahead. When they arrived at Maggie's flat, she helped her up the steps and went to make coffee without being asked. Maggie half sat, half lay across her blue and lemon chintz sofa, listening to the sound of Janine moving about in the small, modern kitchen.

She loved her flat, treating it as her own, personal little haven and she rarely invited anyone back there. Those few people who did get through the door often commented on the unexpectedly feminine style in which it was decorated. Cool lemons and blues covered the sofa chairs, matching the soft yellow carpet and china blue curtains. There was a hint of pink in the striped wallpaper which she had picked out in the cushions and lamps which lifted and warmed the colour scheme.

As Janine walked in with coffee steaming in two bone china mugs, Maggie felt the atmosphere in the usually sunny room thicken with tension.

'About earlier,' she blurted suddenly after they had both sipped their coffee in uncomfortable silence for several minutes, 'I don't want you to think that I ... well, that I could ever ...'

'Fancy me?' Janine finished for her coolly.

Maggie felt her cheeks suffuse with heat and she realised she was blushing furiously. There was something about Janine that made her feel as awkward as a gauche schoolgirl. Since that fateful day when she had kissed her in the office, Maggie always had the uncomfortable feeling that Janine was party to some crucial information of some kind to which she herself had no access. She always seemed to be wearing an expression like a cat who has been at the cream whenever Maggie drew near her.

Worst of all, from her appearance in her dreams to small, shocking incidents such as the one she had instigated today, Maggie had found herself responding in a way which had, until now, been completely alien to her.

'You worry too much, Maggie.'

'But I'm not . . . that way inclined,' she finished, despising herself for her own coyness.

'Really?' Janine arched a disbelieving eyebrow.

'Yes! I mean, no! You know what I mean, Janine, you're just being deliberately obtuse.'

Janine put down her empty mug on a coaster on the coffee table between them. To Maggie's confusion, she leaned across and dropped a dry, sisterly kiss on her forehead.

'The lady doth protest too much,' she smiled mischievously before collecting up her bag and making for the door. She turned as she reached it. 'You should lighten up a little, Maggie, tune in to your innermost desires. It'll be all right, you'll see. No, don't get up. I can see myself out.'

She disappeared though the door with a languid wave, leaving Maggie staring after her in confusion.

It was two weeks before Maggie felt up to returning to the club. Janine had been working away from the office and she found it a relief not to have her around for a while. It had taken all her willpower not to wince every time she sat down and all her presence of mind to keep her attention on her work and off the growing ache between her legs.

After the Jefferson Company fiasco, Maggie had received a rocket, followed by a written warning from her immediate boss. Since then she had tried to keep her head down, working late and coming in early to make up for lost time. After two weeks of this punishing regime, she felt she had earned an evening off so she left work and headed straight for Lady's Lane.

The first person she saw as she went into the gym was Alexander. He was crouched by the rowing machine, adjusting something in its mechanism. Maggie felt her legs turn to water as he glanced up and his startlingly blue eyes met hers across the room. Slowly, he rose to his feet and smiled at her, beckoning her over.

'Ready for a workout, Maggie?' he asked her, his voice like warm honey dripping over her finely tuned nerves.

She sank onto the rowing machine he had just been adjusting, and tried not to shiver in response to the touch of his warm hand which rested lightly on her shoulder. There were two other women in the room, Tina she recognised from the Exhibition Room on her second visit and an overweight blonde who was making heavy work of the bench press. Tina nodded politely to her before going back to her sit ups.

To Maggie's surprise, Alexander showed no inclination to leave her side as she began to exercise. He stopped her to reposition her feet and the touch of his fingers against her ankles sent little sparks of electricity rushing up her calves.

God, but he was beautiful! No matter how many times she saw him, Maggie never failed to be moved by the satisfying symmetry of his features, the strength of his perfectly muscled body which glowed bronze with a healthy, animal sheen.

She tried to concentrate on the exercise, but as her pulse rate quickened, so did the tempo of her desire for him. Suddenly, she wanted nothing more than to be wrapped in his arms and to feel the powerful thud of his heartbeat against hers.

He indicated with a nod that she should finish rowing and move onto the next machine. As she stood, Maggie stumbled against him. Alexander's strong arms came around her and for a second she allowed herself to lean against him, closing her eyes to savour the sensation. She loved the way he smelled, a unique combination of musk and citrus, As he steadied her, she could feel the raw strength of him which was confined by the velvet smooth texture of his skin.

Realising that she was prolonging the moment just a little too obviously, Maggie blushed and moved on. As she took her place on the leg spreader, she could not resist a glance up at him through her lashes. She sucked in her breath as she saw he was watching her, his bright blue eyes hooded, his firm, sensual lips twisted into a half smile.

There was something about that smile that sent a jolt of delicious anticipation through her. He turned away then to attend to the blonde who had reached the end of the circuit and Maggie tried to concentrate on the exercise. It wasn't easy. Every time she looked up, Alexander was in her line of vision.

From every angle he looked magnificent, every line and plane of his well sculpted body visible through the uniform of tight black shorts and T-shirt which was cut away at the shoulders. His golden blonde hair was shaved at the nape of his neck and around his ears, worn longer on the top where it was thick and strong, inviting her to run her fingers through it.

The door of the gym opened and Tristan stepped through. He greeted Alexander cheerfully and made a point of speaking to each of the club members in turn.

'I'll be off then,' Alexander said.

Maggie's dismay must have been written all over her face for Alexander smiled slightly as he glanced over at her. She watched him covertly as he picked up a towel and strode out of the gym, through a door marked 'Private'.

She waited a few moments until Tristan's back was turned and the other women were engrossed in their own routines before slipping quietly through the door after Alexander.

7

Maggie found herself in a narrow corridor, white walled with a terracotta tiled floor. At the end was a swing door with a round window and a notice proclaiming *Strictly Private – Staff Only Beyond This Point*. She hesitated for a moment, then, remembering Alexander's smile and the promise it held, she pushed the door open.

She was in a changing room, obviously used by the trainers if the names on the lockers were anything to go by. First names only, Judd, Tristan, Dean, Bruno. The one marked Alexander stood open. The atmosphere in the windowless room was close in spite of the air extractor fans which buzzed discreetly around her. She could hear running water and walked toward its source.

Rounding the corner, she could see Alexander's naked body through the glass shower screen in the corner. He had his back to her, and the steam swirling around in the cubicle obscured her view of him. Quickly stripping off her clothes, Maggie stepped into the shower with him.

His movements stilled as he felt her presence, but he showed no surprise as he turned to face her. Maggie smiled tentatively and stepped forward, the tips of her breasts almost touching his wet chest in the close confines of the shower.

His chest was completely hairless, so smooth she wondered if he shaved it. Almost shyly, she ran her hands over it and down his arms. The light hairs there tickled her fingertips. Alexander did not respond to her touch, watching impassively as she reached for the shower gel and squirted a generous portion onto her hands.

He stood, statue still as she began to lather his chest and shoulders, moulding the finely drawn muscles of his arms with her hands until he was entirely covered in thick, white suds from the waist up. Only then did she divert her attention downwards to his insultingly unaroused penis.

To her surprise, it barely responded to her careful soaping. Rinsing it off, she dropped to her knees and began to run it gently back and forth between her palms. He was circumcised, the exposed glans soft and vulnerable at the end of an unexpectedly long and slender stem. Lifting it in her hand, Maggie brought her lips to the tip.

She gasped as Alexander suddenly grabbed her by the elbows and hauled her back to her feet. He looked grim, his thick, blond brows drawn together in a frown that completely transformed his normally friendly face. Her actions had obviously displeased him in some way, but he didn't say a word as he gently, but insistently turned her round.

Suddenly unsure of herself, Maggie held her shoulders tense as he began to soap them. She had forgotten how clever his fingers were and she soon felt a delicious languor invade her limbs. Without realising she was moving, she leaned back against him.

There was no mistaking that he was erect now, the slim, hard rod pressed into the small of her back, pointing up her spine. Perhaps he preferred not to be touched, maybe he got his kicks from arousing others, Maggie thought dreamily as his soapy hands described big, slow circles on her full breasts.

She gasped as he suddenly tweaked her hardening nipples, pinching them almost painfully before turning his attention to the wet curls between her legs. All rational thought fled as he meticulously soaped each tender fold of flesh, lingering almost lovingly on her burgeoning clitoris. Her legs felt weightless as she leaned against him and gave herself up to the sensation of his soapy wet fingers against her slippery flesh leaves.

Working up a richer lather, Alexander began to soap the twin orifices of her vagina and anus, pushing the suds deep inside her so that she felt stuffed with delicate, air filled bubbles.

'Oh!'

She groaned as he reached for the showerhead and directed the spray between her legs. The water cascaded over the eager nub before he redirected it upwards. Maggie's knees buckled as she felt the surge of warm water bubble up inside her and pour out again down the insides of her thighs.

Alexander thwarted her attempts to touch herself, pulling her arms behind her back by the elbows and growling, close to her ear, 'Oh no you don't. Come with me.'

He turned off the water and wrapped a thick, white towel round his waist. Maggie took the identical towel he offered her and wound it sarong style, under her arms. Wordlessly, she followed him as he padded through the shower area and headed for double pine doors at the far end of the changing rooms. As he opened them, thick, hot steam billowed out, enveloping them in its heavy, fragrant heat.

Once inside the sauna, Alexander bolted the doors behind them. Maggie felt a curious sensation curl in the pit of her stomach as he turned towards her.

'Sit,' he ordered tersely.

It was against Maggie's nature to obey such an imperiously issued command, but she did it none the less, bruising the backs of her knees against the edge of the slatted pine seat as she stumbled against it. She watched Alexander warily as he paced the small, square room, his expression masked by steam.

Her eyes widened in alarm as he suddenly opened a cupboard and took something out. He handed the object to her, watching her closely as she examined it. It was a small switch, the wooden handle about six inches long from which a handful of what looked like horsehair dangled in long, spindly strands.

'Have you ever used one of these, Maggie?' Alexander asked coldly.

She shook her head, unable to take her eyes off the sinister looking object in her hands..

'In a proper sauna, you would use one of these to beat yourself. It's supposed to increase the circulation.'

He took it from her and examined it minutely, running the tip of his forefinger along the handle and dangling the ends of the horsehair against his palm.

'It's a clever little device, made to redden the skin, not to break it. Yet it packs quite a punch. Hold out your hand and I'll show you.'

Reluctantly, Maggie offered him her hand, palm upward. Alexander smiled slightly, then he flicked the switch across Maggie's palm. He watched her face intently as she snatched it back and curled her fingers over the stinging weal. The sudden pain had taken her breath away and she looked up at Alexander through eyes welling with tears.

'That hurt!' she protested croakily.

'Good. I have to teach you a lesson, Maggie darling. A lesson about trespassing where you have no business and touching a man without an invitation.'

He watched as she absorbed his words and the incredulity and horror crossed her face.

'What . . .? You wouldn't dare!'

Maggie flinched away as Alexander advanced on her, cowering against the warm wall of the sauna as he dropped down on his haunches in front of her. She felt unsure of herself, frightened even, and she did not like the feeling one bit.

'Wouldn't I?' he whispered huskily. 'Aren't you just a little bit curious, Maggie?'

She shook her head even while the invidious thought formed itself in her head that, yes, she would like to know how it would feel to entrust herself completely to this hypnotically powerful stranger.

He laughed, suddenly and kissed her. It was a kiss of such sweet tenderness that Maggie relaxed, all the tension flowing out of her as he tasted the sweet honey of her lips. She was barely aware that he was gradually compelling her to sink to her knees onto the hard, damp floor before him. She jumped as she felt the scratchy stroke of the switch across the backs of her thighs.

'Trust me, Maggie. Take your punishment well and you'll earn a reward.'

His voice was like silk, easing over her trembling limbs as he coaxed her onto her hands and knees in front of him and slowly peeled away her towel. She felt exposed, horribly vulnerable as her breasts hung heavily downwards. She could feel Alexander's eyes on them even before he reached down and squeezed them in his large hands.

'Beautiful,' he murmured, 'like two great udders just waiting to be milked.'

He swung them slightly as he released them and Maggie watched them move ponderously from side to side, unable to tear her eyes away. A wave of shame, the like of which she had never before experienced, washed over her as Alexander slapped them sharply on the underside and her nipples hardened visibly in response.

'You see – I knew you'd like it,' he whispered, close to her ear.

He slapped her breasts again and she moaned softly.

'No!' She jumped as he suddenly grabbed her chin and brought her face up to his. 'I haven't given you permission to enjoy this, bitch! If I find any hint of wetness between your rampant thighs you'll regret it – do you understand?'

Maggie nodded, tears welling in her eyes as she realised that she was already moist, she was becoming aroused by the control Alexander was exerting over her despite her shame and fear.

'Crawl across the room and show me you're dry,' he barked.

Maggie began slowly, concentrating on putting one hand, one knee before the other for fear of falling flat on her face.

'Arse high!'

Her arms and legs were shaking so much she was afraid they wouldn't be able to hold her weight as she pushed her bottom out and up, sure that the gathering fluid between her legs would be plain to his suspicious eyes. Her breasts and knees scraped the wooden floor and she was grateful when she reached the other side of the room.

'I might have known!' His voice was hard, mocking her as he reached down and dipped his finger between her legs, then held it up in front of her heated face so that she see the evidence of her own arousal glistening on it.

She resisted as he pressed it against her lips, giving in with a groan of defeat as he pushed past her teeth and forced her to lick her own love juice from his finger.

'You know what this means, don't you?' he said silkily. 'You want me to punish you, don't you? Say it.'

'No!'

'Yes. You've been a bad, bad girl, Maggie, you know that, don't you? You deserve to be whipped for your lewd behaviour.'

'No! Yes! Oh . . .!'

Maggie cried out as the first stroke of the switch came down on her raised buttocks, swiftly followed by another beside it. Alexander waited for her to catch her breath before delivering a third blow, careful, it seemed to avoid the spot where it landed before.

After only a dozen or so strokes, Maggie's bottom felt as if it was on fire. She was aware of every square inch of her skin and hot tears ran swiftly down her face, plopping into a pool on the floor in front of her. The heat of the sauna clogged her nose and throat, making it hard to breathe and her sex burned in sympathy with her bottom.

'No, please! No more!' she sobbed.

Miraculously, Alexander paused. She felt the gentle touch of his lips against her inflamed skin, soothing her. The burning sensation mellowed into a warm glow as he caressed her flaming cheeks with one hand, smoothing her hair with another.

Maggie had a sudden, irresistibly strong urge to touch herself, to release the pent up tension which had been building in her straining clitoris.

'That's right,' Alexander crooned, helping her into a more comfortable position, 'touch yourself, baby, let me see you come.'

Maggie closed her eyes against him, concentrating instead on the building pressure deep inside her. Leaning against the bench which ran around the room, she opened her legs wide and rubbed her hot fingers around the slick, soft flesh of her vulva. Her clitoris had slipped its hood and quivered eagerly towards the familiar touch of her fingers.

Circling her middle finger around it once, twice, three times, Maggie felt the beginnings of an orgasm start at her core.

'Open your eyes,' Alexander commanded and she obeyed

instantly, holding his intense blue gaze as the waves began to radiate out from her clitoris and she tapped it hard with her forefinger with an increasingly frantic rhythm.

'That's right, baby, make it come, let it go . . . push.'

'Ah! I'm coming! I'm coming!' she yelled, half in triumph, half in anguish as her climax pulsed through her, more intense then she could ever remember, before she collapsed forward into Alexander's waiting arms.

'Ssh,' he crooned, stroking her hair as she calmed down, 'it's all right. You were terrific, Maggie. Just as I knew you would be.'

He licked at the corners of her eyes, tasting the salt of her tears before lifting her up and carrying her out of the sauna.

Antony was ploughing his way through a pile of paperwork when Alexander burst into the room. He took one look at the younger man's flushed, intent face and knew what he wanted. In spite of himself, he felt an answering need stir in his groin.

'You're looking a bit flushed, Alex. Something wrong?'

Alexander ignored him, merely unzipping his trousers and releasing an enormous erection.

'Shut up, Antony, and suck me,' he snapped.

Antony considered telling him to suck himself but already a film of lust was obscuring his reason and he obligingly sank to his knees. His jaw ached, the back of his throat closing up in protest as Alexander mercilessly thrust into his mouth. He was relieved when at last the thick, milky fluid flowed and lubricated his throat.

Afterwards, Alexander zipped his trousers without a word and disappeared into the kitchen, leaving Antony feeling piqued. Ungrateful little sod, using him like that! His own arousal gradually ebbed away leaving a dull, gnawing ache in his balls. He slumped on the sofa and fumed.

'Here – I've made you coffee.'

'Big bloody deal,' Antony growled as he took the mug from him.

He stiffened as Alex sat down beside him and slung a sympathetic arm round his shoulder.

'Don't sulk, Tony – I'll make it up to you.'

'Huh.'

'OK, you sulk and I won't tell you who I've just reduced to putty in my hands.'

Antony was instantly interested, quarrel forgotten.

'Maggie?'

'That's right. Well? That's what you wanted, wasn't it?'

Antony grinned.

'How did she take it?'

Alexander made a rocking motion with one hand, palm down.

'Tricky to start with, but I didn't hear any complaints when I saw her to her car. Janine's been pestering me to set something up between her and Maggie, but apparently Maggie's not been too keen. I think if I was there though . . . maybe I could even get it on film.'

'Terrific. How soon can we put our proposition to her?'

'Wait until after this gig with Janine and see how she reacts to that. I shouldn't mention it yet though – she's probably feeling a bit bewildered right now.'

Maggie was feeling more than bewildered, she was devastated by what she had allowed Alexander to do to her. Every fibre of her rational being told her she had sold out. Yet the memory of his lovingly mocking voice and the feel of his hands, alternately punishing and soothing, told her that she would gladly repeat the exercise.

Lying wakeful in her lonely bed, she relived the experience

moment by moment, analysing her reactions, marvelling at how expertly he had manipulated her. And all without any gain in terms of pleasure to himself. But the most curious thing of all was that, while she had, at times, felt real fear, she had also, paradoxically, felt incredibly safe with him. As if she trusted him to protect her from the very punishment he was meting out. It was all very confusing.

The following morning she was woken by the ring of the doorbell. Ambling drowsily to see who it was, she was surprised to find a huge bunch of red roses waiting for her. After she had signed for them and closed the door on the messenger, she opened the accompanying card. Her heart seemed to skip a beat as she read, *Until the next time – love, Alexander.*

The next time! Maggie was torn between wanting to crush the roses to her breast and throwing them, still in the cellophane, into the bin. They were too beautiful to throw away, so she arranged them between two vases which she placed in opposite corners of the living room.

She was disappointed to find that they were hothouse roses, completely without scent. Like sex without love, she thought suddenly, yet no less beautiful because they weren't perfumed. Again, like sex without love, she smiled ruefully. What the hell, she had joined the Black Orchid Club with a view to expanding her sexual horizons, surely she wasn't going to allow her first experience of a little mild S & M put her off?

Janine was back at work now and Maggie more than ever got the impression that the girl was hiding something. Yet she seemed to be actively avoiding Maggie, as if she had taken the hint after all and had decided that to pursue her would be a waste of time.

A week to the day after the incident with Alexander, a parcel arrived at the office addressed to Maggie. She sensed Bob's curious eyes on her as she laid it on her desk and was unsurprised when Janine appeared in the doorway.

'Presents at the office? Who's the new admirer, Maggie?'

Maggie muttered something non-committal and waited until she was alone before opening the box. For some reason her fingers trembled as she broke the seal and lifted the lid. The contents were shrouded in fine tissue paper on top of which was a square white card inscribed with Alexander's bold script.

'*Wear this for me*,' she read, '*Tomorrow evening – and I'll promise you a night to remember!*' Underneath he had written '*PTO*' so she flipped the card over. On the back he had written, in capital letters, '*TRUST ME?*'

Not on your life! she thought wryly. Very slowly, she peeled back the tissue paper. She gasped as the contents were revealed. What she had expected she wasn't sure – lacy undies, maybe even a dress, but not *this*!

Gingerly, she fingered the black latex material before pulling it out to see what it was. A body suit, soft and supple in finely seamed rubber, lined with red silk. There were studs positioned around the breasts and crotch and as she examined it more closely she realized that these could be snapped apart to release the flaps which were fastened over those areas.

Maggie stifled the urge to giggle. Surely he didn't seriously expect her to wear this thing? Out of the corner of her eye she noticed Bob craning his neck to get a look at what she was holding and she stuffed the ludicrous garment back into its box and shoved it under her desk, out of sight, though she was exquisitely conscious of its presence for the rest of the day.

The following day was a Saturday and Maggie allowed herself the luxury of sleeping until nine. After shopping and dealing with the routine chores around the house she cooked herself a light lunch and prepared to catch up on some paperwork. The white box with the kinky underwear inside it was pushed firmly to the back of her wardrobe, but her mind kept skittering back to it at the most unexpected moments.

It wouldn't hurt to try it on in the privacy of her own bedroom, just for a laugh, to see how she looked. Then she could go to the club tonight and return it to Alexander, telling him that it simply wasn't her scene.

She thought about it while she wallowed in a decadently hot, scented bath, her wet hair piled high on her head, covered by a shower cap. The water caressed her skin as she moved gently under it, enjoying the sensation. She was still thinking about it as she dried her hair and dressed it in a high top-knot in a style far more elaborate than she normally wore.

Carefully smoothing base make-up and a dusting of powder over her face, she selected a dark, smoky-grey shadow for her eyes and startlingly red lipstick and nail polish. The lipstick made her lips look more full, ripe. It wasn't until her meticulously painted finger and toe nails were dry and she had pulled on sheer black silk hold-ups that Maggie took the box out of the wardrobe.

In the harsh electric light, the latex rubber looked shiny, wet. She rubbed her hands over it and found she liked the feel of it, holding it to her face to better absorb the distinctive smell. It was difficult to put on and she had to wriggle into it, easing it up over her hips and breasts until she could slip her arms through the straps and position them on her slender shoulders.

The silk-lined rubber felt warm against her bare, perfumed skin and she found, to her surprise, that she liked the feeling of constriction. The bodice held her in tightly, like a corset. Maggie turned slowly toward the full-length mirror in the corner of the room and gasped at what she saw.

She hardly recognised herself. The bodice had nipped in her

waist to an impossible degree, pushing her breasts up and together so that they spilled seductively over the top of the garment like two ripe melons. Her long legs were shown to advantage by the high-cut legs, her pale skin vulnerable against the uncompromising black of the rubber.

This was a garment which was meant to be worn purely for sex and, encased in it, she looked as if she was made for it too. Hardly taking her eyes off the mirror, Maggie slipped into high-heeled black leather mules which lengthened her legs still further.

It seemed a shame to cover herself with a conventional dress, but she could hardly drive to the club looking like this. The black lycra tube she pulled over it was hardly more decent but at least she no longer looked like a walking sex toy. She smiled as she anticipated the look on Alexander's face when he saw she was wearing his present. Surely he would reward her with the use of his delectable body in the face of such devotion?

The drive to the club took on the guise of an erotic journey as the rubber pulled against Maggie's skin with the slightest movement. Changing gear became something to look forward to and by the time she drew into the car-park, the silk gusset was already damp against her sex and Maggie was primed ready for action.

As she stepped into the bar, Antony came over to greet her. His eyes slid along the length of her body and Maggie wondered if he knew what she was wearing underneath. The idea gave her an erotic charge and she smiled confidently at him.

Alexander is expecting you,' he told her, 'this way.'

He took her by the elbow and steered her toward the Exhibition Room. Maggie felt a *frisson* of apprehension as they headed, not for a discreet cubicle as she had expected, but toward the main doors, into the room itself.

The bed in the centre was canopied and covered in fine white lace. Alexander stood to one side, beside a tripod onto which he was fixing a movie camera. Maggie barely registered his presence for, as the door closed behind her and Antony, she saw a movement in the shadows and a woman stepped into the light.

She was wearing a similar bodice to the one Maggie had on, only she had completed the ensemble with black, thigh-high boots, fishnet stockings and a storm trooper's leather cap, the peak pulled down low on her forehead. Her eyes were hidden by a small, black leather mask. In one hand, she held a long, evil-looking black leather whip which she tapped impatiently against her thigh.

Maggie's eyes skittered nervously around the room to the mirrors which reflected the scene a dozen times around her and wondered how many eyes were watching. Antony squeezed her elbow and gave her a little push toward the bed. The woman spoke and Maggie's blood ran cold as she recognised the voice.

'Don't worry, Maggie, darling, I'm not going to hurt you – much.'

Maggie's lips moved numbly.

'Janine . . .!'

8

Maggie's first thought was to turn tail and run. At a signal from Alexander, both Janine and Antony melted into the shadows and Alexander stepped forward and took her by the hand.

'Don't look so worried,' he whispered, putting his arm around her and leading her into the soft spotlight.

Maggie blinked as she stepped into the diffused glare. She could no longer see beyond the reach of the lights, it was as if she and Alexander were alone in the room with only the lace covered bed before them. Allowing herself to be coaxed down onto it, she pressed herself against Alexander's lean muscled body as he began to kiss her, slowly at first, then more hungrily as she responded.

He was wearing a peach-skin soft, silk shirt in sky blue tucked loosely into black denim 501's. Maggie could feel the heat of him through it as she held onto his shoulders and she delighted in the soft rub of silk against his glossy skin. She wanted the kiss to go on forever, it turned her legs to water and washed away all the doubts invading her mind.

No one had ever kissed her like Alexander did. With her eyes closed, she clung to him as if she were drowning and he were a life raft. At that moment she knew, with extraordinary clarity, that she would do anything for this man, anything at all he might ask of her.

'Do you trust me?' he murmured, his words tickling over her swollen lips.

Maggie could not make her mouth work, her lips felt heavy, bruised. It was all she could do to nod her head.

'You see the camera?'

She nodded again without opening her eyes.

'Do you know what that is for, Maggie? It's so that you can see how beautiful you really are. So that you won't forget that you are mine to command. Do you understand? Look at me, Maggie.'

She opened her eyes with difficulty and saw that his brilliant blue eyes were boring into hers. Gazing at him was dizzying, hypnotic and she nodded again, dazed. His smile warmed her and the last vestiges of fear fell away.

Feeling a hand at her neck, she turned to find Antony on the bed behind her. Now here was a body she knew well and she welcomed the tender kiss he placed on her soft lips.

Antony wrapped his arms around Maggie and pulled her closer to him. He could taste Alexander on her lips and his shaft responded to the well loved stimulus, leaping with delight in his loose grey chinos.

Someone turned on the sound system and the haunting throaty voice of a faceless jazz/blues singer curled around them. He felt Maggie relax against him as he lay her down on the bed. Running his hand over her body, he could feel the lycra move over her bare skin, in erotic counterpoint to the latex rubber encasing her beneath.

Antony felt Maggie tremble as he eased the tight skirt up over her hips. The strip of soft skin at the tops of her thighs looked very white against the black of nylon and rubber which bordered it. He ran the fingers of one hand round the edge of her stocking top, bringing the skin up in little goosebumps.

Covering her pubic mound with one large hand, he squeezed gently, imagining the hot, pulsating wetness encased within the supple, soft rubber. A spasm passed across Maggie's face as he continued to squeeze rhythmically, his fingers inching their way into the cleft of her bottom.

He felt a tap on his shoulder and turned to see Janine's impatient face pressed close to his. He nodded, removing his hand reluctantly and taking the black silk scarf she offered him. Maggie started as he tied it tightly round her eyes and he gentled her with his lips as she began to murmur in protest. As he kissed her, drawing her tongue voluptuously into his mouth, he felt her resistance slowly ebbing away.

She raised her arms and bottom obligingly as he removed her dress and he planted a soft kiss at the corner of her mouth. Drawing back to run his gaze over the length of her body, he narrowed his eyes appreciatively. She presented a delectable sight, her long, black-clad legs pressed tightly together, her white arms still raised above her tense face. He obeyed an impulse to kiss the tender hollow of her smooth armpit and she shivered convulsively.

Antony reminded himself with difficulty that his role was to prepare her for Janine, waiting impatiently in the shadows. Slowly, he began to roll down her stockings, first one leg, then the other, until she lay, naked, but for the black latex bodice which clung lovingly to her womanly form.

The rubber gleamed dully under the diffused spotlight, her restrained breasts swelling, creamy white, spilling over the top. Antony reached forward and ran the tip of his forefinger along the edge of the join of the flap over one breast. Removing it completely, he pressed the top of her breast so that the swell was forced downward, through the peephole.

Her aureole glowed a dark pinkish brown, the nipple standing proud, poking obscenely through. Antony tweaked it, rolling it between his thumb and forefinger and tugging gently until it grew longer and harder. After repeating the process with the other side, he turned his attention to the studs around her crotch.

Until now, Maggie had lain quietly, only moaning softly when he handled her breasts. As she felt his fingers snapping open each stud, one by one, she whispered.

'Oh no! Please . . . please . . . take away the blindfold.'

'Ssh. It's OK. Feel, Maggie, just feel. You don't need to see.'

The dark, thick curls of her mons tickled his fingers as he eased the silk lined rubber gusset away from between her thighs. He sighed, breathing in the hot, honeyed scent of her. As he had expected, she was wet, dripping with anticipation. It was all he could do to stop himself from pressing his face against that warm, moist centre of pleasure.

Janine handed him more scarves. She was impatient to begin, her lust making her tremble as she waited for him to continue. Antony ran the palm of his hand soothingly along the inside of Maggie's arm until he grasped her wrist. Her hand curled into a fist as he bound her to the corner of the bedhead.

Once her arms had been secured, he repeated the procedure with her ankles, tying them to the endposts. He stood back to admire his handiwork. She lay, spreadeagled and helpless, on the white lacy covers like a sacrificial offering. Her nipples and vulva were exposed, vulnerable, her soft mouth slightly open, the full bottom lip trembling visibly as she waited for something to happen.

Reluctantly, Antony stepped back and let Janine take over.

Janine gazed down on the helpless woman on the bed and felt a rush of adrenalin. She had dreamed of this; Maggie, tied and blindfolded, completely in her hands. Maggie, whose treacherous mouth had denied the attraction that her body demonstrated all too well.

She swooped on the quivering lips, fastening her mouth over Maggie's as she squirmed in protest. Her mouth tasted sweet, hot, and Janine closed her eyes for a moment to savour it before drawing back.

Although she could not see them in the darkness, she knew that each of the two way mirrors concealed a watcher and she smiled slowly, playing to the audience. Making a show of sucking her forefinger, she leaned across Maggie and circled it around one tumescent nipple. The skin of Maggie's breast shrunk away from her touch and she increased the pressure.

'No, you don't, my darling,' she crooned, 'don't be coy. Everyone knows you like it. This gives you away!'

She passed her finger along the crease of Maggie's exposed vulva, dipping it into the welling moisture within. She smiled as Maggie groaned and she sensed her shame.

Bending down, she drew a black bag from under the bed and selected a switch from inside. It was tiny, no more than six inches long with thin, feathery strands which kissed the skin as she trailed it slowly across Maggie's breasts.

Maggie gasped as Janine suddenly struck a light blow on the underside of one nipple, swiftly followed by a blow to its twin. Janine waited until the constrained mounds stopped quivering before she recommenced the punishment, whipping the straining nubs until they glowed, bright red and hard.

She saw with satisfaction that Maggie's mouth was twisted out of shape with the effort of keeping in her cries, her lips wet and slack as she took great, gasping gulps of air through her mouth. She bent to take one tortured nipple into her mouth.

It was hot as she lathed it with her tongue, bathing it in saliva and sucking it hungrily. Maggie groaned as Janine transferred her attention to the other nipple, grazing it with her teeth and tugging, none too gently.

Alexander removed the camera from its stand and drew closer, focusing on the action of Janine's tongue. Playing to the camera, she took the nipple between her teeth and pulled, stretching it to the point of tension when Maggie could no longer hold back a cry of pain. Then she let it go, watching through hooded eyes as it sprang back into shape, the flesh shivering as it did so.

Alexander withdrew as Janine walked to the head of the bed and cradled Maggie's head in her palms, massaging her temples with her thumbs.

'Does that feel good? I'm going to make you feel good, Maggie, I'm going to show all those people watching us how much you enjoy making it with another woman.'

'No . . .!'

'Oh yes! And you *will* enjoy it, darling. I promise.'

She returned to the bag beside the bed and selected a long, springy switch with a tiny, rubber paddle attached to the end. Tapping it against Maggie's cheek, she let her feel the series of rapid blows caused by one flick of the wrist. She watched the confusion pass across Maggie's face and smiled.

It was easy to imagine how the other woman was feeling – bound and blindfolded with no way of knowing what was about to be done to her. Janine could almost taste her fear and the flavour of it fed her already raging desire.

Climbing up onto the bed, she straddled Maggie, taking her weight on her knees either side of her waist, keeping her back to her. She paused for a moment to savour the sight before her. The muscles in the tethered legs were held taut with anticipation, the exposed vulva a shocking slash of colour against the black latex.

The hairy outer labia were pulled back, concealed by the constricting black rubber, leaving the vulnerable inner lips exposed. Maggie's unwilling arousal was evident from the sheen of moisture clinging to the tender pink skin and the way in which the swelling clitoris had already slipped its hood. It stood proud, the hard nub inviting attention.

Janine ran her middle finger delicately along the edge of the lips in a light, tickling caress before bringing it up to slowly pleasure the willing bud. Maggie's breathing quickened and moisture began to seep out of her, making her juicy cavity pout invitingly.

Glancing up to make sure that Alexander was still filming, Janine waited until the muscles in Maggie's thighs began to tense as she reached the brink. Picking up the little rubber paddle, she tapped it sharply against the hard bud.

Maggie was unable to hold back the cry of pain as the exquisite, tiny blows rained down on her straining nub. She writhed on the bed, desperately trying to escape the merciless instrument of torture and Janine's cruel fingers which were holding her open. Janine slipped the first and second fingers of one hand around the throbbing clitoris and squeezed it so that it stood high, unable to escape the punishing, light blows.

Faster and faster the paddle came down on that tenderest of places until Maggie cried out in a sound that was part ecstasy, part denial. Janine swooped and took the pulsing bud between her teeth, suckling it as it throbbed and twitched and at last was still.

Janine climbed off the bed and stood, watching impassively as Maggie regained control.

'Well, my sweet, you do love it, don't you? Let's see what else we have to entertain us.'

She reached into the bag and withdrew a large, hard dildo. Antony gasped in the shadows and Janine smiled. He had a good memory! Leaning over Maggie, she stroked the cold instrument down the side of her face, laughing as Maggie shrank away from it.

'Oh, it gets better!' she whispered.

Turning on the power, she held it as it purred gently down Maggie's face.

'No! Oh please, no!'

Janine turned it off.

'Oh yes! But you have to earn it, sweet Maggie.'

Removing her own briefs, Janine kicked them aside and climbed back onto the bed. Resuming her position, she straddled Maggie once again, this time lowering her own moist softness over Maggie's face. At first the unwilling lips forced against her open vulva remained protestingly still. Then, as if deciding that she had no choice, her tongue tentatively pushed through her clenched teeth and she began to lick gingerly.

Janine arched her back and closed her eyes. Her fingers found Maggie's tender sex and rubbed slowly up and down until, gradually, lips and fingers were in unison. Once she had started, Maggie seemed to know instinctively what to do, lapping at Janine with a vigour which almost approached enthusiasm.

She learned fast. When Janine dipped her fingers into Maggie's hot honeyed vagina, Maggie's tongue mimicked the action; when Janine rubbed her hard clitoris slowly, Maggie's tongue swiftly followed. By moving her own fingers, she could direct the novice beneath her into an orchestrated symphony of lovemaking. It was almost like making love to herself, only this was better than masturbation any day!

A fine sheen of sweat began to film her body as Janine felt the first flush of impending orgasm approach. Oblivious now to the audience and the camera, Janine concentrated only on her own pleasure, rotating her hips on Maggie's flicking tongue whilst rolling her tender clitoris between her fingers.

As the first wave of her climax washed over her, Janine reached for the dildo and flicked the 'on' switch. Spreading

Maggie's pubic lips wide with the fingers of one hand, she held the vibrator at the gate of her sex. Slowly, she eased the buzzing machine into her body, working it in up to the hilt as her own orgasm overcame her and she collapsed exhausted, across the bed.

Maggie did not try to stem the tears of humiliation which ran in hot rivulets down her cheeks as she was led by a chain, naked but for the high-heeled mules and the studded leather collar round her neck. When the vibrator had been pulled from her convulsing body and the scarves removed, she had found herself alone with Alexander. There was no sign of either Janine or Antony in the now darkened room and the camera had been pulled away out of sight.

Alexander was silent as he helped her out of the tight rubber bodice, though his eyes looked unnaturally bright, as if he had a fever, and he fastened the collar around her neck attaching the chain.

Now they were going through the lounge bar. Maggie kept her eyes on the carpet and concentrated on putting one foot before the other as the hubbub of conversation ceased. Her cheeks burned with shame as everyone began to clap and she realised that a great many of those present had probably witnessed her humiliation.

She let out her pent up breath with a sigh of relief as they reached the sanctuary of the private lift. Alexander did not look at her as they travelled upward and she remained meekly silent. She could still taste Janine's feminine musk on her lips and tongue and a blush covered her naked skin as she recalled how she had enjoyed pleasuring her. Even the pain the other girl had inflicted on her had been sweet in the end. Her vulva ached as she moved forward, responding to Alexander's light tug on the chain when the lift door opened.

Antony and Janine were waiting for them in the lounge. Janine had obviously just stepped out of the shower. She had changed into a white, silky kimono, her pale blonde hair damp across her shoulders. She smiled slightly at Maggie as she caught her eye, and Maggie dropped her gaze, heat searing her skin.

Alexander led her over to the white leather sofa and made her sit, not on the soft cushions, but on the sheepskin rug in front of it. He looped the chain around the legs of the glass-topped coffee table, tethering her like a dog.

The doors to the cabinet housing the huge, flat screened television had been rolled back. A bottle of dry white wine stood uncorked, three glasses by its side. The apartment was warm, softly lit by several lamps placed strategically round the room.

Alexander poured the wine and, ignoring Maggie, handed Antony and Janine a glass. They sat together on the sofa, Janine between the two men. Alexander's black denim clad leg was lightly touching Maggie's bare shoulder. Without a word passing between them, Antony picked up the remote control and the TV screen flickered.

Maggie gasped as she was confronted by her own bound and blindfolded image. She felt curiously detached, removed somehow from the anonymous, sex-soaked figure which writhed uncontrollably on the lace-covered bed.

It was difficult to breathe as she watched Janine whipping her hard, wanton nipples, poking invitingly through the holes in the black latex body. She watched, mesmerised, as the camera zoomed in on her anguished face, panning to where Janine sucked greedily on her breasts, wincing with remembered pain as she pulled and let go.

Alexander held his glass to her lips and she drank deeply of the crisp, dry wine. She almost choked as her own vulva came into view, spread wide open, dripping with arousal, filling the screen.

'You see how lovely you are – so willing, Maggie, so deliciously succulent!'

Maggie felt a hot blush stain her body as Alexander's honeyed words caressed her ears. His breath was warm as it fanned her face, his lips tickling the tip of her ear. Incredibly, she felt the familiar throb begin between her legs as she watched, unable to drag her eyes away from the screen, as the little rubber paddle beat on her shamelessly straining clitoris. She had never seen that most intimate part of her at the moment of orgasm, and she could not prevent a little cry of distress from passing her lips.

Alexander used the chain attached to the collar round her neck to pull her head round so that he could kiss her. The kiss had no warmth in it and when he pulled his head away, Maggie felt as if she had been branded.

Turning her attention back to the screen, Maggie saw her own tongue darting in and out of Janine's spread sex-lips, a frown of intense concentration between her eyes. The camera lingered, for a moment, on Janine's rapturous face as she worked her hips back and forth over Maggie's mouth. Her eyes were closed, her head pulled back so that the soft white flesh of her throat was exposed in a tender, graceful arc.

For a moment, Maggie felt a rush of pure love for her and yearned to press her lips against the tiny pulse visible in her neck. Then the camera swung to Janine's hands and Maggie saw herself, spread lewdly open, the vibrating dildo held threateningly at the entrance to her sex.

She could feel it now, that cold, hard, foreign object as it violated her. And yet, even as she had abhorred the intrusion, her muscles had contracted around it, drawing it in deeper until it filled and stretched her, the final humiliation.

Maggie watched with increasing horror as she saw Antony help Janine from the bed and lead her away, leaving Maggie alone, tethered to the bed under the watchful eye of the camera, the monstrous dildo still vibrating wildly inside her. The last shot was a close up of her face, mouth wide open, contorted with rapture as orgasm after orgasm wracked her body.

9

There was absolute silence as the film finished and Antony turned off the television with the remote control. Maggie sat staring at the blank screen. Her lungs hurt in her chest, her breath emerging in short, sharp gasps as the image of herself which had just faded from the screen remained imprinted on her memory.

Never had she imagined she was capable of such total abandonment. It shocked her, even while she was excited by it. And to have let herself go to such a degree in front of an audience . . .

'You see, Maggie,' Alexander's throaty voice broke the silence, 'you were made for it.'

He laughed as she turned her stricken face towards him and ruffled her hair as if she was indeed a favourite pet. Maggie felt a rush of pure, unadulterated desire for him. It was his cock that she wanted to replace the cold, unyielding plastic of Janine's toy; his warm, masculine body she wanted to enclose and possess her.

Raising herself up on her knees, she shuffled round as far as the leash would allow, and, oblivious to Janine and Antony, pressed her face against his black denim-covered crotch. She could feel the hardness of him pushing against the stiff fabric as she nuzzled him in a mute plea.

Alexander laughed again and began to unbutton his fly. He was naked underneath and his white, slender shaft sprang suddenly up and slapped her across the face. Greedily, Maggie took it into her mouth and began to suck it hungrily. She felt it thicken and swell as she ran her tongue up and down the underside and round the smooth, circumcised tip.

She gasped as, suddenly, Alexander tangled his fingers in the hair at the back of her head and pulled her roughly away. Her eyes signalled her distress as he brought his face close to hers and said coldly,

'You didn't ask permission, did you?'

Maggie shook her head, tears starting in her eyes as the action pulled her hair at the roots. All reason seemed to have left her, she only wanted to feel him in her mouth again, draw him into her yearning body.

'Please . . .' she whispered.

Alexander bestowed one of his golden smiles on her and she basked in its warmth. Her spirits plummetted as he spoke.

'No, sweet Maggie, I think you've had enough for tonight. Don't be so greedy.'

He kissed the tip of her nose and let go his punishing grip on her hair. Gently, he pushed her away from him.

'I'll tell you what, as you've been so very good, I'll let you watch.'

Maggie frowned, not understanding, at first, what he meant. Following his gaze as he turned away from her, she saw that Antony and Janine were oblivious to them and were kissing passionately at the other end of the sofa. Janine's robe had fallen open to reveal her nakedness and Antony's large, sensitive hand kneaded her right breast as she pressed against him.

As she watched, they sank slowly onto the sheepskin rug, mouths still melded together as Antony shrugged off his shirt and Janine deftly dispensed with the fastening to his trousers. Maggie shifted uncomfortably as her own juices began to flow in empathy with Janine when Antony began to kiss her small, perfectly formed breasts.

Glancing at Alexander, she realised that he was watching, not Janine, but Antony. She tugged experimentally against the chain which bound her to the coffee table, but it held her fast. She did not dare to use her hands to untie herself and she sank back against the sofa, defeated.

The soft leather was warm against her bare skin, the silky, ticklish fur of the rug brushing against her swollen sex. She could not take her eyes off the couple not two feet away from her as their loveplay turned rougher, more urgent, the tender kisses turning into bites, the languorous caresses into mildly punishing scratches and pinches.

Maggie's mouth and throat felt dry and she gulped gratefully at the wine Alexander held against her lips. She watched jealously as Antony flipped Janine onto her stomach and raised her up onto all fours. Janine was sideways on to Maggie, so she had a clear view, in profile, of both her face and her bottom which she wiggled enticingly at Antony.

His erection bobbed in front of him as he scooped her up and turned her so that Maggie could see her pink, moisture-slicked sex beneath the tight, puckered hole of her bottom. Alexander suddenly sprang out of the seat and disappeared from the room.

Antony slipped his forefinger into Janine's open sex, inches away from Maggie's face, and Janine sat back slightly so that she was impaled on it, wriggling her bottom lewdly as Antony pushed it in and out teasingly. Alexander returned with a large, square mirror which he leaned against the television cabinet. It was strategically placed, for Maggie could now simultaneously see Janine's face and her rear, swaying like a cat on heat.

She watched with bated breath as Antony knelt between

Janine's outspread knees, poised to penetrate her. Placing his hands on Janine's hips to steady himself, he eased into her, closing his eyes in concentration as her silken sheath drew him in.

Maggie glanced at Janine's face reflected in the mirror as Antony began to thrust in and out of her. Her eyes were closed, her hair dishevelled, falling over her face. Perspiration stood out on her forehead and her mouth was slack, the pink tongue visible between the open lips.

Antony had leaned over Janine now, grabbing at her dangling breasts for balance. Maggie winced in sympathy as the large hands squeezed uncaringly, the fingers digging into the soft flesh. A movement behind Antony caught her eye and she looked up to find that Alexander was watching her.

He smiled at her beatifically as he slowly unbuttoned his 501s and allowed them to drop to his knees. Maggie's eyes opened wide as she realised what he was about to do. Her own neglected sex throbbed with disappointment as Alexander ran his hands lovingly over Antony's pumping buttocks.

He held a tube in one hand and as Maggie watched, he squeezed a generous portion of white cream into his palm. Unable to tear her eyes away, she watched as he applied it to the crease between Antony's buttocks, working it in carefully and lubricating the tight anal orifice concealed within.

Antony's face was tense, a study in concentration as he drove rhythmically into Janine from behind, barely breaking his stroke as Alexander took him. Maggie watched through a blur of frustrated tears as the scene being played before her rose to a crescendo.

Janine came first, loudly, shrieking as the sensations overcame her. Antony held her fast as she made to pull away from him, kneading her breasts cruelly in his hands to keep her still as his semen pumped into her convulsing body. Finally, he fell across her with a groan, crushing her under him on the rug as Alexander buggered him mercilessly, not letting up until his own climax had come, accompanied by a triumphant shout.

It seemed like a long time before anyone stirred. Alexander levered himself off Antony and turned away, pulling up his jeans as Antony finally realeased Janine. Able to breathe freely again at last, Janine lay prone, panting for a few minutes more. Then she too rose and dressed silently.

No one took any notice of Maggie as they dressed. Janine kissed Antony and Alexander. Only then did she and the two men turn and notice Maggie, still tethered to the coffee table, an unwilling, unfulfilled observer.

'We can't leave her like that,' Antony said to Alexander.

They came to sit down either side of her.

'Poor Maggie,' Alexander crooned, 'why don't you relieve yourself?'

For a moment, Maggie did not understand. Janine smiled at her, that self satisfied, cat-like smile, and went to fetch the large, square mirror. Maggie felt the heat rise in her cheeks as Janine held the mirror steady in front of her, kneeling down behind it and leaning her chin on the top so that she could still see Maggie. She shook her head as Antony and Alexander each took an ankle and, gently, but insistently, parted her legs.

'No! Oh no, please . . . I can't!'

'Ssh! Antony placed his lips against her ear. 'It's nothing. Just do it . . . do it for us.'

'Open your eyes, Maggie,' Alexander said sharply, and Maggie responded to the note of command in his voice.

She could see herself displayed in the mirror, her legs straight, held apart at the ankle by the two men whose golden heads were resting either side of her dark one. Her lewdly gaping vulva looked swollen and red, the tumescent pleasure-bud slipping clear of its hood even as she watched. There was a well of moisture at the lip of her vagina which slowly overflowed and dribbled into the crevice of her bottom.

Maggie swallowed convulsively as she contemplated what they wanted her to do. To bring herself to orgasm in front of so many hot, lustful eyes, the mirror ensuring that there was no escape from the spectacle.

'I . . . I can't!' she whispered.

'Of course you can, here,' Antony kissed her ear and, picking up her limp hand, pressed it against her labia.

The slightly sticky moisture bathed her fingers and they moved, almost of their own volition, along the tender, slippery creases between her legs. Everything in Maggie rebelled at the thought of debasing herself in such a way, yet she could no longer deny the jags of white hot pleasure throbbing at her core.

She felt Alexander's tongue, hot and wet in the whorls of her ears as she began to run her soaking finger either side of her inner lips. She watched, fascinated, in the mirror as her sex opened under her hand like a flower in the sun.

'Beautiful.'

Janine's hushed whisper barely impinged on her consciousness as she settled her back more comfortably against the sofa and dipped two fingers into her hot sheath. Her inner flesh rippled and sucked at her invasive fingers and she worked in another, then a fourth as her legs were spread wider and held slightly off the floor.

She felt hot, the hair on her head sticking to her forehead as someone eased a cushion under her bottom, raising it up so that she could see herself even better. The rose of her anus glistened as her juices overflowed and ran in viscous rivulets down her perineum and between her buttocks.

Uncaring now of the avid gaze of the others, Maggie withdrew her hand and began to circle her own anus with her forefinger. Pressing experimentally at the opening, she was shocked and excited when it yielded under the gentle pressure and she was able to slip the tip of her finger inside.

'Further,' a voice fluttered in her ear and she eased her finger in up to the first knuckle.

Feeling empty, she used the fingers of her other hand to fill her sex. She could feel her other finger through the thin wall between her vagina and her anal passage and she pushed it in further, the better to increase the unfamiliar, utterly incredible, sensation. Her neglected clitoris pulsed and she murmured in frustration.

A male hand reached down and gently removed her hands. She moaned in protest, until she realised that he had replaced the finger in her anus with his own, and a second set of male fingers obligingly penetrated her feminine orifice, leaving her own hands free to play with her quivering bud.

She could not hold on for much longer, sight and sensation were becoming too much. Stretching her labia apart with the fingers of one hand, she exposed her clitoris and pinched it hard between the finger and thumb of the other hand.

It was enough to tip her over. She felt filled to brimming as Antony and Alexander fingered her twin orifices as she rubbed her clitoris, bearing down with all her might until the sensations spiralled through her, so intense that, for an instant, she blacked out.

When she came to, Janine and Alexander had gone and she was lying in the crook of Antony's arm, her head cradled on his shoulder. He was stroking her hair tenderly and smiled down at her as she opened her eyes.

'All right?' he asked and she nodded, made speechless by an emotion very much like love.

She jumped as Alexander reappeared, but he too smiled at

her, dropping onto his haunches beside her and stroking the back of his forefinger down the side of her cheek. She watched dispassionately as he leaned across and kissed Antony, full on the lips.

Without another word, Antony picked her up and carried her to the bathroom where Alexander had run a warm, bubbly bath. Maggie sank gratefully into the silky water and lay in exhausted acquiescence as they washed her and dried her, smothering her in talcum powder before slipping an oversized nightshirt over her head as if she were a child.

Yawning, she realised it must be very late. She leaned against Alexander as they led her into the bedroom. It was dominated by a huge soft bed. Maggie crawled gratefully into the centre, smiling sleepily as she felt Antony and Alexander settle either side of her. She felt warm and safe . . . and loved. She smiled and snuggled into Antony's back as sleep claimed her.

Over breakfast in bed the following morning, Maggie felt as if all that had gone on the night before had been a dream. Yet here she was, sitting in bed with two men making her fair share of a mess with the warm, crumbly croissants Alexander had produced.

In the gentle light of morning there was no sign of the cold, controlling Alexander of the night before. He was relaxed, his beautiful face still softened by sleep as he watched Antony lazily. Antony seemed happy, talking desultorily about his plans for the weekend as he poured them all more coffee.

Maggie felt disorientated as she realised it was Sunday morning. She had no plans of her own and was inordinately pleased when Alexander suggested that she stay with them for the rest of the morning. They lounged companionably in bed until lunchtime and Maggie couldn't decide whether she was pleased or relieved that neither made a pass at her.

'Do you like your job, Maggie?' Antony asked unexpectedly.

'Of course,' she replied automatically, frowning as it hit her that her career had slipped in her order of priorities recently.

'Would you consider a change?'

She turned to Alexander, perplexed.

'Such as?'

'Antony has a proposition for you.'

Maggie looked questioningly at Antony and caught the tail end of the affectionate glance which passed between him and Alexander.

'I need an assistant,' he said, smiling at her.

'An assistant? You mean here, at the club?'

The idea would have been funny if she hadn't sensed the sudden watchfulness of Alexander beside her. Suddenly the relaxed atmosphere evaporated and Maggie felt a curious tension curl in the pit of her stomach. She was careful not to glance at Alexander as Antony went on.

'My present girl, Jackie, works behind the scenes. You won't have met her. She's leaving at the end of the month and I need a replacement.'

'And you think that *I'm* qualified for the job?' Maggie was incredulous.

'It's a live in post,' Antony told her, ignoring her disbelief. 'I think it would suit you.'

'Live in?' Maggie repeated stupidly.

She felt the heat of Alexander's body as he reached out and turned her away from Antony and towards him. As she had expected, his expression was intense and she shivered under his startlingly blue gaze.

'You'd be living here. With Antony and I.'

Maggie replayed the scene in her mind as she sat at her desk on Monday morning. After she had torn her gaze away from

Alexander, she had glanced at Antony for confirmation. He had smiled, nodding encouragingly as if it was the most normal thing in the world to ask a woman to move in with yourself and your male lover. Suddenly she had felt the urge to get out, to get away from their all pervasive presence.

She felt claustrophobic and she knew that, if she didn't step back from the situation and spend some time alone, she would have agreed to anything. Neither Antony nor Alexander had tried to pressure her when she had mumbled her excuses and got up. They both watched her lazily from the bed as she pulled on her clothes.

'I'd better go,' she'd told them awkwardly. 'Thanks for the offer. I do appreciate it, it's just . . . I need some time to think. I'll call in next week and let you know.'

Neither spoke. They both smiled at her and Antony blew her a kiss as she left, covered in confusion.

She hadn't been able to stop thinking about the strange offer since. For the rest of the day she had replayed the evening in her mind. The memory of her reluctant subjugation to Janine, the exhibitionistic tendencies she had never guessed she possessed, the frustration of being made to watch while Antony and Janine and Alexander . . . and the final humiliation of masturbating in front of them.

'Maggie? Maggie I'm beginning to wonder if you're with us these days!'

She jumped as Jim Thurlstone, her immediate boss, tapped her on the shoulder. Seeing him standing there, frowning down at her, she felt like a schoolgirl caught with her hands in her knickers. Mumbling an inadequate excuse, she took the file he handed to her and immersed herself, red faced, in the paperwork which she had allowed to pile up in her 'in' tray.

It wasn't that she hadn't had offers before, she mused the following afternoon. She had lived with a guy once, in fact, but two together? Her mind skittered off to the possibilities and she had to squeeze her thighs tightly together to stop the trembling which had started up between them.

To her profound relief, Janine had stayed out of her way. She didn't know how she would react to that knowing smile for she still hadn't quite come to terms with what had happened between them. Catching Bob's eye at the next desk, she tried to concentrate.

Her concentration span seemed to have shrunk to the point of extinction. She sighed as she sank back in her chair less than half an hour later. After the mess she'd made of the Jefferson job a few weeks before and her increasing distraction, she was aware that she was going to have to watch her back. Hers was a cut-throat industry and Bob, for one, would be more than happy to step into her shoes.

It came as no great surprise to her when she received a summons from on high not two days later. As she left the MD's office, she wondered with strange detachment, why she wasn't devastated. The phrase 'summarily dismissed' skittered through her mind, swiftly followed by the realisation that she didn't, in fact, really care.

She cleared her desk, working on autopilot and nodded courteously at Bob when he offered her his insincere condolences. Little sod was already eyeing her desk, probably trying to decide the best spot for his aspidistra. She grinned suddenly, startling him, and he scurried off muttering some excuse about having to keep his head down in the light of what had happened to her.

Janine came by with genuine concern in her voice.

'But Maggie, what will you do?'

'I don't know yet.'

Janine regarded her shrewdly.

'You don't seem that cut up about it.'

Maggie looked her squarely in the eye and smiled.

'I've had other offers,' she said airily, gathering up her belongings.

She started in surprise as Janine suddenly leaned forward and placed a restraining hand on her forearm.

'I know what you're thinking of, Maggie, but please – think very carefully before you commit yourself.'

'Oh?'

'Yes.' Janine removed her hand and frowned, seeming suddenly unsure of herself. 'I . . . I wouldn't like to see you hurt,' she said unexpectedly, her voice small.

Maggie thought of Janine's little black bag and what it contained and raised an ironic eyebrow at her. Janine had the grace to blush.

'I mean emotionally hurt.'

Maggie was brisk.

'I can take care of myself. Don't worry – I won't rush into anything.' She smiled, feeling carefree suddenly. On impulse she kissed Janine's smooth cheek.

Then she half-walked, half-ran out of the building to her car and headed straight for the Black Orchid Club.

10

Maggie lay back in the warm, bubbling water and closed her eyes. Bliss! Seven a.m. and there wasn't a soul in the club to disturb her. She had exclusive rights to the Jacuzzi and she revelled in the unaccustomed pleasure of her own company.

She had been living at the club with Antony and Alexander for six weeks now and she was beginning to wonder if she was losing her sense of reality. Today she was taking over from Jackie and a new batch of trainers were coming in for her to interview.

Each man had been personally selected by Alexander and Antony; they had conducted the preliminary interviews and weeded out those who were obviously unsuitable. It was her job to decide which of the five shortlisted would be most popular with the other women.

Judd was leaving after spending almost a year at the Black Orchid and Dean was being released after breaking the 'no outside relationships' rule. In addition, Antony had decided that the club membership had grown sufficiently large to consider employing more trainers. So that meant that Maggie could set on all five candidates she was to put through their paces if she so desired.

She smiled to herself and sank deeper into the Jacuzzi. The bubbles gurgled and fizzed around her legs, tickling the inside of her thighs as they rose upward. She was naked, her dark hair piled up on the top of her head and secured carelessly with a cotton scrunchy. She never bothered with make-up this early in the morning, so she didn't have to worry about the warm water splashing her face, trickling down her cheeks with a lover's caress.

Maggie closed her eyes and, taking a deep breath, submerged herself in the warm water. As she resurfaced, she gripped the padded bar which ran around the circular pool and allowed her naked body to float on the surface of the water.

It was so peaceful with only the light chatter of the watery bubbles and the gentle hum of the air conditioning around her. Slowly, Maggie parted her legs, revelling in the controlled pull of her well toned muscles. She had never been so fit, her body so trim and toned as she was now. And her skin – so soft and blemish free.

Since she had moved in with Antony and Alexander she was rarely allowed to bathe herself. Invariably, she would find the water had been run for her and one or other of them would appear, arms full of perfumed soaps and lotions and talcum. All that was required of her was that she lay back in the water and submit to their gentle ministrations.

Alexander was the best, lingering over every process, polishing her skin as if it were the finest, most valuable porcelain. Yet there was never any sexual contact, even though he was often visibly aroused by touching her. And Maggie . . . Maggie had learned never to make overtures to him for fear of making him angry. No, not angry exactly, she mused. She opened and closed her legs in a scissor like action which forced the bubbles to travel between them with more force, languidly enjoying the way they bumped and popped, unobstructed, against her sex.

Angry wasn't quite the right word to describe Alexander's reaction to the few times she had tried to initiate sex with him. Disappointed in her, perhaps. Certainly, she always felt contrite, like a child who has tried to take one more cookie from the jar.

The most unsatisfactory thing about living with Antony and Alexander was that she was only ever allowed to make love with Antony. They didn't seem to mind if she stayed while they made love to each other, she had, on occasion, even joined in. But she was never intimately alone with Alex.

Maggie sighed as she switched off the Jacuzzi and wrapped herself in a huge white towel. Snuggling into its luxuriously soft warmth, she padded back to her private bathroom, part of her office, which adjoined the pool room. Antony was waiting for her when she went back upstairs to the apartment.

'Ready for the interviews, Maggie?'

'Do I get to eat breakfast first?'

'Only a light one, darling – I wouldn't recommend you have sex with five men in a row on a full stomach.'

He poured them both a coffee and Maggie frowned slightly at him. His tone had been ever so slightly cutting and she sensed an air of resentment about him that she had noticed a couple of times before.

'Is everything all right, Antony?' she asked as he handed her a mug.

He looked up and smiled, somewhat ruefully.

'Don't mind me. I got out the wrong side of the bed this morning.'

He left her alone and Maggie reflected that Alexander had not returned home the previous evening. She had a shrewd idea that that was what had put Antony in such a prickly mood. The lounge door opened at that moment and Alexander appeared, as if her thinking about him had conjured him up. As was often the case when he disappeared on one of what Maggie privately termed his French Leave, he was in high spirits, kissing her exuberantly before sinking down beside her on the sofa.

'Phew, I'm exhausted!' he exclaimed.

Maggie slanted a look at him sideways, through her lashes as he helped himslf to coffee. He never seemed to feel the need to explain himself or his actions. Didn't he see how his behaviour upset Antony? She could feel the tension emanating from him as he came back into the room, could feel the effort it cost him not to question Alexander about his movements. Yet Alex merely smiled at him before turning to her.

'I want you to try out each of the guys I've selected for you and mark them on a scale of one to ten. Their general attractiveness, their attitude towards you, their confidence and general level of skill, etc. Remember, you've got to bear in mind the needs of our members – don't judge the guys purely on your reaction to them. OK?'

'I think so. What about if one of them gets out of hand?' She blushed as Alexander raised an ironic eyebrow at her. 'I mean, if I don't want to and he . . . well, you know.'

'Antony and I will be behind a two-way mirror. Any problems, give a signal and we'll rescue you.'

Maggie raised her eyes heavenward. She might have known!

'Won't you two get bored, watching me all morning?' she teased gently.

'We'll find something to do if it gets too monotonous, won't we, Antony?'

There was a slight challenge in Alexander's voice as he turned to the other man, but Antony just shrugged. Maggie had no doubt that Alex would talk him round – he always did.

Later, in the large, luxuriously appointed 'office' she had been given, Maggie began to feel nervous. She leaped up from the comfortable leather chair which sat behind the heavy, masculine looking old oak desk and paced to the other end of the room, her high-heeled mules soundless on the cream carpeted floor

By the second-floor window which overlooked the city, there were two rattan chairs and a glass topped table on which she had placed an assortment of drinks and crockery. A coffee percolator hissed and fizzed on the small counter in the corner, filling the room with the aroma of coffee beans.

Nervously, she drew the butter yellow silk curtains and walked round switching on the softly shaded lamps placed strategically round the room. The large, comfortable, lemon chintz covered couch faced the two-way mirror on the opposite wall and she went over to it and switched off the privacy switch so that Antony and Alexander could see the room.

Glancing at the grandfather clock, ticking sonorously in the corner by the desk, Maggie saw that it was time to begin. Yet still she procrastinated. It all seemed so cold, so clinical, preparing to make love with five men she had never even seen!

She was wearing a cream silk robe, belted at the waist, which brushed the floor as she walked. She was naked underneath and she suddenly felt vulnerable.

'What's the matter, Maggie?' Alexander's voice over the intercom made her jump.

'I . . . I just feel a bit awkward, that's all. Er . . . maybe this isn't quite such a good idea.'

'You knew what the job would entail, Maggie, are you having second thoughts?'

Alexander's tone was cutting and Maggie stopped her pacing and took a deep breath. He was right, she knew what she was taking on. She trusted him to help her if she couldn't handle anything, and there wasn't much she felt she couldn't cope with. And she really didn't want to lose this job – apart from anything else, she loved living with Antony and Alexander. She wanted to please Alex and the idea that he was becoming impatient with her made her reply hastily.

'Of course not.'

'Just get on with it, then, Maggie, there's a good girl.'

Maggie pressed the buzzer on her desk and the heavy oak door opened silently on its well oiled hinges. Maggie's eyes widened in surprise as the open doorway was filled by an enormous, broad shouldered hulk. His skin shone like well-polished ebony, his shaven head as smooth and well shaped as the rest of him. The whites of his eyes showed up in startling contrast to the blackness of his skin and as he treated her to a slow, confident smile, her eyes were drawn to the perfection of his strong white teeth.

He closed the door behind him and Maggie's eyes were drawn to the way his shoulder muscles rippled under the tight-fitting black T-shirt. There was a glint of gold in one earlobe and around his thick, strong neck. As he walked slowly towards her, Maggie's eyes were drawn to the thigh muscles which bulged in the tight blue jeans and the unmistakeable fullness at his crotch.

Her eyes snapped up as he stopped, standing in front of her, waiting. She swallowed, wetting her unaccountably dry throat, her former nervousness forgotten. This was one hell of a guy.

'Hello!' she smiled, holding out her hand, 'and you are?'

'Constantine G. Winchester the Third,' he said, his smile flashing at her look of astonishment, 'but my friends call me Con.'

His voice was beautiful, rich as dark treacle, yet as smooth as a good brandy. Maggie felt the compulsion to make him talk more, just for the pleasure of hearing that strong, well modulated voice. As he enclosed her soft, well manicured hand in his larger, stronger one, though, the attractions of his voice faded into insignificance.

Maggie allowed him to pull her slowly towards him until they stood, breast to breast. Even in her high-heels, she had to crane her neck to look up at him and she was glad when he lowered his head to hers and covered her mouth with his.

His kiss took her breath away, his tongue wrapping itself around hers and drawing it into the hot wet cavern of his mouth. His chest was solid, immovable as her soft breasts were crushed against it and she felt herself being lifted up, off her feet. His sheer bulk made her feel tiny, powerless in his arms as he held her to him with one hand while he opened her robe with the other.

He balanced one trainer clad foot on her desk and literally sat her on his bent knee, cradling her with one arm as he covered one quivering breast with his hand. Maggie sucked in her breath as she contemplated the erotic contrast of his dark hand on her white breast as he knowingly coaxed her nipple to hardness.

She ran her hand tentatively over the smooth dome of his stubble free skull as he bent his head to her breast. The skin felt warm and velvet soft under her fingertips. Maggie closed her eyes as his lips tugged at her responsive nipple, sending little shocks of reaction along the nerves connecting it to her innermost centre of pleasure.

Con pushed the robe off her shoulders and she shivered as it fell to the floor in a silky heap, leaving her skin exposed to the air. It was comfortably warm in the room, yet she felt little goosebumps form all over as he ran the palm of his hand down her side from her armpit to her hip. The rough skin of his palm lightly snagged her skin as he polished her hip bone before gripping her thigh, lifting it up so that her leg was bent at the knee.

Smiling slightly at Maggie, Con used his free hand to unbutton his fly and release his tumescent penis from the constriction of his jeans. Maggie unconsciously licked her lips as the monster reared up and pointed its succulent tip at her. Her mouth watered as she contemplated savouring the musky, salty teardrop which had appeared in its centre, but Con was holding her fast and she had no chance to move.

Easing his jeans over his taut buttocks, he left them stretched around his thighs as he sat her on the edge of the desk and he positioned himself between her thighs, feet planted firmly apart. His large hands parted her sex and he framed the tender, moist pink fold of flesh with his two hands, touching her almost reverently.

Maggie watched with bated breath as he ran his two forefingers along the insides of the outer lips, exposing the glistening flesh leaves within. As he reached the most sensitive point, he squeezed the labia firmly together, making her pleasure-bud tingle in anticipation.

She was disappointed when he removed his fingers, though not for long. His large hands slipped under her bottom and cradled each buttock, forming a warm cushion between her and the cold, hard wood of the desk. Then he was lifting her up, balancing her entire weight in his palms as he held her, poised, the entrance to her body opening above his swaying shaft.

Maggie gasped as he lowered her slowly and she was impaled on the hard rod which filled and stretched her to capacity. Her arms flew around his neck as he took her entire weight on his hands and moved her pelvis up and down, rubbing her clitoris firmly against the fine line of black hair on his lower belly as he did so.

He was so strong, so solid, he seemed immovable as Maggie clung helplessly to him, powerless to resist his determined manipulation of her body. His eyes were closed now, his lips slightly parted. A fine line of perspiration glistened on his smooth upper lip and the cords in his thick neck stood out as he neared his release.

The relentless, ticklish pressure of his belly against her clitoris was driving her wild, her well-lubricated sheath throbbing and burning as the huge cock slid in and out of her. She closed her eyes and concentrated on the sensations building deep within her.

A kaleidoscope of colours exploded behind her eyelids as the rhythmic rubbing brought her to orgasm, her ankles linking behind Con's back as she sought to meld herself further with him. A deep, guttural groan sounded deep in his throat, emerging as a triumphant shout as his seed burst from him and shot upward into her sex, still convulsing strongly around him.

Even in the throes of orgasm, Con stood, feet planted firmly shoulder-width apart, steady as a rock. He held Maggie firmly until the waves had subsided and she clung weakly to him, spent. Then he carefully lifted her up and off his still partially erect penis and put her gently onto her feet in front of him.

Maggie leaned weakly against the desk and watched him as he calmly pulled his jeans back up, tucking his formidable member inside before rebuttoning the fly. He smiled at her, cocking his head slightly to one side as if expecting her to say something.

'Th-thank you, Con,' she said shakily, 'we'll be in touch.'

He seemed to be about to say something then, thinking better of it, he grinned and nodded, striding away from her with the same jaunty coinfidence as when he approached her. Maggie watched him go, admiring the neatness of his muscular behind in the tight-fitting jeans. As the door swung to behind him, she slumped slightly, running her fingers distractedly through her dishevelled hair.

She jumped as the door opened again and another man came through. She hadn't buzzed to say she was ready yet – surely she had time to wash and pee?

'One moment I . . .' she trailed off as she surveyed the man who hovered uncertainly in the doorway.

The contrast between this one and Con was so marked it was almost laughable. It was almost as if they were from a different species. This one was a good foot shorter, about equal to Maggie's own five feet six inches with a skinny, weedy build. His shoulders were rounded, his chest even more so, virtually concave. The white T-shirt he was wearing should have clung to his pectorals, instead it hung loosely across his chest and disappeared into his baggy grey slacks. Maggie guessed he must be here for maintenance, or some other thing that would have to wait until later.

'Sorry,' Maggie smiled politely, pulling her robe more closely around her, 'could you come back later?'

He blinked uncertainly and shuffled his feet. Maggie tried to conceal her impatience. She had an increasingly urgent need to pee and she could feel the residue of Con's semen trickling down her inner thighs.

'I'm rather busy at the moment,' she explained, 'you see, I'm in the middle of interviewing.'

If he thought it odd that Maggie was conducting job interviews dressed in nothing but a silk robe, he did not show it. He virtually wrang his hands together as if gathering his courage to speak to her. When, finally, he did dare to address her, his voice was shrill with nerves.

'Excuse me, but I'm next, Madam.'

Maggie stared at him, fighting with the urge to laugh.

'Um, well, I'm sorry, but I think there's been a mistake. You do know what the job entails?'

'Oh yes, Madam. I think I'm well suited to it, begging your pardon for being so bold.'

His ingratiating manner was beginning to get on Maggie's nerves. Her tone was abrupt as she asked him. 'What's your name?'

'Malcolm, Madam.'

Well, it would be, wouldn't it? Maggie's lips twitched. He had virtually bobbed a curtsey as he introduced himself.

'Pleased to meet you, Malcolm, but I don't think you're quite what I had in mind for the job.'

She expected him to give up at that point, but he was still gazing at her hopefully with his wide, brown, lost puppy dog eyes. She sighed. He really was a most uninspiring specimen. Not only was he nauseatingly self deprecating but his mousy brown hair stuck up in alarmed tufts on top of his head, reminding her of a toilet brush. Losing patience, she abandoned all pretence of charm and snapped.

'Look, Malcolm, I need a shower and a pee and I don't have time to stand here and argue with you. Do you understand?'

His face took on an expression of adoration.

'Oh yes, Madam, but if you'd just allow me . . . may I?'

Maggie frowned. Maybe if she humoured him, he'd go away. She nodded, raising her eyebrows in surprise as Malcolm dropped to his knees and shuffled towards her. She stood stock still as he reached her and pressed his lips against each of her feet in turn.

Glancing uncomfortably at the two-way mirror, she imagined Antony and Alexander watching them. It was a new angle to her to find herself in charge of a man as submissive as this, and she was not sure if she liked it. Malcolm reverently lifted the hem of her robe and began to lick his way up her inner thigh.

Maggie tensed as another droplet of semen seeped out of her and ran down her leg. Malcolm lapped it up, sucking at the soft, damp skin as if the combined juices of her coupling with Con were the sweetest nectar. Whatever his deficiencies as a man in her eyes, Malcolm definitely had a skilful tongue. Maggie relaxed against the desk and obligingly parted her thighs, granting him access to the sticky curls between them.

Closing her eyes on the unattractive sight of Malcolm's hair between her legs, Maggie concentrated instead on the pleasant sensations of his respectful, wet tongue lapping its way along her moist folds. After the punishing encounter she had enjoyed with Con, Malcolm's attentions were soothing against her swollen sex.

He nibbled on her resting bud until it began to spasm, not with the furious, all-consuming tremors Con had evoked, but in a gentle, mild climax which was pleasant rather than mind blowing. Maggie smiled, glad that Malcolm had some talent.

Unfortunately the orgasm caused the muscles of her over-full bladder to relax and when Malcolm very deliberately pressed the tip of his tongue firmly against her urethra, Maggie was powerless to prevent a small trickle of urine from escaping.

Mortified, she clenched her pelvic floor muscles to stop the leakage, but Malcolm seemed determined not to let her go. The urge to pee grew stronger as he teased the tiny hole, probing with his tongue until she could hold back no longer.

Maggie looked down in horror as the steady stream of golden liquid flowed over Malcolm's face and down his neck. His eyes were closed, his mouth open, the expression on his face rapturous. He had unzipped his flies and was masturbating himself furiously. As Maggie finished, his orgasm overtook him and his semen spurted out, mingling with the steaming urine on the front of his trousers.

Repulsed, Maggie lifted her foot and pushed his shoulder with the toe of her mule. Malcolm toppled over, writhing about on the floor in a paroxysm of ecstacy.

'You filthy little worm! Make sure you're out of here when I get back!'

She flounced into her private bathroom and locked the door behind her. Her angry, flushed face stared back at her in the mirror over the basin. Suddenly, she began to laugh. The little man was priceless! How many of their clients, probably stuck with a boorish, domineering partner, would like to get their own back on mankind? And Malcom had obviously loved every minute of the humiliation to which she had unwittingly subjected him.

Taking the time for a quick, rejuvenating shower, Maggie changed into a clean robe, identical to the first, and ventured back into the office. To her relief, Malcolm had disappeared. Someone had been in to clean up for there was a damp patch on the carpet and the sharp antiseptic scent of cleaning fluid hung in the air. Maggie pressed the button on the intercom.

'Next, please.'

11

The next candidate virtually bounced into the room. He was fit, exuding good health in his casual, dark-red sweat top and baggy black track pants, and he was young. Very young.

'I'm Jason,' he introduced himself eagerly, trying not to make it obvious that he was eyeing her up.

Maggie hid a smile as she noticed he already had a hard-on and that the track pants could barely contain his enthusiasm.

'How old are you, Jason.' she asked him, resisting the urge to ask if his mother knew he was here.

Jason's cherubic, boyish face split into a cheeky grin.

'Everyone asks me that. I'm twenty . . . well, all right, I'm eighteen – honestly,' he laughed as he saw her disbelief, 'I could show you my driver's licence?'

'No need,' she said quickly. She was sure that such basic, mundane matters would have been checked out long before he got to this stage. Briefly, she wondered if eighteen was old enough. But there was eighteen, and there was eighteen!

'Do you like women, Jason?'

'You bet!'

'*All* women?'

'Tall, short, fat, thin, blonde, brunette, redhead—'

'OK, OK!' she laughed, 'I get the picture.'

She walked slowly towards him, watching his reaction as she deliberately allowed her hips to sway. It wasn't difficult to adopt the exaggerated roll of the pelvis in the high-heeled mules. Jason stood still, only his eyes following her as she circled him, looking him up and down appraisingly.

He had an open, honest sort of face, smooth jawed, blue eyed with a smartly barbered crop of shiny, clean blond hair. There was a deep cleft in the centre of his chin which hinted at more craggy looks as he aged. His body was well sculpted, his legs long and lean and his chest pleasingly broad. Maggie could smell the faintest trace of fresh, lemony soap as she stood closer to him, noting the way his cock leaped in his trousers in reaction to her proximity.

'Do you like to fuck, Jason?' she enquired, dropped her voice an octave.

His colour rose slightly, but he met her teasing gaze without flinching and grinned.

'You bet!' he said again.

'Hmm. And does your skill match your enthusiasm?'

'Want to try me?'

Maggie smiled and reached up to run her forefinger down the side of his smooth-skinned cheek.

'You bet!' she whispered.

Jason's lips were unexpectedly demanding as they moved on hers and Maggie felt her blood quicken. So he looked young – she certainly didn't feel in the least bit maternal towards him now! Taking him by the hand, she led him over to the lemon chintz couch and pulled him down onto it, on top of her.

Briefly, she wondered if Antony and Alexander were enjoying themselves behind the two-way mirror as she contented herself with savouring the kiss. Drawing Jason's tongue into her mouth, she sucked at it gently, encouraging him to relinquish the self-control she could sense he was struggling to retain.

She lifted her shoulders up off the couch to help him as he

eased her robe down, exposing her soft-tipped breasts. His eyes were hot, warming her skin as he gazed down on her with a mixture of admiration and lust.

'God, you're beautiful!' he breathed.

Maggie hid a smile at the conviction in his voice. In anyone else she might have dismissed the comment as a stock line, but from Jason it sounded fresh and new. As he lowered his head to kiss her breasts, Maggie tangled her fingers in his thick, glossy hair, massaging his scalp as he drew one swelling nipple into his hot mouth.

Tiny shivers of pleasure coursed down her spine and she felt the moisture begin to gather between her thighs in response to the feel of his lean young body pressing against her silk-covered mound. Jason's hands were roaming at will all over her upper body, his mouth planting tiny butterfly kisses along the tender skin of her inner arm from her wrist to her armpit before tracing the line of her collar-bone and running back down the other arm from shoulder to hand.

Maggie helped him remove his trousers and briefs, her mouth curving into a pleased smile as his penis sprang into view. Like the rest of him, it was well formed and hard, the soft protective foreskin already drawing back to reveal the purple headed glans beneath. Maggie would have liked to have tasted that magnificent specimen, but she was aware that time was short.

Her brief was to try out each candidate's satisfaction quotient from a woman's point of view. Any pleasure they derived from the exercise should be purely coincidental, not arrived at through any direct action from her.

With that in mind, she pushed his head gently lower. He needed no further encouragement to open her robe completely and spread her softly quivering thighs.

Maggie gasped at the first contact of his tongue on her

swollen vulva. This sensation was completely different from Malcolm's tentative, nervous licks. Jason ran his tongue around the tender folds in bold, confident strokes, as if he were settling down to a particularly delicious meal.

As the centre of her pleasure zone responded, she arched her back and bore down, inviting him to deepen his exploration. He did not disappoint her. She groaned as his hard, seeking tongue found the straining nub and flicked hungrily back and forth over it.

A delicious warmth slowly radiated out from that tiny point, suffusing her with a sense of well being that only truly good sex could imbue. Jason had found her blossoming opening with one finger and he gently moved it in and out as he continued to diligently stroke her outer sex with his tongue.

Maggie wrapped her long legs around his neck, holding him to her as the familiar waves began to break and the heat rose up and consumed her. All her attention was focused on that small core of her femininity as it pulsed and throbbed against the pressure of Jason's eager tongue.

She smiled at him as he raised his head. His eyes were glazed, his chin smeared with her feminine secretions and he was smiling. Dipping his head, he blazed a trail of kisses in a line from her pubis to her throat before claiming her mouth.

Maggie wrapped her legs around his waist and urged him to possess her. He leaned his forehead against hers for a moment as the tip of his swollen cock nudged against the entrance to her welcoming sex. He slipped inside her with a sigh, resting there for a few seconds before beginning to slowly withdraw.

Gradually, he built up his rhythm, exquisitely slowly at first, then gaining momentum. Maggie matched his movements, bringing her bottom up from the sofa to meet him, drawing him into her and tightening her intimate muscles as he withdrew.

His smooth skin grew hot under her palms as he began to quicken his pace, building to a crescendo. They rolled together, slipping off the couch and onto the soft carpet. For a moment, Maggie was on top, then he rolled her over again onto her back, holding her buttocks in his hands as he thrust into her.

Maggie could feel little thrills of sensation rippling through her as the movement of his thick, hard shaft stimulated the walls of the silky sheath which enclosed him. She closed her eyes and concentrated on the delicious friction, digging her fingernails into his shoulders as his breathing became faster and more shallow and his movement became frenzied. He cried out as he came, collapsing on top of her and covering her face with kisses.

'God, you're fantastic!' he gasped, his voice quavering.

Maggie cradled his head against her breast as she waited for his breathing to slow and his temperature to return to normal. She was touched by his gratitude, moved by his innocence. His sexual style owed more to enthusiasm than finesse, but it was energetic and honest and she knew this was an experience she would look forward to repeating.

At last, they peeled apart and he used her bathroom to freshen up while she called for a cold drink. He took a coke from her gratefully and drank it quickly. Maggie sipped at hers, watching the muscles in his throat contract as he swallowed.

He grinned at her as he handed her his empty glass. 'Thanks – I needed that! Have I got the job?'

Maggie smiled.

'We'll be in touch,' she told him.

His face fell, a picture of disappointment.

'Oh.'

Maggie could not let him leave like that. She stepped forward and kissed him on the cheek.

'I'm sure we'll meet again,' she murmured, her face turned away from the two-way mirror so that only he could hear.

Jason's face split into its usual happy grin and he hugged her.

'Be seeing you, then,' he said and he left with as much spring in his step as there had been when he first came in.

Maggie took a few minutes to compose herself. She knew now why Alexander had decided to watch the proceedings. No doubt it gave him a kick to see her take five men one after the other. She shivered. If only she knew what went on in his mind!

After she had washed, she buzzed the intercom and took a seat by the curtained window so that she would have time to appraise the next candidate before he saw her. The door opened and a young, long-haired man swaggered through it. His hair was a dirty blond colour, his eyes, when he turned them on her a faded blue. He was wearing tight, brown leather trousers and a white, wide-sleeved cotton shirt, unbuttoned at the front to his navel.

'Hi babe, I'm Darren,' he drawled.

Maggie winced. He looked and sounded like a parody of a seventies rock star. A complete turn off.

'Hello. Won't you sit down?'

She indicated the other rattan chair and he strolled over and perched awkwardly on its edge. His eyes skittered from her face to the window and round the room. He linked his hands loosely in front of him, brought them up to his chin, then dropped them again. Finally, he seemed to be able to bear the silence no longer.

'Well, are we goin' to get it on or what?'

Maggie considered telling him to get lost and go and do 'or what'. She didn't have the energy. Standing up, she raised her eyes heavenward at the two-way mirror before turning back to Darren, unbelting her robe and letting it fall to the ground. Then she stepped out of her shoes and waited.

His faded blue eyes grew rounder, fixed on her naked breasts as he leaped to his feet and tore off his clothes. He had a good body, Maggie noted dispassionately, probably better than young Jason's. So why didn't the sight of him, naked and erect, do anything for her?

Darren's hand on her bare skin were cool and knowing. As if following a tried and tested ritual he had learned off by heart, he smoothed the skin of her neck and squeezed her breast, kissed her half-heartedly and stared soulfully into her eyes as he led her over to the sofa and slowly laid her on her back.

Maggie's mind wandered to the meal Alexander had promised to cook that evening, one of her favourites. She frowned slightly as Darren thrust one hand between her closed thighs and twiddled about for a minute. Satisfied that she was wet – he wasn't to know that she had already been with two men and could hardly be otherwise – he bent her legs at the knees and thrust into her, making her wince.

His face was intent as he drove in and out of her and Maggie realised he had probably forgotten who she was. So intent was he on reaching his own climax, he didn't notice her grimacing frantically at the two-way mirror.

'Yes! Oh yes!' he yelled as he reached the peak.

Maggie fought the urge to giggle. He rolled off her and they both dressed in silence. There was a bubble of smug self-satisfaction about Darren which she was longing to burst. Her chance came soon enough.

'When do I start work, then, darlin'?' he asked her casually as he zipped his leather trousers.

'You don't.'

'Huh?'

'I think you have been labouring under a misconception, *darling*. This is an exclusive club for very discerning ladies. Not a knocking shop set up for the benefit of our male employees.'

'Whaddaya mean?'

Maggie ignored the belligerent scowl and continued. 'You're not up to it, my dear.'

'I've never had any complaints before.'

'No, but then sheep can't speak, can they?'

They both jumped as Antony's voice came from behind them.

'Wot's that supposed ter mean, then?' Darren took a step towards Antony then, eyeing his superior physique, obviously thought better of it.

'It means it's time for you to leave. And try to learn a few manners before you next approach a lady.'

Darren swung towards the door, his high colour signalling he was offended. As he reached the door, he turned back to Maggie and spluttered.

'I'll tell you wot your trouble is, darlin' – you're frigid!'

'Get out,' Antony said, his voice dripping boredom.

'I didn't enjoy it anyway, bleedin' lesbian!' was Darren's parting shot as he slammed out of the door.

Antony turned to Maggie and raised an eyebrow at her.

'Are you all right?'

She nodded, then couldn't keep back the laughter bubbling in her throat. Antony joined in.

'Frigid!' he said.

They put their arms round each other and laughed until the tears were running down their cheeks. When they had recovered, Antony brushed the hair out of her eyes tenderly. Holding her gaze, he asked, 'I'm sorry, I don't know how that boor got through.'

Maggie shrugged. 'Don't worry – I've dealt with far worse

than him on the outside. It was probably Alexander's idea of a joke.'

'You could be right. If you're OK, do you feel up to the last interview?'

'Is this one civilised?'

'I'd say he is.'

Maggie laughed.

'Fancy him yourself, do you?'

Antony let her go and wandered back to the door.

'Mind your own business,' he replied good naturedly.

'Well, so long as he *is* half way decent, perhaps he could join me for some lunch – I'm starving!'

'That shouldn't be a problem. I'll have something sent up.'

Maggie went to brush her hair and thought longingly of the Jacuzzi. She felt grubby and wished there was time to freshen up before she met the final candidate, but already she could hear the door opening and the sounds of heavy male footsteps coming into the room. For the first time in a long time, she wondered if she would be able to muster the enthusiasm required to put him through his paces. Laying down her brush with a sigh, she went back into the office to greet him.

'Hello, sorry to keep you waiting, I . . .'

She trailed off as she saw the man who had come in and was looking out of the window. He had pulled back the curtains and bright sunlight streamed in, outshining the lamps. He turned slowly at the sound of her voice and all Maggie's tiredness fled as she was caught by his dark eyes.

He was wearing clean, but well-worn denims with heavy soled tan leather boots and a wide belt. His denim shirt looked soft from many launderings. It clung lovingly to the breadth of his strong shoulders and was open at the neck, revealing the merest hint of crisp, dark chest hair.

Raising her eyes to his face, Maggie saw that he was smiling at her and she felt the heat rise in her cheeks. He had a firm, well-shaped mouth which lifted slightly more on the left than the right when he smiled. His nose was slightly hooked, but perfectly proportioned, his eyes, so dark they were almost black, widely spaced and framed by thick, black lashes.

His skin was tanned, the tiny laughter lines radiating out from the corners of his eyes looked paler, as if he had spent a lot of time squinting in the sun. And his hair was as black and glossy as an American Indian's, falling in a thick widow's peak over his forehead and curling wildly round his ears.

Recovering herself slightly, Maggie moved towards him and offered him her hand.

'How do you do? I'm Maggie.'

'Brett,' he said, clasping her slender hand in his capable fingers.

Maggie felt the tremors tingling up her arm and swallowed, hard.

'I hope you don't mind, but I've ordered lunch. It's been a hectic morning.'

She blushed as she realised what she had said and he smiled at her again. Maggie warmed to him and indicated with a wave of the hand that he should sit on one of the rattan chairs. As he did so, she thought of Antony and Alexander snooping behind the two-way mirror and knew *this* time, she wanted some privacy.

Casually wandering over to the two-way mirror, she blew a kiss at its opaque surface and flicked the privacy switch. Alexander was going to be furious! Serve him right for letting Darren slip through the net. She smiled to herself as she thought how she had outwitted him for once. Just then there was a knock at the door and one of the kitchen staff appeared with a hostess trolley. Thanking her, Maggie wheeled it into the room and locked the door behind her.

'It's just salad and baked potatoes, I'm afraid,' she apologised as she lifted the covers off the trays.

'Looks good to me,' Brett responded, relieving her of one tray.

Maggie couldn't take her eyes off him as he took a hearty forkful of fat, juicy prawns, dripping in mayonnaise and put it in his mouth. He chewed slowly, as if savouring every bite, his eyes never leaving Maggie's. She felt as if she could be eating sawdust, her mouth and throat were so dry, her heart beating irregularly. Despite her frequent escapades, it had been a while since she had felt this much desire for a man.

'How did you find out about the Black Orchid Club?' she broke the tense silence, wetting her lips with the cool, clear mineral water which had been sent up in a jug.

'A mate of mine worked here before he came out to Australia.'

'Australia?' That explained the deep suntan. 'What were you doing out there?'

Brett shrugged.

'This and that. Cattle herding, mostly.'

A vivid picture of him astride a horse, yielding a lasso like an old-fashioned cowboy pushed its way into Maggie's head and she smiled. The image suited him.

'What is it?'

'Nothing. Just that you struck me as being the outdoor type.'

'Really? And is that a good thing?'

His voice was thick, like double cream. It trickled over her senses, affecting her concentration, drowning her in sensuality.

They had finished eating. Brett seemed to be waiting for her to make a move, but, for once, she didn't know the best place to start. She felt sticky, unclean and she knew she wanted to come to this man fresh.

'Look,' she began, 'I feel awfully hot and sweaty. I'd really like to take a bath – would you mind?'

She hoped he wouldn't think she was rejecting him, would be happy to come back later. He smiled slowly at her.

'Sure. Would you mind if I joined you?'

Maggie's eyebrows flew up in surprise. She thought of the Jacuzzi. There'd be plenty of hot water and there was a lock on the inside of the door. It would be the perfect place to be alone. Her lips curved into a smile of delicious anticipation.

'Be my guest,' she murmured huskily.

12

Maggie switched on the Jacuzzi and poured a thimbleful of her favourite, scented bubble-bath into the swirling water. The taciturn maintenance man would not be pleased with her when he had to drain the system, she thought wryly. Too bad!

Taking out a large box of matches, she lit the scented candles which were held in glass fronted iron sconces screwed to the walls and extinguished the harsh electric light. She looked around her with satisfaction.

The water in the Jacuzzi was frothing gently, large, iridescent bubbles rising up and disappearing with a soft 'pop' the minute they touched a hard surface. A subtle, musky scent filled the room, laying heavily on the still air. The candlelight flickered as the door to her bathroom opened and Brett stepped through.

He had taken off his boots and the belt of his jeans and he stood, barefoot, looking round him. His expression was inscrutable and Maggie felt her heart quicken. She watched silently as he slowly unbuttoned the denim shirt and shrugged it off.

His chest was broad, carpeted in a light covering of curly black hair which arrowed down the line of his belly and disappeared into his jeans. He held her eye as she stood across the pool from him and began to slip the buttons of his jeans through the stiff buttonholes. He was wearing plain black cotton boxer shorts underneath and he made no move to remove them, merely staring quietly back at her.

The tension in the room was palpable as Maggie slowly

slipped her robe off her shoulders and kicked it aside. Brett's eyes flickered briefly over her naked, candlelit body, before returning to her face. Maggie was aware that her nipples had grown hard, her legs weak as she anticipated the feel of his strong, hair-roughened arms around her, longed for the touch of his cool, firm lips on her skin.

Very slowly, she walked to the edge of the Jacuzzi and sat down on the edge. He watched her as she slipped into the water with one graceful, fluid movement, closing her eyes for an instant as she sank up to her neck into the warm, bubbling water.

When she opened them again, she saw that he had dispensed with his boxer shorts and was moving towards her. Proudly naked, his erect penis swayed invitingly as he plunged feet first into the pool, submerging his entire body under the water.

Maggie giggled as she felt him brush against her ankle as he resurfaced, water streaming down his face, his black hair plastered against his skull. Without feeling the need to speak, they relaxed against the padded side of the pool, wet shoulders touching, both enjoying the sensation of the bubbles burbling around them.

The illicit bubble-bath had caused the Jacuzzi to overflow, huge, frothy masses of white bubbles rising up into the air so that soon only their heads were above it. Maggie could feel the constantly moving water washing away the remains of her encounters with Con and Malcolm and Jason and Darren. She felt clean again, renewed.

She jumped as Brett's wet hands slithered around her equally wet waist, lifting her up and towards him. His naked body pressed against hers, the wet skin slippery and soft. She could feel his hardness nudging at her outer thigh as he turned her and crushed her foam covered breasts against the hard, hairy wall of his chest.

Maggie welcomed his kiss, tasting the warm, sweet water

on his lips and tangling her fingers in the damp curls at the nape of his neck. His tongue probed against her teeth and she drew it in, liking the taste of him and eager for more.

They were almost completely submerged now, mountainous walls of white foam climbing around them. The candlelight shone dully through the bubbles, enclosing them in a wet, frothy cocoon, a secret world inhabited only by their seeking, hungry bodies.

Maggie allowed the water to buoy her up so that Brett's head was level with her hard-tipped breasts. She sucked in her breath as his lips touched first one, then the other, suckling gently until she felt the erotic pull deep inside her. His teeth grazed her nipples as he pulled away and lifted her, his large hands spanning her waist as he pressed his face against her navel, delving into it with his tongue.

Looking down, Maggie could see the crisp, dark hair of her pubis, almost entirely obscured by the clinging foam, inches away from his busy tongue. She parted her legs slightly in invitation, imagining how the soft pink folds of her inner flesh, streaming with warm water from the Jacuzzi, would now peek out at him.

She braced herself against the padded bar as he tilted her pelvis, one strong hand supporting her buttocks. With the fingers of his free hand, he gently parted the pouting lips of her vulva and spent a long moment gazing at the intricately formed flower within.

Maggie felt her cheeks grow warm as his scrutiny continued, sighing in a mixture of relief and ecstasy as he gently entered her with two fingers. She sank down on them, grinding her hips against his, searching for his lips with her own.

Brett hooked one of her legs around his waist and she brought the other up to join it, crossing her ankles behind his back. The foamy bubbles hissed and popped against her skin as she lay back in the water, her shoulders resting against the padded bar and welcomed Brett into her body.

They made love slowly, almost lazily, indulging in long, hungry kisses. Maggie loved the feel of him moving inside her, filling her up, his strong arms supporting her in the water. As his tempo gradually increased, she closed her eyes, laying back her head in the water. She could feel her hair floating like a halo around her head. Her ears filled with water and the bubbles creeped up, over her face, splashing her nose and mouth.

She sensed the moment that Brett reached the point of no return and she opened her eyes. He was staring straight at her, his mouth set in a grim line. Gathering together all his will power, he waited until the deep ripples of delight had begun to course through her body before allowing himself to join her. They both reached the peak together, clinging to each other as each was overcome and they sank, slowly, into the warm water.

Maggie held her breath, holding tightly to Brett's reassuringly bulky shoulders as they resurfaced. He lifted her up, away from the foam and she felt the water course down her face and drip off the ends of her hair.

'I think we'd better get out of here before we drown in this stuff!' he murmured against her ear.

Maggie laughed.

'OK, can you reach that switch?'

He looked in the direction in which she was pointing and waded over to it. Immediately, the bubbles stopped and the foam which had been stirred up by the activity in the water began to pop and hiss.

As they both climbed out of the pool, they were covered in foam. Laughing, Maggie handed Brett a large, white towel before rubbing herself down with an identical one.

'Allow me.'

Brett took the towel from her and began to pat her shoulders gently. He had wound his own towel around his waist. Maggie sighed as he began to blot the water running in rivulets between her breasts, obligingly shifting her weight so that he could press the soft towelling against her streaming sex.

When he had finished, Brett wrapped the towel under her arms, sarong style, pulling her to him as he tucked it in. His kiss was warm, friendly, even and Maggie returned it in full measure. She felt pleasantly tired and leaned against him, grateful for his strength. 'Shall we go back to my office?' she whispered.

He nodded and they meandered slowly through the foam-filled room to the relative normality of the office beyond.

Brett was still very much on Maggie's mind when she went down for work that evening. After they had dressed he had stayed to drink tea and chat and she had found herself liking him more and more. When finally he had left, reluctantly it seemed to Maggie, she had gone back to the apartment to face Alexander.

He had been furious with her for defying him by switching the privacy button on the two-way mirror. She didn't care. Although she had the uncomfortable feeling that she would be made to pay for her insubordination at some point, she was indifferent to his cold fury now.

Tristan called her over as she checked out the gym.

'Hilary wants to speak to you,' he told her. 'I said you'd find her in the bar.'

Maggie nodded and went in search of Hilary. She was one of their regular clients, the kind that Maggie liked – discreet, but uninhibited. She spotted her as soon as she went into the bar. In her late forties, Hilary was slim and chic, her red-gold hair cut in a severe crop which on most women of her age would look cruel, yet on her it emphasised the fragile bone structure of her face.

She smiled as Maggie joined her, her intelligent blue eyes crinkling at the corners.

'Hello, Maggie,' she said, her light, musical voice easy on the ear. 'Drink?'

'Thanks.'

The barman poured her a dry martini and the two women chatted companionably about nothing in particular for a few minutes. Maggie was beginning to wonder why Hilary had asked to speak to her when the older woman casually mentioned her daughter.

'I didn't know you had a daughter, Hilary,' she commented.

'Emily is twenty-one. She's a lovely girl, a bit plump, perhaps, but I keep telling her she'll fine down as she gets older.'

Hilary trailed off, chewing on her lower lip in a characteristic gesture that Maggie recognised. She had a feeling that this daughter had something to do with Hilary's seeking her out and she waited patiently for the other woman to continue. She seemed to be trying to make up her mind about something. At last, she turned to Maggie and laid an exquisitely manicured hand lightly on her arm.

'I hope you don't think this is out of order, but ... I was wondering if I could book a man for Emily on my membership card?'

Maggie opened her mouth in surprise, but Hilary did not let her reply.

'I know it sounds like an odd request, but you see, I'm so worried about her! She's so shy and unsure of herself. I know she would like to have a full social life, but she had an unfortunate experience some years ago and ... well, I think she's frightened.'

'That's only natural, though, surely? When she meets the right man—'

'But that's just it, Maggie,' Hilary interrupted with some agitation, 'Emily won't let any man close enough to her to find out if he's remotely the right one! I thought that a professional man . . . someone who knows the situation. The first time is so important and I want it to be right for Emily.'

After the initial shock, Maggie began to see more and more sense in Hilary's words. If Emily had been put off sex at an impressionable age then it was important that her first time was perfect.

'Fathers have been introducing their adolescent sons to prostitutes for years,' Hilary said, a trifle desperately, 'and as this is such a progressive sort of club . . .'

'Have you spoken to Emily about it?' Maggie asked as Hilary trailed off again.

'Sort of.'

'And?'

'And she didn't completely veto the idea. What do you think, Maggie? Could you arrange something?'

Maggie immediately thought of Brett. His patient, tender strength would be ideal in a situation such as this and he would be moving into the club at the weekend. He was perceptive enough to know how to handle a woman like Emily. She smiled at Hilary.

'Don't worry about a thing. You bring Emily here next Monday evening when it's quiet – I know just the man for the job!'

Emily hovered on the threshold of the Black Orchid Club and tried to screw up enough courage to go in. Though her mother had assured her repeatedly that she would be in full control of the situation, it didn't seem to help to know that she could call a halt at any time. She didn't have to do anything she didn't want to.

Yet did she want to lose her virginity to a nameless gigolo who was being paid to have the honour? Emily shuddered as she thought how close she had come to losing it five years before, in a brutal, careless encounter. Perhaps her mother was right, it would be far better to place herself in the hands of an experienced, older man.

Besides, Hilary had assured her that all the men here were hand picked and were utterly gorgeous. And it wasn't as if she couldn't reject the one this Maggie had picked for her if she didn't fancy him.

A platinum blonde passed her on her way in and glanced at Emily strangely. She blushed, embarrassed at being caught hovering uncertainly on the doorstep. Taking a deep breath, she followed the woman inside.

She gave her name to the frighteningly well-groomed receptionist and waited while she spoke to someone on the intercom. A door opened to her right a few minutes later and a smart, dark-haired woman, dressed in a sharp business suit, walked towards her, smiling.

'Emily? I'm Maggie. Would you like to come this way?'

Emily nodded mutely, and followed the woman, stiff with nerves, through heavy oak double doors. Confronted by a long, marbled floored corridor bordered by floor to ceiling mirrors, Emily almost turned tail and ran. She could not avoid her reflection as she trotted behind the elegantly turned out woman in front of her.

In her bedroom mirror at home she had been satisfied with the blue, indian cotton two-piece with its romantic tucks and flounces and the ties which laced at the front of the gypsy style, off the shoulder blouse. Now, though, seeing herself reflected from every angle, she realised her figure looked decidedly lumpy, her white, smooth-skinned face round, like a full moon under her upswept brown hair.

She tried to keep her eyes focussed on her low-heeled leather pumps as she walked, concentrating on controlling her growing dismay. After all, what did it matter if the man her mother had booked for her found her physically attractive? So long as she liked him, he was being paid to make love to her.

'Are you feeling all right?'

She started as Maggie spoke to her and swallowed hard.

'Perfectly. Thank you.'

The woman smiled sympathetically at her and ushered her through a door marked 'Private'.

'This flat belongs to Alexander, one of the chief trainers. He doesn't use it very often as he has made other arrangements, but it's kept clean and tidy and we felt you might be more comfortable in here.'

Emily nodded and looked around her. They had stepped into a living room, quite small, but cosy. The twin sofas, arranged around the fireplace, were covered in a dark-red damask and looked brand new. There was a small coffee table between them on which a selection of magazines was displayed. Glancing at them, Emily saw that they were all current.

By the window there was a compact, circular table, covered in a dark-pink cloth flanked by two dining chairs. It was set for dinner; two place settings and a silver bud vase with a single pink rose in the centre. Straight ahead, she could see a small kitchen. A delicious smell wafted through the open door and tantalised her tastebuds, reminding her that she had been so nervous about tonight, she hadn't eaten since breakfast.

To her right, beyond the fireplace, was another open door through which she could just see a large double bed. Emily felt the heat rush into her cheeks as she quickly looked away. Until that moment, she had almost begun to relax, the small flat gave the appearance of being so homely. But the sight of the bed had reminded her sharply of her true reason for coming and all her misgivings rushed back.

'Dinner's almost ready,' Maggie said gently. 'I'll stay until I've introduced you to Brett, by that time your meal should be served.'

Brett. Emily was conscious that she was holding her breath as there was a light tap on the door and Maggie went to open it. She didn't know what to do with her hands, they suddenly felt too large and she folded them carefully behind her back. Vaguely, she was aware of Maggie speaking, of a man walking into the room.

'Emily? Emily, this is Brett.'

A pair of polished black lace-up Oxfords came into Emily's line of vision as she stared at the floor. Slowly raising her eyes, they travelled up a pair of long legs clad in loose-fitting black chinos. She saw the soft, dark hairs on the backs of his hands as he clasped them loosely in front of himself. Noted the long, sensitive fingers and the masculine, knotted veins standing out on the insides of his wrists.

Moving up, there was a conservative, moss green cashmere sweater, worn over a white shirt with a plain grey tie. Emily's eyes stopped at the tie. So far the man had looked singularly unthreatening and she was almost afraid to look at his face. Then he spoke.

'Good evening, Emily,' was all he said, but there was such gentleness in those three words that it gave her enough courage to raise her head and look him full in the face.

It was a strong face, well tanned under thick black hair which looked newly barbered. It was shaped around his small, perfectly formed ears and only slightly ventured onto his broad forehead. Emily guessed that, when it grew, it would flop forward and probably irritate him. His eyebrows were thick, but not bushy, and the eyes which gazed back at her were as dark as any she had ever seen.

His nose suited him, not conventionally handsome, but just right. He smiled at her, a slightly crooked, ironic little smile and she forced her own cold, stiff lips to respond.

'How-how do you do?' she managed to respond at last.

He took a step towards her and she was unable to stop herself from flinching. He immediately stopped, turning instead towards the kitchen as if that had been his intention all along. As he removed a tray from the oven, Maggie touched her arm.

'All right?'

Emily glanced back at Brett and tried to imagine how it would feel to be enclosed by those strong, finely muscled arms. She shivered.

'Yes,' she whispered.

Maggie looked quizzically at her, but said nothing. As Brett came back into the room bearing a covered dish, both women watched him. He laid it carefully down on the table, on top of a placemat and turned his smile on them both.

'Voila!' he announced, as if he'd cooked it himself.

'I'll leave you two to eat,' Maggie said.

Emily glanced at her. She could have sworn she heard a note of regret in the older woman's voice. But no, Maggie was smiling indulgently at her.

'Have fun,' she said lightly as she walked away.

For an instant, Emily thought she would call her back, but Maggie was already in the corridor. The door clicked softly shut behind her, and then she was alone with Brett.

13

'Are you hungry?'

Emily dragged her eyes away from the closed door with difficulty as Brett spoke. It was a perfectly normal, unthreatening question and she fought her rising panic to answer him with a nod. He pulled out her chair for her and, seeing her hesitate before moving towards it, moved back to his side of the table.

Heavens above, here she was expecting to make love with this man, and she couldn't even bring herself to risk brushing against him when she took her seat! It was never going to work.

'Um . . . I don't know that this was such a good idea . . . I—'

She raised her hands, palms upwards in a small gesture of helplessness as she struggled, and failed to find the right words. Glancing nervously at Brett, she saw that he was regarding her levelly, his dark head held slightly on one side, as if waiting for her to answer an unspoken question.

'What I mean is . . .' she continued, her voice rising on a note of desperation, 'I've changed my mind. This has all been a ghastly mistake!'

There – it was said. Emily held her breath, her eyes fixed on her own hands, folding and unfolding over each other, as she waited for his inevitably angry response. When it did not come, she chanced a glance at him and saw that he was still watching her, his face relaxed.

'No problem,' he said softly. 'You're calling the shots, Emily – remember?'

He smiled at her startled expression and she felt some of the awful tension ebb away.

'You . . . you mean you don't mind?'

Most men she knew would have hidden their hurt pride under loud bluster, but Brett merely stared calmly back at her, his dark eyes untroubled.

'Of course not. It would be a shame to let good food go to waste, though. Won't you at least stay and eat with me?'

Emily glanced at the covered dishes and felt her mouth water. It did smell delicious.

'Why don't you put on some music while I pour the wine and light the candles?'

He picked up a bottle from the dumb waiter beside the table and Emily watched as he deftly dispensed of the cork and poured the ruby red liquid into two large, crystal glasses. He seemed so unconcerned by her rejection of him that for one contrary moment, she felt piqued. Smiling to herself, she went over to the CD player.

What kind of music would he like? she wondered. There was a large, eclectic selection ranging from Country music through to Soul, Classical and Heavy Rock. She wavered for a moment between Grieg and Sinatra, plumping in the end for Harry Connick, Jr. As the first track began, she took her place at the table and picked up her wine glass.

Brett was looking at her strangely.

'What?' she asked, alarmed, 'What is it?'

He smiled in the face of her agitation and raised his glass to her.

'You chose one of my favourite albums,' he told her.

For a moment she thought, cynically, that he was taking the mickey, but then she saw the respect in his eyes and she smiled.

'I saw him play live when he came over to England last,' she told him. 'My mother loves that kind of thing, but it wasn't until after I heard Harry sing that I understood why!'

'Yeah, he's a one off. It takes courage to fly in the face of the modern scene at his age.'

'They say he's Sinatra's successor, don't they?'

'About time they found one!'

They laughed and some of the tension between them disappeared. Brett uncovered the shiny silver dishes and they helped themselves to rich, fragrant Boeuf Bourgignon and fluffy vegetable rice. Emily ate hungrily, washing it down with large gulps of the full-bodied red wine with which Brett kept topping up their glasses.

The music ebbed and flowed around them, its bluesy, upbeat style making her feel happy, combining with the wine to make her feel mellow. Brett was a stimulating companion, eager to argue good naturedly with her when they discovered they had both read the same book, but disagreed about its merit.

'But you couldn't possibly be qualified to comment – you don't know how a woman would think in that situation.'

'Don't be so chauvinistic! Men feel too, you know and I don't think there are such fundamental differences as feminists would have us believe.'

'Oh really? So how would you say you're like a woman?' she scoffed.

'For a start, men look for relationships in the same way that women do.'

'This is a funny setting for you to put forward that view! After all, aren't the women here trying to conduct their sex lives as they would if they were a man?'

'Maybe. But I think that's great. Why shouldn't women learn to take as much as they give? It doesn't make them any less feminine.'

Emily pushed away her empty plate and sat back in her chair, replete. She regarded Brett a little hazily over the rim of her wine glass. He too had finished his meal and was busy uncorking their third bottle of wine.

'So what made you come to work here?' she asked curiously.

Brett shrugged.

'I get free bed and board, unlimited access to the gym and the 'work' isn't so hard.'

'Don't you like hard work?'

A shadow passed across his eyes and Emily wished the sarcastic words unsaid.

'I'm sorry – that was unbelievably rude of me.'

She reached across and touched the back of his hand as it rested on the table. The crisp dark hair tickled the pads of her fingers and she pulled her hand away, as if she had inadvertently touched something hot. Dragging her gaze back to her wine glass, she felt the heat rise in her cheeks.

'It's OK. I know how it sounds. The fact is, I had an accident a few months ago. Nothing too serious, I just need to take things easy for a while. Build myself back up.'

Emily looked up in surprise.

'You look adequately built up to me,' she said, without thinking, blushing even more furiously as she realised that now he would think she had been ogling his body.

He laughed, softly.

'I'm getting there. Would you like a sweet? I believe I saw chocolate mousse with pears at the back of the fridge.'

'Chocolate is my passion!' she announced, swallowing uncomfortably as Brett merely raised an eloquent eyebrow at her.

She watched him as he walked into the kitchen. The loose-fitting black trousers hid the outline of his legs, skimming his buttocks and giving the merest hint of their shape. Emily liked the way he walked, loosely, as if he was comfortable within his own skin. Confident. Yes, that was it. There was an air of confidence about him that she found appealing, erotic.

Emily brought herself up short. They had agreed to keep things light and she was determined to stick to that agreement. She would not let herself be fooled by the mellowing effect of the wine and the music, lulled into a false sense of security by Brett's hitherto undemanding company.

She had let herself be fooled before, thinking that this time it would be different, that she would be able to go through with it. Once or twice she had even got as far as kissing, touching, feeling . . . Then the clear, horrific image of that other man's leering face would intrude, his cruel, hurting hands would replace those of the man she was with and it would be over.

'Emily?'

She jumped as Brett's warm, concerned voice enveloped her and she looked up at him, unable to hide the sudden panic which had gripped her. He frowned slightly as she stared up at him, wide eyed. He withdrew the hand he had automatically reached out to her, using it instead to pick up the glass dish he had placed on the table in front of him.

'Chocolate mousse?' he asked in a voice which made the innocuous phrase sound like 'multiple orgasms?'

Emily smiled and took the dish from him, forgetting to flinch as her fingers brushed his.

The CD had run its course and Brett got up to change it. Emily smiled in delight as she realised he had selected a compilation of classical tracks which she loved. Brett returned the smile as he regained his seat.

The rich, dark chocolate mousse slid seductively down Emily's throat, chased by the cool slipperiness of the pear. Her eyes were caught by the movement of Brett's throat as he ate, imagining him feeling the same sensations. As she raised her eyes to his, she caught her breath.

He was watching her mouth, his expression intent. As he felt her gaze on him, he met her eye and all the easy friendliness between them disappeared in an instant. Emily watched, mesmerised, as he slowly reached out his hand and touched the corner of her mouth with his forefinger.

Her lips parted slightly at the slight pressure. As he withdrew his hand, she saw that he had wiped away a smear of mousse from her lips. As she watched, he slowly brought his finger up to his own mouth and inserted the tip between his lips. Her breath hurt in her chest as she watched the movement of his lips as he sucked on his own finger.

They rose from the table with one accord and moved into the small space between it and the red damask sofas flanking the fire. Emily fought to make her mind remain blank, concentrating only on Brett as he reached out and took her hand.

Suddenly the room seemed full of him. He towered over her, a good six inches taller than her even in her ridiculously high heels. Emily's mouth felt suddenly dry, her heart beating unevenly in her chest. She moved her lips once, twice, but no sound would come out as he slipped his other arm around her waist.

She held herself rigid as he began to waltz slowly with her on the spot. He was only holding her loosely, a casual, impersonal embrace as he moved her, like an automaton, backwards and forwards. Her fingers touched his shoulder and felt the hard steel of muscle under the soft cashmere. She could feel his hand splayed across the small of her back. Their other hands were loosely clasped, no other part of them was touching. Yet she could feel the animal heat of his skin, smell the clean, slightly musky maleness of him. She shivered.

Brett must have sensed her sudden, atavistic fear, for he

made no attempt to draw her closer, even when the melody slowed and coiled around them. Neither did he respond when she tentatively tried to move away, he simply kept shuffling his feet, coaxing hers along with him and did not loosen his grip on her.

Emily tried to concentrate on the slow, steady rhythm. Forward, side, together, back, side, together ... The wine had numbed her usual heavy nervousness, relaxing her tense muscles and creating a pleasant, rose tinged fog in her mind. She was no longer hungry and she felt warm, slightly drowsy from the heat of the fire. It, combined with two matching lamps burning on either side and the flickering candles on the table, provided the only light in the room.

Slowly, infinitely slowly, Emily found herself drawn into the warm circle of Brett's arms. She flinched as the tips of her breasts brushed against the broad, unyielding wall of his chest, but she did not pull away. More than anything, she found she wanted to lay her head in the tempting curve of his shoulder.

As if reading her thoughts, Brett leaned slightly towards her, so that her cheek was inches away from his chest. Breathing slowly and deeply to calm her racing heart, Emily rested her head lightly against him. He placed the hand he was holding on his other shoulder and held her tenderly round the back of her head, his other hand motionless at the small of her back.

Emily closed her eyes and sighed. She felt so safe, so secure in this curiously sexless embrace, she didn't want to move. Brett's heart was beating against her cheek, its strong, steady beat reassuring. The arms which enclosed her, though strong, were not compelling and she did not feel the usual panic of entrapment.

Gradually, she became aware that he was stroking her hair,

winding the soft curls which framed her face round and round his fingers before smoothing them round her ears. Soon, his fingers ventured in a featherlight caress to the nape of her neck and she shuddered, not with fear this time, but in reaction to the warm chills which ran down her spine.

Of its own accord, Emily's neck arched back and she opened her eyes to find herself caught in his dark, fathomless gaze. Her legs felt curiously weak and she leaned against him, aware for the first time of the hardness of his thighs beneath the innocuous black fabric of his trousers.

Her mind skittered to what might even now be stirring between those thighs and she began to pull away, but Brett held her fast by the nape of her neck, bringing his other hand up to cup her face.

Emily stood, completely still, as he gazed down at her, seeming to study every aspect of her face. He smoothed an errant curl away from her forehead and traced a line from her temple down her cheek to the corner of her mouth with his forefinger. Her bottom lip trembled as he lightly ran his finger over it and she felt an answering flutter low down in her stomach.

'So beautiful,' he whispered softly.

Emily automatically began to demur, but he stopped the self deprecating words from ever being uttered by placing his fingers against her lips.

'Ssh!'

He reached up and untied the scarf which held her hair in place. It tumbled down in a dark cloud against her face, to her shoulders and Brett ran his fingers through it, drawing it back, away from her face.

Emily's eyes widened as she watched the pupils in his dilate and he lowered his head to hers. Her first instinct was to turn her face away, to avoid the inevitable demands of his lips and tongue. Brett caught her small chin between his thumb and forefinger and gently coaxed it round.

He leaned his forehead against hers and stared into her eyes. The tips of their noses touched and his warm breath, wine sweet, caressed her tremulous mouth. Infinitely patient, he waited until the unwanted panic had subsided and Emily relaxed against him. Still he held her chin as he brought his lips to hers.

It was a kiss like no other that Emily had ever experienced. She had braced herself for a hard, demanding onslaught, but it never came. Brett brushed his lips over the fullness of hers so lightly that they tingled, before he planted a tiny, butterfly kiss at the corner of her mouth. Slowly, his eyes still holding hers, he worked his way along her mouth in a series of minute kisses.

Using his thumb, he gently pulled down her lower lip so that the soft, wet flesh inside was exposed. Emily's eyes fluttered to a close as he ran his tongue along the intimate, tender flesh before covering her mouth with his.

Even then, the kiss was gentle, though, strangely, it was not tentative. He seemed to be drawing out the pleasure of his first taste of her, savouring the warm, honeyed sweetness of her mouth while pressing her more tightly against him. Emily's lips parted slightly as he applied the lightest pressure against the forbidding barrier of her teeth and she welcomed the heat of his mouth over hers.

She frowned as he slowly pulled away, her eyes flying open as a rush of cool air came between them. He was looking at her quizzically, silently asking if she wanted to continue. Emily trembled slightly in his arms, aware that her breasts had swollen in their lacy restraint, and that a liquid fire was smouldering in her secret places.

She wanted him to carry on, cursed him for breaking into

the sensual thrall in which he had enveloped her. Now she had time to think, the cold, irrational fear curled up from her toes and took hold, beginning to consume her.

A frown passed fleetingly over Brett's dark face before he reclaimed her mouth. Emily resisted him for a few seconds before slipping mercifully back into the realms of sensation. The cool, searching lips were nothing like the rough, snarling mouth of the man who had attacked her. The long, sensitive fingers now playing up and down her spine were as different as they could be from those cruel, hurting hands which had haunted her for so long.

Emily whimpered, deep in her throat and Brett pulled away again, scanning her face with tender, caring eyes. As if reading the fear, reflected in her pupils, he kissed her eyelids closed, covering her face in kisses as he bent her back over his arm, exposing the long white column of her throat.

The whimper turned into a gasp of pleasure as his cool, seeking lips travelled down from her chin to the sensitive hollow at the join of her collar-bone. She felt his tongue dart out and caress the soft skin there before he turned his attention to the line of her jaw. Travelling from one ear to the other, he explored the sensitve skin beneath her jawline with lips and tongue, tickling and tantalising until Emily was desperate for him to return to her mouth.

With a small groan of frustration, she caught his face between her two hands and brought it up to hers. She felt his lips curve into a small smile of satisfaction as she initiated the kiss. This time, it was more urgent. His lips were more demanding on hers, pushing them back against her teeth. Yet instead of frightening her, as it might have mere minutes before, the urgency of the kiss only served to increase the hard core of pleasure building deep in her womb.

She was more than ready for the intrusion of his tongue,

tentatively at first, then probing deeper as she drew it in. He tasted of good red wine and rich chocolate and she sucked on him, relishing the echo of the meal they had just shared.

Gradually, Emily became aware that by his holding her more closely against him, she could now feel the evidence of his arousal that he had been careful to conceal from her before. It nudged her thigh, a swollen, demanding animal, independent of its owner. She pulled away abruptly.

'I . . . the music . . . You change the music while I go . . . er . . . while I go to the bathroom.'

She did not give Brett a chance to react, she had rushed through the open bedroom door and into the small *en suite* bathroom locking the door behind her.

Once inside, she went into autopilot, using the lavatory and flushing it before washing her hands at the little sink. Catching a glimpse of her reflection in the mirror tiles, she stopped in her tracks. She hardly recognised herself! Her cheeks were flushed, her hair dishevelled. Her hazel eyes looked unnaturally bright, her lips full and red. And this was the effect a kiss could have on her?

Emily stood and stared at her reflection for a few minutes, waiting for her heartbeat to slow. She began to feel ridiculous. Kissing Brett had been wholly unlike anything she had ever experienced before, a delicious, enjoyable experience which she hadn't wanted to end. It was only when she felt the hardness of him, the impossible, masculine *size* of it . . .

Where was it she had read that size didn't matter, it was what one did with it that mattered? Emily giggled, a trifle hysterically. She was sure that was advice given to the under-endowed, not a generously sized man like Brett!

Emily bit her lip. Perhaps there was some truth in what the magazines said. That other man had used his tool like a battering ram, an instrument of torture. From what she knew of him, she couldn't imagine Brett hurting her. Unless he was a complete Jekyll and Hyde.

She jumped as there was a soft knock at the door.

'Are you all right in there?'

She smiled at the concern in his voice, sorry that she had caused it.

'Yes, I . . . I'll be out in a minute.'

She listened as his footsteps receded before holding her cold hands under the warm flow of water, absorbing the heat.

When she went back into the lounge, Brett was sitting on one of the sofas, his dark head resting against its back, his eyes closed. Emily stood quietly and watched him for a moment. He had taken off the green jumper and loosened his tie. Several crisp, black curls escaped over the open collar of his shirt. Their wine glasses sat, refilled, on the coffee table and another classical CD was playing.

Less inhibited now that his eyes were closed, Emily's gaze roved to the apex of his thighs which were spread casually, bent at the knee. She could see no sign of that hot tumescence which had so worried her before. Watching him sitting, relaxed and confident on the sofa, Emily felt a mule's kick of need, the like of which she had never felt before.

It startled her to realise that she wanted him. Yet she did not know how to overcome the fears that blighted her desire. Trust. She had to trust him. Emily took a deep breath.

Slowly, so as not to alert him to her presence, she crept across the room until she was standing between his outstretched thighs. She watched with bated breath as he opened his eyes and saw her standing there. He smiled and reached up to grasp both her hands in his.

Emily allowed herself to be pulled onto his lap, wrapping her arms around his neck automatically to regain her balance. He dipped his head and nuzzled the warm swell of her breasts under the indian cotton blouse, breathing in the woman-scent of her before reaching up and pulling her head down to meet his.

As his mouth fused with hers, Emily felt the unfamiliar warmth spread from the centre of her through her body, causing her arms and legs to grow heavy and her eyelids to droop. She entangled her fingers in his thick, dark hair, clinging on as he dazzled her senses, stroking the soft, sensitive skin of her mouth with the tip of his tongue, drawing out responses she had never dreamed she was capable of.

She barely noticed when his hand edged upwards from where it rested at her waist and began to fondle the underswell of her breasts. As he gently disengaged his mouth from hers, Emily found to her surprise that she was panting lightly, gasping for breath as she sought to bring her racing heart under control.

Brett had unfastened the thin ties at the modesty-preserving neck of her blouse and Emily looked down at herself through half-closed eyes. Against the floral prettiness of the gypsy style top, the creamy swell of her breasts looked shocking. Swollen with passion, they fought against the restraint of the dainty, lacy black bra, on the verge of spilling out over the top.

Emily's first instinct was to reach down, to cover herself, but even as she thought it, Brett's dark head blocked her view and she felt the gentle rasp of his tongue in the dark valley between her breasts. She gasped as he gathered up one trembling globe in his hand and brought it up to meet his lips.

The first touch of his tongue against her hardening nipple sent sharp needles of sensation jabbing through her body, down to her hot, moist centre. Caught between panic and need, Emily groaned, unable to stop herself from thrusting forward, inviting him to enclose the aching tip of her breast with his seeking lips.

And as her straining nipple was drawn into the hot, wet cavern of his mouth, Emily allowed her tightly pressed thighs to relax and fall apart and she released a long, shuddering sigh of surrender.

And in that searing instant he was drawn to ... the ...
... her ... and ... she ... the ... of ... her fingers
... her ... of her ... to her ... the ... the ...
... ...

14

Brett's fingertips worked a tantalisingly slow path from her knee under her long, flowing skirt along the outside of her thigh. Her legs were bare, the skin warm and soft and his fingers glided smoothly across the naked skin.

Emily felt the goosebumps rise on her flesh as he reached the uppermost part of her groin before returning to her knee. This time he worked his way up her inner thigh. With infinite slowness, he raised his head from her breast and sought her mouth as his fingertips reached the uppermost part of her thigh and his hand enveloped her lace-covered mound.

As he squeezed gently, experimentally, Emily opened her eyes and was caught by his intense dark gaze. He held her eye as if gauging her reaction as he slipped his forefinger into the elastic of her briefs and stroked the moist curls within with the back of his finger.

Emily's breath caught in her throat, her eyes widening with alarm as he began to deepen the caress. Instantly, he stopped, returning to the gentle stroking movement as he turned the main thrust of his attention to her mouth.

It opened in sweet surrender under his and Emily's eyes fluttered to a close. She clung to him, her fingers digging into his shoulders as he plundered the secret recesses of her mouth, his fingers curling possessively over the damp curls at the apex of her thighs.

A small sound, half protest, half agreement, escaped her lips as he suddenly removed his hands and mouth, bringing his arms about her, one around her shoulders, the other beneath her knees. She held onto him tightly as, with one sure, graceful movement, he rose, sweeping her up into his arms as if she were weightless.

'Hush,' he whispered against her hair, 'trust me.'

And she did. Leaning her head against the hard pillow of his chest, Emily allowed him to carry her out of the living room and into the bedroom beyond, kicking the door shut behind him. He lay her on the bed, gentling her with kisses as she murmured a half-hearted protest.

The bedroom was dark, lit only by two dim lamps at either side of the bed and by the diffuse light of the full moon which filtered through the uncurtained window. The moonlight illuminated the hard planes of Brett's face, casting eerie shadows across his features as he rose and stood at the end of the bed.

Emily's mouth felt dry as she watched him slowly unbutton his shirt and shrug it off, discarding it carelessly on the floor. Moonbeams silvered his smooth skin as she feasted her eyes on the broad sweep of his shoulders. The cords of his neck were prominent, disappearing into the thick, curly mat of dark hair which covered his pecs and tapered down in a perfect 'V' towards his navel.

His stomach was flat and hard, the tracery of well-toned muscles visible under the taut skin. Emily's eyes followed the line of hair down to where it disappeared into the waistband of his trousers. He was hard, an unmistakable tumescence stretching the fabric. Emily's eyes darted back up to his and she swallowed against the unwelcome spasm of alarm which gripped her.

The expression in his eyes reassured her, for while they were intent and knowing, she could still see the gentleness which was so much a part of him, in their depths. Gentleness and strength – it was a powerful combination. Emily's lips curved slowly into a smile.

She felt she should participate in some way, should perhaps remove her own clothes, but a residue of shyness remained. Besides, she wanted to concentrate on the spectacle of Brett's belt sliding slowly, inexorably through the belt loops before he began to unbutton his fly.

He was wearing boxer shorts underneath, black cotton, which barely contained his masculinity. Dark hair curled on his tightly muscled thighs and Emily's fingers itched to reach out and touch him. Would his body hair be coarse and rough, or silky soft? Still she held back, unsure how to behave, afraid that if she moved the old fears would return with a vengeance and stop her wanting him.

For she *did* want him. More than anything she could ever remember wanting, she wanted to possess Brett, wanted to feel the beautiful body which was now standing, motionless, in front of her, melding with her own.

She held her breath as he came round to the side of the bed. It dipped under his weight as he sat next to her, leaning on one bent elbow and regarding her for a long moment, his expression inscrutable. She lay, motionless as a rag doll as he began to undress her.

First he removed her blouse, pulling it up over her head and casting it aside. He dispensed nimbly with the inadequate black bra, running the palm of his hand lightly over the hard nubs of her breasts before turning his attention to her skirt. She lifted her hips obligingly as he pulled it down and it went to join the rest of their clothes on the floor.

She was naked now but for the black lace panties. They felt damp between her thighs as Emily squirmed under his scrutiny. Then Brett dipped his head and began to kiss downwards, from her neck. By the time he reached her navel, she knew that she was beautiful.

Every kiss, every movement of his darting tongue convinced her of his desire. Her skin burned in his wake, her limbs trembling with the strength of her reaction to him. She lay motionless, her breath coming in short, shallow gasps as he caressed the soft, sensitive skin between each of her toes with the tip of his tongue.

Tentatively, she gathered up her own breasts in her hands and was shocked by the rigid swell of her nipples, pressing into her palms. Brett sucked lightly on her big toe and she felt tension knot in her stomach. She wanted to feel him close to her, wanted to press her female softness against the long, lean length of his body.

'Brett,' she whispered, 'hold me . . . please.'

Her voice sounded hoarse, deep, completely unlike itself as he slid up the bed and took her in his arms. She buried her face in the moist musky depths of his chest and closed her eyes. Her fingers shook as she laid her hand on his chest. His hair was coarse, yet surprisingly soft. One neat, male nipple pressed against her palm and she cautiously rubbed it, pulling her hand away as if stung when it responded by growing hard.

'It's all right,' he murmured against her hair, as if sensing the imminent return of her fears, 'I'm not going to hurt you.'

'Do it now then, Brett, now, quickly, before I change my mind again!'

'Wait . . . there's more, Emily, so much more!'

'Please!' her fingers worked feverishly at the button of his boxer shorts. 'There'll be time afterwards for all the rest!'

'Emily . . .'

'I need to have you inside me! Before my body closes against you . . . Oh!'

Her fingers closed around the hard, silky column of his penis. It stirred slightly against her palm and her wide eyes were drawn to the naked crown. Tentatively, she ran her thumb across the tip, surprised and delighted to find the skin there velvet soft, newborn.

Brett's breathing sounded shallower and she flicked her eyes upwards, gauging his reaction. He was regarding her through narrowed eyes and there was a tension about the way he held his jaw which gave her a little thrill of power.

It had to be now. Even while she lusted after him, she could feel the tiny, insidious tendrils of fear curling in her stomach, reaching out and invading every part of her. Aware that she must seem desperate, she drew him closer to her, rubbing the tip of him against her bare thigh as she lay back on the pillows.

Brett rolled over and levered himself up onto his hands, placed either side of his head. He watched her face as he knelt between her tremulously parted thighs and nudged gently at the entrance of her body. Emily closed her eyes.

She felt his fingers coaxing her moist flesh leaves apart, running softly over the sensitive folds, sending little shivers along her quivering nerve endings. Her mouth and throat felt dry in the prelude to panic she had dreaded. She gasped as he entered her, smoothly, without force, and her well-prepared body opened and welcomed him in.

Emily's eyes opened as he began to move slowly in her. A liquid heat seemed to be consuming her from within, travelling in swirling waves along her veins until she glowed. Brett covered her parted lips and kissed her deeply, his large hands cradling her head in their palms, gentling her.

With each long, controlled thrust, his penis scraped deliciously over her untutored clitoris, making her juices flow faster, easing his way. She had never dreamed it could be like this! Lingering, gentle . . . essentially loving.

Brett's pupils had dilated so that she could no longer see the iris. Her own face, rapt, was mirrored in them as he almost imperceptibly increased the tempo. As the friction caused little ripples of sensation to run along her inner flesh, Emily instinctively drew up her knees and wrapped her legs around his waist, drawing him deeper into her.

His face was intent, the muscles of his shoulders as she dug her fingers into them, held taut. A fine sheen of perspiration filmed his forehead as he levered the upper half of his body up off the bed, away from her. Now Emily could see the fusion of their bodies as she glanced down between them. Unable to drag her eyes away, she saw how their pubic hair meshed together, saw the strong white column of his penis, glistening with the moisture of her body, as it withdrew and plunged in.

She gasped as she felt the ripples of sensation come faster, building slowly, inexorably to a crescendo. Clenching her teeth, she drew him down against her, needing to feel his weight, anchoring her as she drummed her heels compulsively against his thrusting buttocks.

'Oh! Oh my God! Oh . . .!'

She thrashed her head from side to side as white light exploded inside her head and her entire body was wracked by uncontrollable shudders. In response, Brett thrust faster and harder into her, his voice joining hers as they sped together into a vortex of feeling, abandoning all rational thought on the way.

Emily had lost all track of time. Gradually, her heartbeat slowed and her temperature returned to normal. Slowly, it seeped into her consciousness that her legs felt cramped and that Brett's body, still wrapped around her, was heavy and damp. She stirred slightly in mild protest.

He opened his eyes and took his weight onto his elbows. His eyes smiled as he looked down at her.

'Well,' he said, his voice hoarse still with reaction.

Emily smiled weakly, still not quite able to believe what had happened between them.

'Well indeed!' she whispered.

Brett removed himself gently from her and coaxed her under the duvet. Pulling her into the circle of his arms, he kissed the top of her head.

'Are you all right?'

'Hmmm!' was all she could manage.

Her limbs felt heavy, as if she had just endured a marathon session in the gym. Between her legs, where the result of their union now seeped warmly onto the sheets, there was a slight, but not unpleasurable soreness.

Emily lay, her head pillowed on Brett's chest, her arms about his waist and examined her feelings. To her surprise, she found none of the regret, no uncomfortable realisation that she had make a mistake, which she had expected to find. She felt . . . replete, yes, that was it! But she had the feeling that the sensation would only be temporary. As if she had just consumed the most delicious, the most exquisitely prepared hors d'oeuvre which had primed her palate for the main meal to come.

She stirred impatiently, levering herself up onto one elbow so that she could look down into Brett's face. Feeling her gaze upon him, his eyelids flickered, then opened. He smiled at her quizzically.

'Are *you* all right?' she asked.

'Sure.'

'Then could we move on to the main course?'

Emily blushed even as she said it. He would have had to have read her mind to know what she was talking about, yet his firm, well-shaped lips curved into a wicked grin as he reached for her.

It was as if, having superceded that first, awful experience when Emily was young, all her fears and inhibitions which had kept her chaste for so long had been swept away. Her body vibrated with a life of its own, independent of her thinking mind, eager for new experiences, further explorations into sensuality.

She lay still, her eyes closed to block out any visual stimuli which might detract from what she felt. Brett's lips were warm against her still damp skin as he sought out every tiny, sensitive patch of skin, helping her to discover erogenous zones she never knew existed.

Emily shivered, unable to anticipate where she would next feel the rasp of his tongue. First it was behind her ear, then in the hollow beneath her hip bone. Her toes curled against the cotton sheets as he traced a path from her collar-bone to her navel, making the goosebumps stand up on her skin.

The first touch of his lips against her swollen sex sent a jolt of electricity through her from head to toe. She could feel the slippery folds of flesh open up under his possessive mouth, inviting him in. Her back arched, he found the small, hard bud which was at the root of her pleasure. In her mind's eye, she imagined it slipping out from under its demure hood and thrusting itself, lewdly demanding, at him.

Emily opened her eyes and looked down. All she could see of Brett was the top of his dark head against the whiteness of her skin, her spread thighs framing his face. His hands kneaded the muscles of her legs, making them ache pleasurably.

She had a sudden, overwhelming urge to stretch. Reaching up to the bedhead, she arched her back higher, lengthening her spine as far as she could. Her lower legs rested on Brett's broad back and she placed her weight on them, pointing her toes downwards as she pushed forward.

Brett's hands came beneath her, supporting her bottom whilst at the same time he took her straining clitoris between his teeth and nibbled on it gently. Emily went wild as her orgasm exploded, bolt after bolt of lightning, coursing through her veins, suffusing her with heat.

Brett held her still, his lips pressed hard against her throbbing nub as the waves at last subsided, leaving her drained. She whimpered slightly as he lay down beside her, curling up with her back to him. He put his arms around her and moulded his body to hers, spoon fashion. Emily had never felt more comfortable in her life and, with a small sigh of contentment, she closed her eyes.

When she woke about an hour later, Brett had rolled over, onto his back. One arm was flung out at right angles to his body, the other still cradled Emily. He was sleeping heavily, his strong, symmetrical features relaxed, his dark hair tousled.

Emily ran her eyes over him greedily, examining him more fully than she would ever have dared had his eyes been open. Those eyes were fringed with the thickest, longest lashes she had ever seen on a man. They looked incongruous, somehow, the only feminine feature on a totally masculine face as they shadowed the area under his eye.

His skin was a smooth, sun warmed brown, stretched tight across his bones. There was a slight bump half way down his nose, but his lips, soft skinned, yet firm, were perfectly formed, the lower slightly fuller than the upper.

Tentatively, Emily reached out and ran a finger along his jawline. It was strong and firm, like the rest of him, and she could feel the sharp rasp of his beard as it pushed stubbornly through his pores. He looked like the type of man who had to shave twice a day, she mused, her eyes running over the black shadow.

His breathing was still deep and even so Emily dared to look further. Gently, so as not to disturb him, she peeled back the covers to expose his nakedness. Beneath his jaw, his neck ran in a thick, strong column to the place where his collar-bones met. Touching him lightly there, with the tips of her fingers, Emily watched his Adam's apple move in automatic contraction.

Obeying an impulse, she dipped her head and pressed her lips against it before moving down to kiss the hollow at the base of his throat. The skin there was warm and slightly damp. She darted out her tongue and tasted the salty tang of it, nervously, as if biting into forbidden fruit.

Glancing quickly upwards, she saw that still he slept, one arm thrown out, unmoving. Her eyes ran across the breadth of his shoulders, liking their symmetry, the beauty of the smooth, polished skin. Further down that glowing flesh was all but covered by the thick, silkily coarse hair that covered him like a gossamer blanket. His flat, male nipples showed through, dark pink and hardening as they were exposed to the slight chill of the room.

Once again, Emily followed her instincts and kissed him, there. And down, down his mid-line to where his taut, flat stomach quivered under her lips. Keeping her eyes averted, for now, from the swelling column which nudged her chin impertinently, she ran her lips around the circle of his waist to his left side.

It was there she found the scar, puckered, still livid, about four inches long, though thin, and winding upward towards his armpit. Emily paused, frowning, remembering how he had told her he had been in an accident. Gently, she placed her cheek against the damaged flesh before nibbling her way back to his navel.

His breathing had quickened now, become more shallow, but still he did not open his eyes. Emily wondered if he were truly still asleep, or whether he faked it. Bypassing the more obvious of his masculine charms, she traced a line up the soles of his feet, from his heels to his toes. He didn't flinch, though his closed eyelids flickered.

Emily smiled and trailed her fingers lightly round his ankles, rolling her thumbs on the bone and walking her nails slowly up his shins. His large, hair roughened thighs tensed as she kneaded them, slowly working upwards to his cock which twitched, once, in anticipation.

He was not asleep now, of that she was certain, yet he kept his eyes firmly closed against her. The sudden tension in his muscles told her he was alert, waiting for her next move. Her hand reached out and hovered, unsure. She held her breath as her hand lowered and closed around the strong, pale column which rose from the thick nest of hair between his thighs.

It was warm, the skin unexpectedly soft as she lightly ran the palm of her hand along its length. Brett appeared to be holding his breath too, now, and Emily felt an answering pull deep inside her as he let it out on a jagged sigh and shifted slightly under her hand.

Growing in confidence, Emily touched the pink, velvety helmet and ran the tip of her finger round the edge before following the tiny crease with one fingernail. She squeezed gently, milking him, before enclosing him in her hand and running it up and down, moving the skin over the swollen column.

Tearing her eyes away, she scanned his face. A slight frown etched a line between his eyebrows, his mouth was drawn into a thin line, his jaw clenched in concentration. There was a light film of sweat across his forehead and on his upper lip and Emily swooped to run her tongue along it, the unexpectedness of the action making his lips part in a gasp.

Emily took advantage of his surprise and covered his mouth with her own, kissing him deeply. The inside of his mouth was hot, his tongue as it met hers, hard and demanding. Emily let go of his cock and braced both hands either side of his head against the pillows. Her arms turned to liquid as the kiss went on and on, so she straddled him, one knee either side of his waist. Although only their lips touched, Emily could feel the scorching heat of his skin, it glowed and gave off warmth, drawing her down to him.

They pulled apart, gasping for breath. His eyes were open now, boring into hers. Emily could feel the lips of her nether mouth pout and open in response to the expression in his eyes. Without so much as a butterfly caress from his fingers, the moisture gathered there and made her ready to receive him.

Slowly, never breaking eye contact, Emily reached down between her legs and parted the lips of her sex. The skin felt hot and slippery under her fingers as she lowered herself onto him and sheathed the tip of his shaft. They stayed like that, poised, for several seconds. Then slowly, excruciatingly gradually, Emily sank down on him.

First the tip disappeared inside her, then, inch by inch, he was enclosed by her hungry passage. His eyes seemed to glaze over as she took the last of him in and sat astride him, absolutely still. His cock seemed to swell even more, filling her up, his hairy balls tickling at the puckered mouth of her anus.

He reached up for her, but Emily shook her head. She wanted to watch his face, see his every nuance of expression as she rode him. She wanted to watch him as he came.

She shifted her weight slightly so that she was leaning back, her back arched. Brett's eyes were drawn to where her hardening clitoris thrust forward, clear of the russet curls of her mons. His eyes were hot on her as he reached down and guided her own hand down to it, pressing the tip of her middle finger against it.

Emily flushed hotly and shook her head, resisting.

'No!' she whispered.

Brett smiled gently and moved her finger slightly. Emily closed her eyes as the small action sent butterflies fluttering through her stomach. Gradually she forgot he was watching her, barely noticing when he took his guiding hand away.

She felt the perspiration break out on her skin as she grew warmer. God it was good! To masturbate herself whilst so full of him. She began to move her hips, gently at first, then more savagely. Rising up on her knees, she withdrew from him until only the tip of him was inside her, before sinking back down again.

The cords on Brett's neck stood out as she repeated the action, more quickly this time. His eyes were riveted on her circling finger as it caressed her clitoris and he watched as his own cock came into view before being swallowed up again.

Emily could feel the pressure building, building, deep within her. Instinctively, she began to tap rhythmically on her straining nub. Tap tap tap, harder and harder, faster and faster until she was thrashing the tiny bud. She cried out as her climax exploded, bucking her hips and closing her eyes despite herself.

Brett was close to joining her, she could feel the dam was about to burst. With an effort, Emily opened her eyes to watch him. His eyes were fixed on her face, but he did not appear to be seeing her. Sweat plastered the hair to his forehead, his lips were dry, his breath coming in short, sharp gasps.

Emily concentrated on keeping to the rhythm she had built up, quickening her pace as she saw that he was about to come. His lips moved, wordlessly, as the first, warning spurt of semen hit the entrance to her womb, then he threw back his head, arching his neck as he lost control.

Emily pressed her lips against his throat as his seed flooded her and trickled back out again, squeezing her muscles tightly to milk every last drop of him. And when at last he slumped, spent, she collapsed on top of him and smothered his face with kisses.

'God! You're wonderful!' he whispered hoarsely as his mouth sought and found hers.

They cuddled up close and held each other as the storm between them subsided, leaving in its wake a delicious lassitude. After a few minutes, Emily stretched and yawned. She could feel Brett's eyes on her.

'What? What is it?' she asked as she saw his expression.

He shrugged and pulled his eyes away, telling her that he was unhappy. Suddenly her new found confidence rushed away, leaving her feeling exposed and raw.

'Wasn't it . . . I thought it was good?' she asked, her voice pitifully small.

Brett sat up and stared down at her in the encroaching dusk.

'It was wonderful, Emily – how can you doubt it?'

He stroked her hair with a tenderness which brought tears to clog her throat.

'Then why . . .?'

'It's nothing. Just that I wish . . .'

'What? What do you wish?' she pressed him impatiently, hoping against all hope that his thoughts mirrored her own.

He smiled, self-mocking, glancing away as if marshalling his thoughts.

'I just wish we had more time. Sorry.'

Emily could not stop the grin which spread across her face as he spoke aloud the words she had not dared utter.

'Sorry?' she echoed.

'I shouldn't say that, I guess.'

'We have a weekend place, a cottage in Cornwall,' she said, her words rushing into each other. 'We could go there, just the two of us, for as long as we wanted . . . Oh! But of course. It's me who should be apologising, asking such a thing of you.'

'Emily?'

'You've agreed to work here, haven't you? I'm only your first assignment.'

Reality, like a bucket of ice-cold water, dampened what was left of her ardour. Emily felt like a fool, allowing herself to get so carried away. Forgetting that this wonderful night had been bought for her by her mother. By credit card.

Brett was still smiling softly down at her and she frowned questioningly at him.

'You're so beautiful, Emily, so very lovely. I think I'm already half-way in love with you.'

'Brett . . .!' she was half shocked, half exhilarated by his earnestly spoken words.

'And that after only one night!' he laughed softly. 'With more time together . . . could we go to this place now? Tonight?'

Emily stared back at him and knew she would do anything, go anywhere to find out if he was right, if what had flared between them these past few hours was more than a simple conflagration of their hormones. And at that moment she knew that she *wanted* him to be right.

'But . . . don't you have a contract?' she whispered.

Brett smiled slightly.

'I'm my own man, Emily. Any contract can be broken.'

He waited until she nodded before branding her with his kiss.

15

'Where is Brett?'

Maggie looked up in surprise as the line of men in front of her stirred. Not one met her eye as she passed her gaze over each of them, which was unusual in itself. Normally there was a continuous, easy banter during roll-call and no one had ever failed to answer any question she cared to ask them. Something was up. Maggie frowned as she realised that since she had, reluctantly, left Brett with Emily the night before, she hadn't caught a glimpse of him.

Dismissing the line up, she made her way to her office where she was met by a very agitated Hilary.

'Hilary! Whatever are you doing here this time in the morning?'

'You might well ask!'

Maggie glanced at her in surprise as she opened the door. Two hectic spots of colour stood out on the woman's normally pale cheeks and she could not seem to stand still. A burning cigarette was clamped between her fingers in defiance of the club's no-smoking rule.

'You'd better come in.'

Once inside, Hilary paced to the window and back again before confronting Maggie. She waved her cigarette around as she spoke, as if to emphasise every word.

'I entrusted my daughter into your care!' Hilary launched into speech, clearly upset.

'I didn't see Emily when she left, I—'

'I don't suppose she wanted you to see her!' Hilary interrupted. No doubt she thought you would have tried to stop her leaving if you had.'

'Didn't it go well?' Maggie asked, worried that her instincts in choosing Brett for Emily had been wrong.

'Go well?' Hilary's voice rose an octave. 'Go well? Yes, it went all right. Too bloody well!' She broke off, as if she had explained enough.

Maggie felt completely bewildered. Frowning, she said, 'I'm sorry, Hilary, but I'm not following you.'

'Emily telephoned me this morning, early. She's in Cornwall at our weekend cottage with this . . . this man you introduced her to!'

Maggie went hot, then cold as the implications of what Hilary was saying sank in.

'With Brett? But they can't be. Brett's under contract to the club.'

'So much for that!' Hilary snorted, her normally musical voice flat with agitation. 'This Brett character clearly has no sense of responsibility. And you've let him run off with my daughter!'

'Now Hilary,' Maggie said soothingly, 'let's have a cup of coffee together and talk this through. Believe me, I'm just as stunned as you are.'

Hilary allowed herself to be steered towards the lemon chintz sofa, crossing her legs elegantly as Maggie rang for coffee to be brought up. She seemed a little calmer as they sipped in silence. By the time she placed the little cup and saucer back on the coffee table, she had regained much of her usual poise.

'I owe you an apology,' she said unexpectedly, waving away Maggie's polite protest. 'No, I do. Emily is quite old enough to be responsible for her own actions. It was ridiculous of me to accuse you of negligence! And if the man had been holding her against her will, she would have hardly phoned to tell me, would she?'

Maggie smiled slightly at the thoroughly unlikely idea of Brett kidnapping Emily. The smile was wiped off her face as Hilary continued.

'I think it was all this talk of being in love which panicked me. I mean, she's spent one night with this man, and already she's hinting at wedding bells and happily ever after!'

'What?'

Maggie thought of Brett, naked, dripping wet and half-drowned in bubbles in the Jacuzzi. Anger, regret, jealousy – all shot through her in quick succession. She closed her eyes, briefly. When she opened them again, she saw that Hilary had dropped her elegant, cropped head into her hands and was crying softly.

'Hilary?'

Maggie instinctively went to sit beside her on the sofa, laying one hand on her shoulder in an awkward gesture of comfort.

'I'm sorry. It's just that I was so worried. Emily's all I've got, she's my baby. She's never done anything like this before!'

She began to sob quietly and Maggie put her arms around her shoulders, drawing her head under her chin. Patting her back comfortingly, she waited until the worst was over, wrapped up in her own thoughts. Gradually, she became aware that Hilary's head had dropped to her breast and rested there.

Maggie stroked the short, red-gold hair. It crackled with life under her fingers, picking up the sunlight which streamed through the window so that it looked as if it had caught fire. Fascinated, Maggie touched her lips against the top of Hilary's head. Her hair felt like silk against the soft skin of her lips, lightly fragranced like fresh peaches.

Slowly, without a word passing between them, Hilary's head turned so that her face was buried in the warm valley between Maggie's generous breasts. Maggie was wearing a soft cream silk blouse over a lacy camisole which laced with ribbons up the front. Her breasts swelled as Hilary's mouth brushed across them, the nipples thrusting wantonly against the flimsy confines of the inadequate camisole.

Beneath the tight red skirt and lace panties, Maggie felt a familiar stirring. She hadn't expected this, not from Hilary, yet she welcomed it, eager for another taste of a woman's softness. This time there would be no coercion, no casually inflicted pain, just a slaking of the lust which was quickly gaining hold of her. Reaching under Hilary's head, she cupped her chin in her palm and raised her head.

Hilary's face was very pale, her usually immaculate make-up streaked with tears. Her mascara had smudged slightly and Maggie wiped away the black stain with the pad of her thumb. A few fine lines around her eyes was the only clue that she was past the first flush of youth, and the years sat lightly on her. The wide blue eyes sparkled with her recent tears, the small, soft mouth tremulous as Maggie's eyes rested on her lips.

'Undress for me, Hilary,' she whispered.

Hilary stood immediately and began to unfasten the buttons on the jacket of her soft lilac suit, her eyes never leaving Maggie's face. The jacket slipped off her shoulders and she threw it carelessly at the coffee table where it slithered to the floor. The short, tight skirt eased over her slender hips and was kicked aside.

Underneath, Hilary wore an oyster coloured, full-length bra slip in silk satin. Beneath that, nothing. Maggie's eyes were drawn to the shadow between her thighs which was tantalisingly visible through the thin fabric.

Hilary's long legs were bare, disappearing into plain, high-heeled courts dyed the same pale lilac as her suit. She wore a heavy perfume which Maggie vaguely recognised. It reached out to her, enveloping her in its heady scent.

Without a word, Maggie stood and shed her own blouse and skirt, facing Hilary dressed in nothing but her lacy white camisole and matching briefs, black hold-ups and strappy high-heels. Both women smiled before stepping forward.

Hilary felt light in her arms as they kissed, their tongues already parrying hotly. Running her hands down the other woman's arms, Maggie admired the taut flesh, kept young by exercise and careful diet. She knew the rest of her body would be in the same condition and felt a thrill of delicious anticipation as she imagined the exploration to come.

They broke apart to shed what remained of their clothes until they were both naked, apart from Hilary's shoes and Maggie's hold-ups and sandals. Each pair of hungry eyes raked the opposite body. Hilary's breasts were small, almost conical in shape, crowned by nipples of the palest pink, hardened like two small buttons. Beneath her breasts, her stomach was gently rounded, the skin perfect but for a fine tracery of stretch marks which did nothing to detract from her beauty.

The soft, curling hair between her legs was the same bright gold as that on her head. They were of a similar height in their high heels and as they each stepped forward again, as if of one accord, Maggie's full, softly rounded breasts swayed against Hilary's.

Maggie gasped as their nipples touched and Hilary's slim arms came about her waist.

'Oh yes!' the older woman murmured, increasing the press–ure so that Maggie's breasts were flattened against her, the hard tips grinding against the smooth buttons of her own.

Maggie felt the rasp of Hilary's fiery pubic curls against the more mundane black of her own and she thrust her hips forward, increasing the contact. They kissed, slowly, taking their time, tasting and savouring each other. Hilary's mouth tasted slightly of peppermint and something sweeter, like honey. Maggie sighed into her mouth.

When they broke apart, they stared, wonderingly, into each other's eyes. Then Hilary turned and led Maggie by the hand to the couch. Smiling slightly, she lay back on the pillows, her legs hooked at the knee over the arm and a cushion pulled beneath her bottom so that her smooth-skinned buttocks were raised for Maggie's pleasure.

Maggie's eyes felt heavy as she ran them over the supine figure of the woman in front of her. Her lips tingled from their kiss, her tongue eager for a richer honey.

'Open up for me, darling,' she whispered.

Hilary slowly spread her legs and displayed herself. Beneath the vibrant curls her flesh was paler than any Maggie had ever seen. The outer lips pouted invitingly, the flower-like labia opening before her eyes. She was very aroused, the petal-soft skin glistened wetly in the sunlight.

Lower down, the skin puckered to a darker pink at the forbidden orifice which stretched open as if, like her vagina, it yearned to be loved. Maggie sank to her knees at the end of the couch and delicately dabbed her tongue against the moist crease of Hilary's exposed sex.

Hilary sighed jaggedly and reached down to touch her clitoris. Maggie watched with lust-drugged eyes as it peeked from beneath its protective hood, responding to the knowing caress of Hilary's expensively manicured fingers. She imagined those long, lilac-painted fingernails scoring lightly along her own yearning flesh leaves and stood up.

Smiling at Hilary's inquisitive expression, Maggie straddled her on the couch, her back to her face. Slowly, she spread her legs and lowered herself down so that they were sixty-nined. Hilary's nether lips closed about her tongue as she made the first long, luxurious sweep from her bud to her opening and back up the other side.

As she had expected, Hilary tasted like the sweetest, most fragrant honey and Maggie closed her eyes, the better to enjoy the feast. Meanwhile, Hilary's tongue was far from idle: it probed and plunged, licked and sucked. Her small white teeth nibbled at Maggie's outer labia, coaxing the lips wider apart so that Maggie felt she must be able to see right into her womb.

Bringing her forefinger into Hilary's sex, Maggie wetted it before lubricating the tight anal opening. Hilary groaned, the sound muffled by Maggie's body as Maggie slowly inserted the tip of her finger. Hilary's sucking grew more intense as Maggie worked her finger in and out, gently at first, then more boldly as the sphincter of muscle yielded and relaxed.

Hilary's pleasure bud quivered against her chin as she used her tongue like a miniature cock, thrusting into her succulent sheath until she cried out her release. The suddenness of her climax interfered with the rhythm of her tongue so Maggie sat up and, before the spasms had reached their peak, she straddled Hilary's upturned jewel, placing one foot firmly on the floor at the end of the couch, the other lightly on Hilary's belly. Squatting, she reached down and opened her own labia, slick from the juices which had mingled with Hilary's saliva.

Her breath was coming in short, shallow gasps which were almost painful to her as she covered Hilary's sex with her own. The other woman's flesh was hot and slippery against hers and Maggie ground herself against Hilary's pulsating love bud so that the waves of pleasure coursing through it transmitted themselves to hers. Within seconds, Maggie was coming too and their hot, feminine juices combined, running into one another as they rubbed against each other in a frenzy of lewd delight.

It was many minutes before either Maggie or Hilary regained some semblance of normality. Hilary stirred beneath her, alerting Maggie to the fact that her weight was probably becoming too much for her. She moved, reluctantly, though her own muscles were beginning to cramp.

Hilary shifted on the sofa to make room for her and Maggie slid along so that they were lying, hip to hip, breast to breast on the narrow couch. They kissed, languidly, their foreheads pressed together. It was Hilary who first realised they were not alone.

Alerted by her sharp intake of breath, Maggie sat up to face the intruder. Or rather, intruders. She relaxed, a slow smile spreading across her face as she saw Jason and Con in the open doorway.

'How long have you two been there?' she asked, absently caressing Hilary's small breast.

Jason reddened and dropped his eyes while Con grinned broadly. A glance at the two pairs of regulation sports shorts told her that they had been watching for some time – long enough for the black lycra to have become stretched to its very limit.

Glancing at Hilary, Maggie saw that she was eyeing Con speculatively and she remembered that the other woman would not have met two of her newest recruits.

'Come closer,' she invited, 'let me introduce you to Hilary. Hilary – this is Jason,' she smiled, encouragingly, at the younger of the two men, before announcing grandly, 'and this is Constantine G. Winchester the Third.'

Hilary's eyes barely passed over Jason, her attention was rivetted on Con as he towered over them.

'My, what beautiful skin,' she murmured and Con flashed his whiter than white smile at her.

'Why don't you guys strip off and join us?' Maggie invited, as casually as if she had been offering them coffee.

She turned back to Hilary without waiting to see if they did as she asked. Taking her into her arms, she gently coaxed her down onto the white, furry rug on the floor. The small button nipples hardened again as Maggie pressed them against the tips of her own and they knelt, facing each other as they kissed.

From the corner of her eye, she watched Con kneel behind Hilary, his big, dark hands trailing a path from her shoulders to her waist and back up again. Jason was obviously watching him, eager to learn, for she felt his narrower hands perform the same action on her own skin.

His eager, youthful cock pressed against her back as he began to kiss the top of her spine. Little sparks of electricity ran down her back as Jason kissed her and Hilary kneaded her firm, brown-tipped breasts. Although she could not see his hands, Maggie guessed from Hilary's expression, and the small mewls of delight which escaped through her pouted lips, that Con had reached down between her spread buttocks.

Hilary's face was rapt, her eyes closed, her soft lips parted. She had arched back her head so that it rested on Con's strong chest. Maggie leaned forward to press her head against the elegant sweep of her neck. A small droplet of perspiration ran down Hilary's neck and Maggie caught it with her tongue.

Craving the salty moisture, she licked a path downwards, between Hilary's neat breasts and on towards her navel. Jason supported Maggie's hips, dragging her back slightly on her knees so that her buttocks were held fast against his rising tumescence.

As she darted her tongue greedily into the deep crevice of

Hilary's narrow navel, Con lifted Hilary up and impaled her on his hard stem. Maggie watched, mesmerised, as, inches from her face, the thick, black column disappeared into the pale pink flesh, re-emerging shiny and wet with Hilary's fluids. She pressed her lips down to where the two bodies joined so that every time Con withdrew, she could lick the length of his wet shaft.

Jason's hands played over her back, reaching down into her bottom cleft where his fingers sought her moist centre. Maggie parted her legs obligingly, welcoming his hand working over her hot, hungry flesh as she feasted alternately on Hilary's bulging vulva and Con's thrusting shaft.

Hilary was making small, grunting sounds as she neared her climax. Con's big, black-skinned hands covered her small breasts, his lips fastened on her arched neck as the first spasm rocked her.

Maggie pressed in closer, eager to share in the tumult which she could feel building between them. Her tongue found Hilary's quivering pleasure bud and flicked at it, drawing it out.

As Maggie pleasured Hilary with her tongue, she raised her own bottom still further. Jason entered her with one swift, sure thrust. His skin was warm and damp against hers, but Maggie barely noticed him, she was so engrossed in what was going on in front of her eyes.

She sensed the moment when Con began to come. Hilary's sheath spasmed as the hot, milky fluid shot into her, mixing with her own juices. It seeped out around his still hard shaft and clung to Hilary's red-gold pubic curls. Maggie lapped at the honeyed concoction oozing out of Hilary's body until Con withdrew, grown soft at last.

Pulling away from Jason, Maggie whirled round and flung her arms around his neck. The disappointment on his face told her he thought she had had enough of him and she smiled wickedly. The dismay turned to relief as she drew him down and wrapped her legs around his waist.

Holding him close to her, she rocked her pelvis in time with his urgent thrusts, stimulating her clitoris against his smooth, soft skin so that by the time he climaxed, she too was at the brink. As he came, with one final, triumphant thrust, Maggie went over the edge, crying out as the hot waves of pleasure washed over her.

Antony took one look at Alexander's angry, set face and shivered. Maggie had been careless not to check the privacy switch on the two-way mirror was off. From the moment she had taken Hilary into her arms, he had felt Alexander's anger building.

Now she was kissing young Jason with such obvious enjoyment and Alexander's rage was almost palpable in the small cubicle. His skin was white around the mouth, his startlingly blue eyes stormy as he flicked them over Antony.

'Undisciplined bitch!' he spat.

Antony fidgeted uncomfortably.

'Maybe she hasn't realised yet,' he defended her weakly, but Alex wasn't listening.

He had turned back to the scene in the office and was watching as Hilary, Con and Jason all took their leave of Maggie. Antony shrugged slightly. Maybe it was about time Maggie too found out that loving Alexander wasn't all roses.

Frowning, Antony looked away, remembering how it had been in the beginning, when Alexander had turned up for a job as a trainer, one of the first at the Black Orchid Club. It hadn't taken him long to lure Antony into his manipulative web of seduction. Not that he had shown much resistance. Antony smiled ruefully.

No, the good things about being in Alexander's thrall far outweighed the bad. It was just that one had to put up with certain . . . requirements. As Maggie would very soon find out.

Antony stood up as Alexander did and followed him out of the cubicle.

Maggie stretched languorously as she pulled on her robe. There was a pleasant ache between her legs caused by Jason's youthful enthusiasm and the taste of Con's sperm and Hilary's softer musk coated her mouth. She felt replete, soaked in sex. She smiled to herself. How licentious she had become!

In her private bathroom, Maggie ran a deep, hot bath, pouring in a generous portion of floral fragranced bubble-bath. She hummed happily to herself as she brushed out her hair into a soft, dark cloud and piled it up on top of her head.

The mirror began to steam over as she creamed her face and neck, tissuing it off before splashing her face with warm water. The bubbles had risen to the brim of the bath now. Turning off the taps, she stepped in.

She sighed as she sank her entire body into the sweetly perfumed water. It washed over her, caressing her over-sensitised skin as she leaned back on the inflatable cushion and closed her eyes.

She gasped as hard, male hands suddenly reached down and hauled her out of the water. Her eyes flew open as the draft from the open door whipped her wet skin and she found herself caught in the coldly furious blue eyes of Alexander.

'Alex! What are you doing. Oh!'

She found her feet dangling inches from the floor as he lifted her up. His gaze was a flinty, icy blue and Maggie's eyes flickered nervously to where Antony stood in the doorway. The light was behind him, so his features were in shadow, but there was a peculiar tension in the way he held himself that sent shivers of alarm chasing across her skin.

Alexander never said a word, half dragging her over to the toilet where he sat down on the closed seat and pulled her, face down, across his lap. Maggie struggled desperately to right herself, but her arms and legs were flailing helplessly, her movements ungainly and uncoordinated.

Antony came to sit on the edge of the bath, his knees spread, one either side of her head. It was he that spoke.

'You're wasting your time, Maggie. Lie still or you'll just exhaust yourself.'

Maggie's frantic struggles stilled in response to his reasonable tone and she strained her neck upwards to see his face. Alexander's hand came down on the back of her neck and forced her head back down so that all she could see was the cream carpet, spattered with the soapy water which was dripping from her wet body.

Her legs dangled helplessly, her toes barely touching the ground as Alexander dragged her further over his knee, the harsh denim of his jeans burned the tips of her breasts as they fell, without ceremony, over his knee.

Even then, Maggie hadn't realised his intention and the first short, sharp crack of his bare hand on her backside made her jump and yelp in protest.

'Hold still, Maggie, what's the matter with you?' Antony's bored voice came from above her.

'He hit me!' she shrilled indignantly, struggling vainly against Alexander's restraining hands.

There was another sharp smack as his open palm once again came down on her squirming bottom, swiftly followed by another and another. The sound of his hand against her wet skin seemed magnified in the small room, echoing off the walls.

And it hurt. No matter how much Maggie fought against it, there was no escape. Her bottom began to burn as he spanked her mercilessly. Tears started in her eyes and ran, unchecked, down her face. Why was he doing this?

Raising her eyes in a mute plea to Antony, she saw that he had unzipped his fly and was slowly masturbating himself. He smiled slightly at her, almost kindly, before nudging at her trembling mouth with the tip of his cock.

Maggie tried to turn her head away, but Alexander's fingers tangled cruelly in her hair at the back of her neck and held her still. Inch by inch Antony eased his erect penis past the barrier of her lips and teeth and into the hot, wet cavern beyond. Maggie gagged as Antony's stem pumped in and out of her unwilling mouth while the spanking went on and on.

Suddenly, Alexander's fingers entered her from behind. She heard him laugh derisively and realised that she must be wet. A wave of shame swept over her and she closed her eyes against it. That she should have derived pleasure from this . . . this humiliation! The tears trickled down her cheeks as Alexander ruthlessly manipulated her clitoris so that, in spite of herself, her legs opened wider, her bottom pushed higher in the air as if to meet her punishment half way, welcoming it.

Antony was close to the edge now, his thrusts became more urgent, even less considerate of her as he used her mouth. Alexander took his hand from the back of her neck and reached down to toy with her dangling breasts. She felt hot, her vulva pulsating wildly as he pulled and tweaked at her nipples.

As Antony began to ejaculate into the back of her throat, Alexander delivered a series of short, sharp slaps to the undersides of her breasts and she came, thrusting her hips back onto his rough fingers as her limbs went out of control.

She had barely had time to recover as Antony withdrew from her mouth and Alexander pushed her off his lap, as if she disgusted him. She lay on the floor at their feet, staring up at them through her tears. Antony nonchalantly re-zipped his trousers before stepping over her without so much as a glance at her tear-streaked face.

Alex hunkered down beside her and studied it dispassionately.

'Tears suit you,' he said huskily, 'we shall have to see that you shed some more.'

Maggie stared up at him resentfully. Her rear-end burned painfully still, her breasts ached and her jaw felt as though it had locked in place. She gasped as he suddenly grasped her chin between his thumb and forefinger and pulled her head up.

'It's time you learned the rules, Maggie darling. Have your bath, then come up to the apartment. I haven't finished with you yet.'

Rebellion flared in Maggie's breast.

'I could walk out the door!' she said, her voice shaking, 'I could leave. You can't stop me!'

Alexander let go of her and stood up. He towered over her, still lying naked at his feet and smiled at her in the strangest way.

'Of course,' he said after a long silence, 'you may leave whenever you wish. But I don't think you will.'

He laughed then, a small, cruel laugh which sent ice through Maggie's soul. She did not dare to move as he stepped over her and left her alone in the small bathroom.

She lay there as if frozen for several minutes, wondering what he meant. Eventually she began to shiver and her arms and legs began to cramp. Slowly, gingerly, she eased herself into a sitting position. She winced as her sore buttocks scraped against the carpet. Using the side of the bath to lever herself up, she climbed into the now tepid water.

Sinking into it, she touched herself gently between the legs. Her vulva was still swollen, her pleasure bud unsheathed. Tiny aftershocks ran through her and she closed her eyes. And at that moment she knew, with chilling certainty, that Alexander was right.

The Black Orchid Club had become her home. She would never leave.

16

Antony greeted her quite normally when she returned to the apartment.

'Ah, Maggie! You're just in time for lunch.'

She glanced around her nervously as she took her place at the table and Antony put a plate of homemade lasagne in front of her. She helped herself to salad and fresh, crusty French bread, realising as she did so that the table was only set for two.

'Alexander isn't able to join us I'm afraid,' Antony said, as if he had read her mind.

The awful tension which had been tying Maggie's stomach in knots began to ease as she ate. Whatever else Alex might be, she could not deny he was an excellent cook. Since she moved in with him and Antony she had never had to lift a finger in the kitchen and everything that had passed her lips had been delicious.

She felt Antony watching her and raised her eyes to his.

'What? What is it?'

He smiled enigmatically and shook his head.

'I like watching you eat.'

'Oh? Why?'

'Because you eat the way you make love – with gusto!'

Maggie laughed and bit into her bread. It turned to sawdust in her throat, almost choking her as Antony continued, his tone ominous.

'And without discipline.'

'I don't understand you,' she protested after she had slaked her sudden, inexplicable thirst with a tall glass of mineral water.

'No. But you will. Don't look so worried,' he soothed as Maggie was unable to hide a shudder, 'it's for your own good. Everything has to have rules, after all, and very often it is those very rules that, ultimately, lead to the most enhanced enjoyment.'

He smiled slightly at her anxious bewilderment and raised his glass to her.

'Have you finished?'

She nodded.

'Good. Then come with me – I have something to show you.'

They went into the bedroom and from the top of the wardrobe, Antony dragged down a large, flat, leather case like an artist's portfolio. He motioned for her to sit and she perched on the edge of the bed. A curious nervousness curled in the pit of her stomach, keeping her silent. She could not guess what the portfolio contained, but she had the distinct feeling that she was not going to like it.

She watched in silence as Antony unzipped the case, then untied the purple ribbons holding together the contents. He spread them open on the bed and looked at Maggie, his expression intent.

'You were drawn to Alexander from the moment you first set eyes on him, weren't you?'

Maggie nodded, dropping her eyes before the inexplicable light burning in his steely grey eyes.

'He has that effect on people. That's how it was with me. You love him, just as I do, and in the name of love, you let him hurt you. Oh, I know you think you're too clever to be drawn into Alexander's little games,' he laughed, almost bitterly as she murmured a protest, 'but you're not Maggie, any more than I am. And, though you haven't accepted it yet, like me, you are lost already. Look.'

Reluctantly, Maggie dragged his eyes away from her own folded hands and looked at what was on the bed. Her eyes widened and she gasped. There were photographs, huge, glossy black and white photographs professionally lit. Antony had spread some half dozen over the bed so that image after image assaulted her shocked eyes. Quietly, he slipped off the bed and left the room, closing the door gently behind him.

After a few minutes, Maggie picked up the nearest photograph and pulled it onto her lap. It was a man, back to the camera, his arms tied high above his head, wide apart, to a support which was out of shot. He was naked, standing with his legs apart, his face half turned to the camera, but in shadow, so his features were indistinct.

There was something familiar about the broad sweep of his shoulders, the smooth, strong length of his back . . . Antony! There was a tension in the way he held himself, the muscles bunching under his skin as if he was anticipating pain. Between his legs, his testicles were just visible. They looked horribly vulnerable.

The second photograph was posed at the same angle, though now the man was slumped, his legs bent at the knees, his head lolling forward, so that his face was out of sight. Maggie gasped, bringing her fingertips to her lips as she saw the clearly marked, raised weals across his back and buttocks. They had been carefully criss-crossed over his velvet smooth skin, applied with a precision that chilled her. Slowly, she traced the marks with her fingertips before reaching for the next shot.

Head and shoulders only, this time. Antony's face, tense with concentration, his eyes closed and a frown etched between his brows. His lips stretched around the wet, bulbous head of an anonymous penis.

Picture number four, head and shoulders again. This time Antony's head was thrown back, the strong arc of his neck exposed. The fair hair was dark with sweat, plastered against his brow. His mouth was open, as if he was crying out, his face suffused with the most exquisite expression of pain. Though the picture shocked her, Maggie realised she had never seen him look more beautiful and, to her dismay, she felt a familiar tingle between her legs.

The next photograph she picked up was a lovingly recorded close-up of a male arse, presumably Antony's. His fingers were also in shot spreading his own buttocks and exposing the perfect tattoo on his inner cheek, the Black Orchid. His anal opening appeared as a dark, forbidding cavern, glistening as if recently oiled.

And finally, a woman, naked but for thigh-high leather boots, gleefully inserting the biggest dildo Maggie had ever seen into that gaping arsehole.

'Pretty pictures.'

She jumped as Antony's hot breath caressed her ear. She hadn't heard him come back in and she dropped the last photograph, feeling ludicrously guilty for studying it so thoroughly.

His lips twisted in an ironic little smile and he gathered the photographs up, laying them carefully in the silk-lined port-folio and putting it back on top of the wardrobe. Then he turned and smiled at Maggie with such sweetness that she felt tears start in her eyes.

'You see?' he said softly.

Maggie wasn't sure that she *did* see, but she nodded,

smiling gratefully at him as he handed her a martini. He watched her closely as she drank, waiting patiently for the inevitable questions.

'But why?' she blurted eventually. 'He treats you so badly, yet still you love him.'

'Alexander isn't like other men, Maggie. He'll never give you what you want, but he'll keep you hanging on, just in case the possibility arises. He's a control freak. A puppet master. And we're his loving puppets.'

Maggie considered this for a few moments.

'And is that enough for you?' she asked after a while.

Antony shrugged slightly, a faint colour creeping along his cheekbones.

'It has to be. Ask him for more than he's willing to give you and you'll end up with nothing at all.'

A look of sheer desolation shuttered his eyes for a moment and Maggie instinctively leaned across and pressed her cheek against his. He enfolded his arms about her and turned his face so that their lips collided. They kissed, languidly at first, lovingly, but then something caught fire between them and grew so that Maggie found herself clinging to him, rubbing her thigh invitingly against his aroused crotch.

She gasped as he suddenly pushed her away.

'No!' he shook his head and sought to bring his ragged breathing under control. 'You haven't been listening!'

Maggie laughed nervously and tried to get closer to him, but he pulled away.

'I don't understand – we've slept together before, countless times. You're aroused, I'm aroused – what is the problem?'

'Alexander hasn't given permission.'

Maggie stared back at him, not sure if she had heard correctly. She withdrew to the far side of the bed and shook her head.

'Hang on a minute . . . you mean, all those other times . . . it's all been on Alexander's instructions? You must be crazy!'

'Not crazy, Maggie. I just play the game. As you must, if you want to stay here.'

'I'm not sure I do!'

'Maggie, Maggie! Think before you do anything rash. You've liked these past few weeks, haven't you?'

She nodded, reluctantly.

'And you've never been left without fulfillment when you've wanted it?'

'No, but—'

'There you are then! Alexander can be generous too.'

'What about what happened earlier this morning?'

The humiliation of being dragged from her bath and spanked was still with her. And Antony had had no small hand in her punishment! She glared at him with remembered resentment.

'You got greedy, Maggie. Think about it – all the sensual experience your avid little heart desires, *so long as you play by the rules.*'

'Alexander's rules.'

'Quite.'

Maggie stood up and paced to the door and back.

'So far you've said a great deal about what Alexander wants and nothing about yourself. How do you feel about my coming here to live with you?'

Antony shrugged slightly, tracing the pattern on the duvet with his fingertip as he avoided her eyes.

'What I feel isn't important.'

'Of course it is!' Maggie cried passionately, dropping to her knees in front of him and forcing him to look at her.

'*You're* important, Antony. Surely you believe that?'

Her display had startled him, but now he smiled, almost pityingly, at her.

'I made my choice, Maggie, just as you have. What Alexander says goes. And it's not often that I wish things different.'

He suddenly pulled her against him and kissed her, savagely. Maggie's lips were pulled back against her teeth and she tasted blood before he broke away. Shaken, she paced over to the window. All she could see was a never ending vista of rainwashed rooftops, the only signs of life provided by the pigeons.

'He said he hasn't finished with me yet,' she said when she could trust herself to speak, 'what was that supposed to mean?'

'The time has come, Maggie darling, to demonstrate your commitment to our exclusive little *ménage à trois*. Don't look so anxious – I promise you if you're good, you'll learn to enjoy all of Alexander's little games. Eventually.'

'Have you explained everything to her?'

Antony looked up from the book he was reading as Alexander walked into the lounge.

'I tried to.'

Alex smiled, the beautiful, toe-tingling smile which always melted whatever resistance Antony might feel towards him. He looked magnificent tonight, the white, pure cotton shirt taut across his shoulders, the black trousers melded to his hips and legs like a second skin. Antony sighed. But Alexander's concentration was all on Maggie for now and he knew better than to try to push himself in where he was not wanted.

'Where is she now?'

'She's sleeping.'

'Let her sleep. Tomorrow we'll start in earnest.'

Maggie felt groggy as she woke up. Antony was smiling down at her, a tray in his hands.

'Come on, sleepy head!' he whispered, 'breakfast is ready.'

She struggled to a sitting position and breathed in the rich, dark smell of fresh coffe.

'Hmm! Thanks Antony. What time is it?' she squinted at the bedside clock and swore mildly. 'Why on earth didn't you wake me up? Roll-call is in five minutes!'

She started to clamber out of bed, but Antony stopped her with a hand on her arm.

'You've been relieved of all your duties for the time being.'

Maggie rubbed at her bleary eyes and stared at him, uncomprehending.

'What do you mean, for the time being?'

'Until your training is complete. Now eat up, there's a good girl, we've a busy day ahead.'

Maggie gaped after him as he left her with the tray, her appetite gone. Her training. Of course, what had happened yesterday was just the beginning. Fleetingly, it occurred to her that there was still time for her to back out. She could get up out of this bed, get dressed and walk out of the door into the normal world.

She bit into a warm, crusty roll, spraying crumbs all over the tray. Melted butter trickled across her tongue and she closed her eyes for an instant. Who needed normality? If she left here now she might never find out where the outer parameters of her own nature lay.

'I've run you a bath,' Antony told her when he came back to collect the tray.

Maggie meandered into the bathroom and sank down into the warm, oily water. It embraced her in its all pervasive fragrance, rippling over her blemish-free skin and coating it in moisture. If this was part of the 'rules' she figured she could manage to summon up the appropriate show of obedience!

Antony was waiting for her when she emerged, still damp, wrapped in a towel.

'Come over here, Maggie,' he called.

She padded softly to the big, white leather couch. On the glass-topped coffee table in front of it, Antony had spread a pristine white towel. On the towel he had laid a large bowl of clean water, a cake of soap, a small glass flagon of oil and, mostly alarmingly of all, a pair of long-handled silver scissors and a cut-throat razor.

'What . . .?'

'Hush, don't look so worried. Have you never shaved your pussy before?'

He held out his hand and beckoned her forward. Reluctantly, she lay down on the sofa, on her back. The soft hide felt cool under her bare skin as Antony pushed towel covered cushions under her hips, raising up her buttocks until they were level with his eyes. She kept her knees pressed demurely together as he stroked the soft curls of her mons absently with the back of his hand while he reached for his equipment.

Antony frowned slightly as he turned back to her.

'Now, that's no good, darling, is it?' he chided gently as she stubornly kept her thighs together.

'I . . . I feel stupid!' she confessed, hot colour suffusing her cheeks.

It was all so clinical, somehow, so . . . cold.

'Think of me as your doctor,' Antony suggested, inadvertently making her feel worse, 'I have seen it all before, you know! Come on – open up for me.'

Reluctantly, Maggie parted her thighs, presenting herself to him. She was rewarded by his smile.

'That's better. Wider now – put one foot up, on the back of the sofa and rest the other on the floor.'

Maggie obliged, feeling horribly exposed as he picked up

the scissors. She closed her eyes as he began to snip, pulling her hair between the first two fingers of one hand and trimming, as a hairdresser would.

'Try to relax, darling. I'm really rather good at this!' He stopped cutting and began to work up a lather with the soap. Maggie had to admit, he seemed to know what he was doing as he worked up a lather in her foreshortened curls. He avoided touching her vulva, concentrating instead on the more densely covered mound of Venus.

She flinched at the first touch of the cold metal of the razor against her skin.

'Hold still!' Antony commanded impatiently, 'I don't want to nick you.'

Maggie hardly dared to breathe as he carefully denuded her of pubic hair. After each scrape of the razor, he cleaned it in the water and ran his fingertip across the naked skin, testing the result. After a few minutes, he rose and went to change the water.

Stealing a glance down at herself while he was out of the room, Maggie saw the pink, tender skin of her mound, denuded now of its protective carpet of hair. It looked strange, curiously vulnerable. She bit her lips nervously as Antony returned.

'Now for the best part!' he said, his voice floating like silk across her raw nerves.

Maggie held her breath as he carefully parted the outer labia. There was a small frown of concentration between his brows as he systematically lathered the sparse hair, working the creamy substance into her shrinking skin. The razor felt cold as it rasped over her tender skin.

Her exposed vulva felt unprotected as the edge of the blade moved slowly along its edge. She breathed a long, jagged sigh of relief as Antony laid aside his equipment.

'Lovely,' he murmured, continuing in a more businesslike tone, 'go and use the bathroom now, before I oil you.'

Maggie rose obediently and went to do as she was bid. Once she had finished, she paused to study herself in the floor to ceiling mirror tiles. Where before there had been a perfect triangle of tangled curls at the apex of her thighs, now there was only pink, tender skin. The crease in the centre was clearly visible, barely concealing the hood of her clitoris which peeked through.

Slowly, Maggie shifted her feet apart a few inches. Her labia hung down a little below the protective outer lips, her most private, inner flesh exposed. If she bent the knees, oh so slightly, and tilted her pelvis forward, the entrance to her womb came into view, dark and inviting, shockingly accessible.

She jumped as Antony called her, squeezing her thighs tightly together as she went back into the living room.

Back in position on the couch, Maggie gave herself up to sensation as Antony began to anoint her freshly-shaved pubis with heavy, fragrant oil. She sighed as he worked his way down to her vulva, feeling her lips open and swell, anticipating his touch. Smiling to herself, she reflected that the slippery folds of her labia had not needed to be depilated, yet Antony seemed to be concentrating his attention there.

Gradually, her skin grew warm and slick, her own musky fluids mixing with the aromatic oil. Her legs felt heavy, weighted, as he described a circle around her awakened bud. It quivered, anticipating his touch on its hard tip. When he did touch her there, Maggie knew it would be seconds before she came.

She groaned, her eyes flying open in dismay as he suddenly stopped. He smiled regretfully at her as he dried his fingers on a towel.

'Not yet, my darling,' he told her. 'Not for a long while yet.'

'But—'

'Hush! Lie still now while I fit your restraint.'

The blood rushed in Maggie's ears as he reached down, under the table, into a box she hadn't noticed before. He seemed to consider for a moment, before selecting from its contents. The contraption he withdrew made her gasp.

'This should be about right. Will you stand up please?'

He gave her his hand and helped her to her feet. She stood before him, dazed as he fastened a thin black leather strap, hung with metal rings, around her waist. He smiled up at her almost whimsically as he clipped something onto the ring at the front of the belt. Another leather strap, but this time it was attached at the other end to a small mesh pouch, similar in shape to a cricketer's box.

Maggie's eyes widened as he held it up for her to see. The flexible frame was covered in soft rubber which clung to the skin of her groin as Antony eased it into position. Another leather strap hung from the bottom point of the inverted triangle and this was passed between her legs, fitting snugly across her perineum and along the deep cleft between her buttocks.

Once this was fastened to a metal ring at the back of the waistbelt, Maggie's sex was completely confined.

'What on earth is this in aid of?' she demanded, wriggling ineffectually against the straps.

'The pursuance of your better nature, Maggie,' he replied infuriatingly.

He hadn't finished yet. Maggie watched, appalled as he strapped two wide leather bands around her wrists, her mouth opening in shock as he linked them together behind her back.

'Antony—'

'Quiet. Have patience.'

He gave her out-thrust nipples a playful tweak and, in spite of her growing unease, Maggie felt an answering pulse throb between her legs. The next strap was fastened to the same ring by her navel which held the chastity belt in place. Only this had two wide banded circles of leather attached which slipped over her breasts like a brassiere and fastened at her back and in a halter round her neck.

Antony ran his finger lightly underneath the straps which outlined her breasts and tightened them slightly, from behind, so that the two firm white globes were squeezed slightly.

'Is that comfortable?'

His warm breath tickled her ear as he murmured into it from behind. Maggie's throat and mouth felt dry as she whispered, 'Yes.'

No sooner had she spoken than Antony tightened the breast restraints, pushing them closer together and squeezing them forward.

'And now?'

'Th-that's a little uncomfortable, Antony – oh!'

He pulled tighter so that now her breasts were held in tension, on the brink of pain. Maggie bit down on her lower lip and concentrated on not letting the tears which had sprung to her eyes to overflow.

'Now, let's have a look at you.'

Antony stood back to admire his handiwork, his eyes lingering on the distorted outline of her breasts. Stepping forward, he rolled her nipples between finger and thumb until they stood out, two hard, treacherous little pebbles.

'That's better. But we mustn't forget the shoes – Antony brought them especially for you. Wait there.'

He disappeared into the bedroom and came back with a shoe box. Inside were the highest heels Maggie had ever seen. Antony helped her step into them, steadying her by a hand at her elbow as she teetered wildly in them.

'Come see yourself,' he pushed her gently towards the bedroom. He had left the bedroom door open and Maggie could see herself, as she walked, in the mirrored doors of the wardrobe. She hardly recognised herself as the trussed, wild-eyed creature who swayed seductively in the impossibly high heels.

'Beautiful. Alexander will be pleased. Over here, on the bed.'

Maggie did as she was told, partly because she did not know what else to do and partly because, she had to admit, she was intrigued as to what would happen next. She sat, compliant, as Antony brushed out her long, thick, dark hair, arranging it about her shoulders like a glossy cloak. He brushed it until it shone, then he smoothed it back from her neck and kissed her.

His fingertips played, featherlight, down one side of her neck as his lips caressed the other. Maggie closed her eyes as he stroked the tender skin at her throat. She moaned softly as she felt the kiss of fur against it and realised that he had slipped a lined leather strap around her neck.

A feeling of inevitability overtook her as a chain was clipped to the back of the necklet and she was fastened by it to the tall, ornate bedpost. The chain was long enough for her to lay her head down on the pillows, but not for her to get up from the bed.

Antony was winding a black silk scarf into a blindfold. He kissed both her eyelids before trying it firmly round her head. Maggie struggled to see even a chink of light and little tremors of panic fluttered in her stomach.

'Don't worry – I'll not be far away. I'll bring you lunch, later.'

Antony kissed her lingeringly, lovingly, on the lips. Then he left her. Maggie sat rigidly, trying to penetrate the sudden still silence. She was glad the room was warm, but wished Antony had stayed with her, or at least left a radio on. She had never felt so utterly alone.

Easing herself gingerly down the bed, she lay her head on the soft pillows and prepared to wait for Alexander.

17

Alexander didn't come. Maggie dozed lightly, waking with a start as Antony touched her shoulder. He removed the blindfold, but did not untie her hands, instead he fed her, bite-sized pieces of tender steak au poivre, crisp, green salad, doused in heavy, fragrant oil.

She sipped at the full-bodied red wine with Antony patiently dabbing at her chin as it overflowed. When she had finished, he carried her, still bound, to the bathroom where he unclipped the snug-fitting box so that she could relieve herself.

Maggie felt a blush stain her cheeks as she perched on the lavatory, conscious of Antony's persistent presence. When she had finished, he washed her with a warm, soft flannel and made her bend her legs apart so that he could massage in some more of the perfumed oil.

As before, he teased and tantalised her until her flesh was slick with moisture, her limbs suffused with heat. Then with a quick, regretful flick at her yearning bud, he quickly strapped the device back on and carried her back to the bedroom.

In all this time, Antony had barely said a word to her, except to ask her to move this way or that. When he left her again, Maggie could have wept for loneliness. At least he hadn't re-tied the black silk scarf around her eyes, but her arms were tired from being held in the same position, behind her back. And the moist, tender flesh of her sex pulsed and throbbed, aching for fulfillment.

She lost track of time, dozing lightly every so often. Something about the quality of the silence told her that night had fallen and still she was alone. They weren't going to sleep with her then, not tonight.

Maggie imagined Antony and Alexander together in the big bed in the flat downstairs. Had they forgotten all about her? She had anticipated humiliation, maybe even pain, but this isolation was far, far worse. At least when Alex was using her she had his full attention. Tears of self-pity welled in her eyes and seeped out from the corners, running down the sides of her nose and into her mouth. At last, she slept.

At the breakfast time, she pleaded with Antony to release her hands.

'Please – just while I eat breakfast, while you're here! It's not as if I could do anything while you're watching me!'

He had ignored her questions about his whereabouts last night and he ignored this outburst too. Patiently, he spooned warm, creamy porridge between her stubbornly resisting lips and helped her wash it down with strong coffee. Once again, he carried her to the bathroom and washed and oiled her, making sure she was teetering on the brink of orgasm before he strapped her back up.

'This isn't fun any more!' she complained in a small voice as he laid her back down on the bed.

His lips brushed briefly across the top of her forehead.

'It isn't supposed to be fun,' he murmured softly.

Maggie heard his footsteps reach the door, then it closed behind him with a click. She couldn't bear it. Her arms and legs began to tremble, her restrained breasts quivering with emotion.

'Antony! Antony come back!'

She waited, listening for the sound of his footsteps returning. When he had not responded after several minutes, a red mist of impotent fury overcame her and she began to yell, 'Let me out of here! Antony! Alexander! You miserable bastards – come back here now!'

Incredibly, the door opened and Antony reappeared. He was carrying a suitcase and didn't so much as glance in her direction as he marched over to the wardrobe and began stuffing her clothes in it.

Maggie watched with increasing dismay as her suits and blouses, her skirts and jumpers were all shoved carelessly into the case.

'What are you doing?' she asked in a small voice.

Antony paused and flicked her a cold glance.

'You wanted to leave.'

'No! No, I just don't like this . . .'

'So you don't want to play any more?' Antony sneered. 'Are you going to take your ball home, then? Grow up, Maggie – this is an adults' game. Either you play by the rules or you leave, right now. What is it to be?'

Maggie stared back at him with wide eyes, feeling foolish.

'I'll stay here,' she whispered.

Antony regarded her intently for a few moments, then he nodded once, satisfied.

'Good,' he said curtly.

Maggie watched as he re-hung her clothes and left without so much as another glance in her direction. When he had gone, she crawled underneath the duvet and curled herself into a ball.

She must have fallen asleep for she was woken by the sound of voices in the next room. Scrabbling up clumsily, onto her knees, she strained her ears, listening. It was Alexander . . . and Antony and a woman. The door opened and her suspicions were confirmed.

'Oh!'

The woman seemed to pause in the doorway, obviously having just seen Maggie trussed in the corner.

'It's all right, Camilla. Maggie is being taught how to please me,' said Alex.

The woman giggled.

'She must be very stubborn!'

Antony strode across the room and, without a word, he lifted Maggie and took her through to the bathroom where he performed the usual ritual of washing and anointing her. He traced the tracks of her tears with the pad of his thumb and tutted. The warm flannel was wiped gently across her face. Then she was carried back to the bedroom.

This time, though, she felt, not the familiar duvet under her bare buttocks, but the cold, hard surface of the sturdy modern dressing table. Antony looped the chain over the back of the mirror.

Alexander's unsmiling face swam into view. He was admiring the straps which criss-crossed her body, emphasising her breasts and shielding, though not fully concealing, her sex.

'Beautiful,' he announced. 'Maggie, you are a sight to behold.'

Taking her chin firmly between his thumb and forefinger, he forced back his head and covered her mouth with his. Despite her discomfiture, the kiss melted her insides, making her arms strain against their bonds as they tried to respond to her instinct to hold him. She opened her eyes as he pulled away, opening her mouth with his thumb and caressing the soft, wet skin inside her lower lip.

His other hand closed over one straining breast and squeezed and kneaded, tweaking her nipple into hardness before affording its twin the same treatment. She moaned softly as his hand roamed the soft, undulating curves of her stomach and hips before coming to rest on the mesh box which covered her sex.

Suddenly he stepped away.

'Very good,' he said coolly, totally unaffected, it seemed, by touching her.

Maggie watched with dismay as he turned his back on her and went over to the bed where Antony and Camilla were slowly undressing each other.

'Alex – Alexander please! Untie me. Don't leave me like this . . .'

She trailed off as he flashed her an irritated glance.

'Shut her up, Antony.'

He turned to Camilla and took her in his arms, kissing her passionately. Antony stood up and walked over to her, dressed only in his underpants. Without a word, he picked up the silk scarf which had been tied round her eyes in the beginning. Maggie shrank away, afraid that he was about to blindfold her again. She gasped as she saw that his intention was far worse.

Tears sprang to her eyes as her lips were pushed back against her teeth and she tasted the silk, still salty from old tears. Antony smiled coldly at her, and she knew that, despite all his reasonable words, he was jealous of her. She stared after him as he went to join the couple on the bed.

Surely they weren't going to make her watch them make love to this woman? Touch her, kiss her, taste her as they had her so many times? It was horrible, more demeaning than any spanking or physical punishment could have been. To not even be able to touch herself as she watched . . .

It was then the realisation dawned on her. Of course, Alexander meant to punish her for taking her pleasure without his permission. This was his way of teaching her self-restraint – by forcibly keeping her chaste!

Maggie bit down on the gag. Already her sex-lips were swelling, yearning for a human touch. She tried to avert her eyes from the three naked bodies which writhed on the bed in front of her, but everywhere she looked there were mirrors, reflecting them back many times over.

'Open your eyes, Maggie!'

They snapped open at Alexander's command and she trembled before his furious gaze.

'Watch, and learn. You're to be the star turn at the next party night, Maggie, so you'd better pay attention now.'

A coldness crept into her limbs as his scowl turned into a mocking smile. Party night was two days away. Alexander was plotting something and she was quite sure she wasn't going to like it. For now though, she didn't dare to disobey him. Leaning her back against the cold surface of the mirror, she settled back to watch.

'Turn over, Camilla, onto your back. Show Maggie how gorgeous you are.'

The woman had soft, white blonde hair which kissed the tops of her shoulders. The pansy blue eyes which stared impassively back at Maggie were slightly glassy, as if she were drunk, or drugged. As Alexander smoothed his hand across her flat belly, she preened, thrusting out her full, rosy-tipped breasts, and pouting her lower lip. Her skin was very pale, covered in a light smattering of freckles.

'See how compliant she is?' Alexander said lovingly.

He delivered a sudden, light smack to the undersides of Camilla's breasts. Maggie could not take her eyes off them as they quivered in response. The woman did not utter a sound, though her wide, reddened lips parted slightly on a gasp. She lay back on the pillows, absolutely still as Alexander ran his hands down her body and closed over the light blonde fleece between her thighs.

Obligingly, she drew up her knees as he parted them and Maggie's eyes were rivetted on the shockingly exposed pink skin of her sex.

'You see – juicy already!'

Alexander dipped in his finger and brought it to his lips. Maggie's thighs began to tremble as he began to work his finger along the tender creases. Camilla's soft moan reverberated off the walls and roared in Maggie's ears. Alex smiled at her wickedly as he circled the tiny pleasure bud with the tip of his finger. Maggie watched, mesmerised, as the moisture welled in the lips of Camilla's open sex in response.

An answering wetness gathered between her own thighs and she sought to squeeze them together. She was prevented by the mesh box which held her slightly apart. Maggie's vulva began to throb needily as Camilla's breathing grew faster and she raised her hips up off the bed, subsiding with a groan as Alexander denied her the final release.

He signalled to Antony who pushed a cushion under the woman's hips. Now her tight little anus was also exposed. Alexander smeared some of the moisture from her vulva down the crease and round the puckered entrance. It opened under the pressure of his fingertip and he began to work his way in.

'You like this, don't you, Maggie? You have a very responsive little arse – perfect for taking a man. Oh yes,' he smiled in response to her small, muffled mewl of protest, 'it's time you experienced that singular pleasure. And you will. On party night.'

He turned his attention back to Camilla and began to kiss her passionately. Antony manoeuvred her onto her side and entered her from behind. If she had been able to speak, Maggie would have cried out. Alexander's words had chilled her to the bone. Nothing he could have said could have filled her with more dread. She had hated being displayed in the Exhibition Hall, she knew she could not bear to perform such intimate acts on a stage, in front of a live audience.

She felt Alexander's eyes on her and she stared defiantly back at him. Too late, she realised from the sudden light in his eyes that her resistance excited him. She shrank back against the mirror as he stood and advanced towards her.

He was very aroused, his long, slender cock jutting out from his body. Reaching behind her, he unclipped her hands and brought them round to her lap. She closed her eyes as she breathed in the scent of him, citrus and musk.

Loud groans came from the bed and they both glanced at Antony and Camilla. She was up on her hands and knees now, doggie fashion, and Antony was pumping his hips frantically, his face twisted into a rictus of delight. Alexander turned back to Maggie, obscuring her view. Without a word, he took her hand and placed it on his cock.

Maggie's hand closed reluctantly around him and began to move up and down along the shaft. He felt very hot, as if his release was close. His lips passed across her bound mouth in the lightest of kisses. That kiss was her undoing. Suddenly, she wanted to pleasure him, wanted to make him forget the woman on the bed.

Staring into his eyes, she ran the pad of her thumb around the soft collar of his glans, lightly tracing the outline of the damp groove with the tip of her thumbnail. Judging her moment, she moved the mobile skin across his shaft up and down several times.

A bolt of triumph made her flush as the first, violent spurt of semen burst from him, followed by another and another. The warm, sticky fluid hit her bare stomach and trickled downwards to where her naked, hairless sex was confined by leather and mesh.

When, at last, he was finished, he sighed and drew away from her. Maggie had been so caught up in his pleasure, she hadn't noticed Antony and Camilla leave. Alexander went over to the bed and smoothed the sheets. Maggie watched, wide-eyed, hardly daring to hope as he returned to her.

First, he unhooked the chain and lifted her down, leading her over to the bed by hooking his finger inside the belt of her leather harness. Then he removed the wrist cuffs, the neck restraint and the breast straps. Her breasts sprang free and swayed under the force of their own weight. The mesh box was next and, finally, the silk scarf which gagged her.

When at last she stood naked in front of him, Alexander ran his eyes appreciatively across the body, from her neck to her toes and back up again, where they lingered on her shaven mound.

'Part your legs,' he ordered.

Maggie automatically did as she was asked. Her swollen flesh leaves felt heavy between her legs and she knew she was wet.

'Bend slightly at the knees – that's right. Thrust your hips forward – Lovely! Your inner lips hang down below the outer ones. I think we'll keep you shaved, Maggie, it's a shame to conceal such a delightful asset.'

Maggie shivered, silently begging him to touch her. He smiled and she was sure he had read her thoughts. Suddenly, he reached out and pinched her protruding sex-lips, pulling her towards him. Her arms went about his neck and she clung to him as he worked his fingers across the slippery folds.

It didn't take long. Abstinence and denial had made her desperate and within minutes the familiar, weak heat was flooding through her. As the first waves of orgasm broke, Alexander cupped the palm of his hand softly against her pulsing sex so that she quivered against his hand as she sagged limply against him.

She barely noticed when he lifted her up and lay her down next to him in the large, soft bed. He cradled her in his arms and murmured endearments against her hair. When she had calmed, he lifted her chin and stared intensely into her eyes.

'Are you ready to give yourself over to me now, Maggie?' he asked softly.

Maggie's heart leaped as she imagined him taking her, possessing her now.

'Oh yes!' she whispered fervently.

'Body and soul?'

'Body and soul.'

He smiled and tucked her head under his chin.

'Good,' he said, simply. 'Then tomorrow night Antony and I will take you out to test your resolution.'

It was a few minutes before Maggie realised that she had been given all she was to be allowed to enjoy for tonight. Contenting herself with that, she snuggled against Alexander's warm strong body and drifted into sleep.

Maggie looked about her nervously as they found a table. When Alexander had told her they were going out to dinner, she had expected a romantic restaurant, perhaps with candles on the table. Not a greasy spoon on the edge of the bypass.

The deathly lull in conversation which had heralded her arrival between Antony and Alexander was only just beginning to ease. The coffee bar was manned by a middle-aged, greasy man in a grubby, blue and white striped apron which strained across his pot belly. He stared across at her, slack lipped and Maggie turned away.

An old man propped up the bar, his baggy, stained trousers held up precariously by a pair of stringy braces. His rheumy eyes followed Maggie as she reluctantly slipped into the seat beside Alexander, diagonally opposite Antony. A lone trucker sat to their left, so intent on demolishing his groaning plate of pie and chips he never once raised his eyes from his plate.

On the far side of the room, a rowdy group of bikers sprawled about the place. One, slightly more presentable than the rest, was watching Maggie's dress ride up her legs as she slid awkwardly into the moulded plastic seat which was bolted securely to the ground, too close to the Formica-topped table. She pulled ineffectually at the hem of the red lycra tube, keeping her eyes downcast.

Why had Alexander selected this particular dress for her tonight? Though it had long sleeves and finished high at her throat, it clung to every curve, leaving nothing to the imagination. The tight skirt ended mid-thigh, leaving the smooth silken sweep of her stockinged legs exposed

In a dim, smoky nightclub she could have got away with it, but here, under the harsh electric lights in the early evening when the daylight still lingered, she looked and felt like a tart.

She felt Alexander's cool fingers at the nape of her neck, under the candyfloss curls Anthony had teased into her dark hair.

'All right, Maggie?' he murmured, close to her ear.

'No!' she whispered furiously, keeping her head down to hide her face from the men opposite who were now openly ogling her. 'I'm going to sit next to Antony.'

'No.' Alexander stopped her by closing his hand over her wrist. 'I don't want you to turn your back on your admirers, Maggie. It would be unforgivably rude.'

Maggie was prevented from replying by the arrival of a waitress. The incongruity of finding a waitress in a transport café was enough to make Maggie's head snap up. The girl was very young and slender with long, stringy blonde hair, but her eyes were old. She looked bored as she flipped over her pad and held her stubby pencil poised.

'We'll all have egg and chips,' Alexander told her without

consulting Antony or Maggie. 'And baked beans, fried bread and sausage.'

He turned on his most devastating smile and the girl blushed. Maggie studied her covertly. She didn't have a bad figure under the unappealing pink gingham nylon overall, but she couldn't imagine her exciting Alexander's jaded palate. Nevertheless, he made the effort to compliment the girl with his eyes, no doubt making her day.

'Would you like tea?' she simpered.

'Lovely,' he replied, not turning his attention back to Maggie until she had disappeared, with an exaggerated roll of her hips, behind the counter.

'Don't fidget, Maggie.'

She shot him a resentful look and he laid one hand on her knee, squeezing it gently under the table. Maggie wished he would remove it, the man who had been staring at her earlier had noticed and she was embarrassed by the familiarity. She glanced across at Antony. He was staring out of the window at the traffic, his mind obviously elsewhere.

When their food arrived, Maggie pushed it half-heartedly around her plate, her appetite gone. Antony and Alexander both dug in with a relish which surprised her, swilling down the greasy food with copious amounts of tea. Maggie's tea was congealing in her cup. It was dark brown in colour, little globules of fat swimming on the surface.

'Not hungry, Maggie?' Alexander asked innocently.

He laughed as she scowled at him and helped himself to her sausage. Maggie couldn't wait for them to finish eating so that they could all leave. There was an old-fashioned juke box in the corner of the café and someone was feeding coins into it. Before long the strident tones of Meatloaf filled the confined space with sound.

Maggie felt someone watching her and raised her eyes

cautiously. The young biker was still watching her and as their eyes met, he smiled knowingly at her. Maggie's stomach trembled. Underneath the oily jeans and the heavy leather of his jacket, he looked clean and well built.

His brown hair was cut brutally short to reveal one ear pierced several times, glinting with gold. His hands were square and knotty, as if he used them to make his living. She jumped as she felt Alexander's voice in her ear.

'You've guessed which one it's to be, then?'

'What?'

She turned towards him in horror, her stomach roiling in protest. He surely didn't mean what she thought he meant? She stiffened as Alexander's hand moved up her leg, smoothing her skirt even further up her thigh. Her throat felt dry as she tried, and failed, to pull her eyes away from Alexander's hypnotic gaze. His blue eyes bored into her, like chips of ice, as his fingers brushed against the gusset of her white cotton panties.

Oh God, no! She couldn't be becoming aroused, not here, with all these people looking on! Alexander smiled as if reading her mind and something inside her shrank away from him.

'Please,' she whispered hoarsely, 'please stop!'

He didn't reply. Instead, he swooped on her unsuspecting lips and crushed them under the weight of his kiss. Maggie could hear the catcalls and whistles from the bikers in the corner as she clung weakly to Alexander's shoulders.

She felt dizzy, helpless, her body totally out of control. One part of her burned with shame at his casual humiliation of her, while another, darker side revelled in it. This must have been how Antony felt when he had allowed such compromising photographs to be taken of himself – completely in Alexander's thrall. Gradually, reality receded and she became oblivious to everything but Alexander's sweet breath on her face and his teasing, sure fingers stroking between her thighs.

'Oh, my Maggie! How sweetly you become aroused! It's almost too easy to instruct you.'

His words sounded distant as he murmured them against her lips.

'Please,' she whispered, abandoning all pretence of pride, 'please take me home and make love to me.'

He smiled. She felt his lips curve against hers.

'I will, darling Maggie, I promise I will. Soon. When you've proved how much you love me.'

She frowned, pulling away from him slightly.

'How do I prove it?'

'By doing exactly as you are told.'

He cupped her face in his hands and stared into her eyes for a long moment. Then he twisted her head slightly, so that she could see the men in the corner.

'You see the young one, with the earrings? The one you were eyeing earlier? I want you to go over to him and tell him he can have you for a tenner.'

Maggie froze with shock and she pressed herself against Alexander's side. The man with the earrings seemed to have lost interest in her, he had turned so that his profile was presented to her and was smoking a long, thin cigarette while he listened to his mates' loud conversation. Maggie closed her eyes.

She couldn't do it. Walk up to a complete stranger in a transport café and try to sell him her body . . . no! She just couldn't!

Alexander's eyes were cold as she tried to tell him.

'Surely you can understand.'

'I understand you don't want to keep your position at the club. That you only pretend to love me.'

233

Cold fingers of panic travelled up and down Maggie's spine. Alexander was regarding her coolly, leaving the ultimate decision to her. She glanced at Antony. He gave a small smile of such sweetness she wanted to cry. She didn't want to leave him, knew that her life would be empty, meaningless without them.

'Well?' Alexander prompted her, glancing impatiently at his watch.

'I . . . but where. I mean . . . I couldn't . . . *in here* . . .?'

'Not in here, you silly girl. Do you want to get us all arrested? There's an alley at the side. It shouldn't take you more than ten minutes.'

An alley. Oh God! Maggie saw that dusk was encroaching, but it was still light enough to see what was going on outside. Alexander pressed something into the palm of her hand. Glancing down, she saw that it was a condom.

'Make sure he uses this – it's extra strength, for safety's sake.'

Maggie felt an hysterical urge to laugh at this unexpected show of concern for her. So incongruous in the light of what he had asked, no, *told* her to do.

Her legs shook as she eased her body out from behind the table and began to walk uncertainly towards the man. Her red stilettoes clicked on the stained grey linoleum and half a dozen pairs of eyes turned on her expectantly.

Maggie kept her eyes trained on her quarry. He took his feet off the table as she approached and sat up, a suspicious gleam lighting up his brown eyes. She stopped in front of him and breathed deeply, in and out, trying to ignore the lewd remarks which flew around her. A hand brushed lightly across her bottom and it was all she could do not to flinch.

'Yeah?' The man frowned up at her.

Maggie bit her lip. Supposing he laughed? Or got angry? She bent down so that she could whisper in his unadorned ear.

'I'll go outside with you for ten pounds.'

There, it was said! The man's face was a picture as she straightened and looked expectantly at him. He recovered himself quickly and she saw that the very suggestion had given him an erection.

'Ten pounds?' he repeated, to loud guffaws from his mates.

'How about me for a fiver, darlin'?' someone suggested and Maggie shuddered.

She looked back at Alexander for reassurance and blinked. The table was empty. Frantically her eyes flew round the café, but neither he nor Antony were to be seen. The bastards! How could they go and leave her here, surrounded by these grinning, leering yobs? For the first time in her life, Maggie felt true fear. It trickled down her spine and curled round her waist, lodging in the pit of her stomach.

'Let's go.'

She jumped as the man she had propositioned took her by the elbow. For a moment, she thought about running, but he was bigger than she had expected and she was hampered by her impossibly high-heels and tight skirt. Making out with a stranger in an alley was all very well when she had thought Antony and Alexander were mere yards away, but unprotected, that was a different matter entirely.

Surrounded by so many people, Maggie concluded she had best just get on with it, and trust that he would be satisfied with a quickie in the alley. She did not allow herself to dwell on what could happen if his mates followed them.

Maggie forced her legs to move as the man pushed her impatiently towards the door. She tried to close her ears to the crude remarks which followed them, concentrating on putting one foot in front of the other as they reached the door.

It was cold outside and she shivered in the inadequate dress.

Crossing her arms over her breasts, she followed the man down the alley at the side of the café.

'This'll do.'

He pushed her against the wall, though he wasn't rough about it. Wordlessly, she handed him the wrapped condom. He laughed shortly.

'You're a real pro, aintcha?'

Maggie remembered reading somewhere that prostitutes never kissed their clients on the lips, so when he moved towards her, she twisted her head to one side. She bit her lip as his hands roamed at will over her breasts and hips before grabbing at her hem. She heard something rip as he hoiked her skirt over her waist.

He fumbled with the waistband of her tights and she felt a ladder run down one leg as he rolled them down to her knees. Her briefs followed and she momentarily closed her eyes. He was breathing heavily now, his breath hot on her neck as he dispensed with the zip on his jeans. He didn't bother to pull them down, merely opening up the fly and slipping his swollen cock over the top of his underpants.

He swore as he fumbled with the condom, throwing the wrapper onto the ground. It swirled with the rest of the litter in the little eddies of wind which whistled round their ankles. Empty crisp packets, cigarettes butts and soft drink cans. The alley acted like a wind tunnel, the acrid smell of urine caught in its gutters.

Maggie braced herself against the damp brick wall as his cock nudged between her legs. He sighed as it found its mark and slipped up, inside her. His thrusts were hampered by his position, but he leaned both palms against the wall, either side of her head for balance, his face a mask of introverted concentration.

He gave an almost primaeval shout of triumph as he came,

unconscious of Maggie's wince of pain as her tender rear was knocked against the sharp brickwork. He grinned as he withdrew, nonchalantly unrolling the used condom and throwing it to the ground.

Maggie pulled up her underwear, avoiding his eye. When he had rebuttoned his fly, he took a roll of money from the back pocket of his jeans and peeled off a ten pound note. Maggie took it, her eyes downcast. She had no choice – she hadn't brought her bag and she would need some cash for a taxi.

'Thanks darlin',' the man said, 'that wasn't bad.'

Maggie kept her eyes fixed on his legs as he turned and walked away, whistling through his teeth. As soon as he had gone, she ran her fingers through her hair and smoothed her dress. Her lower lip trembled as she fought to keep from crying with reaction. Her tights were torn beyond repair, so she quickly took them off and guiltily added to the litter in the alley. All she could think of was getting out of the alley before some smart aleck decided she might want another 'customer'.

At the entrance to the alley she glanced cautiously left and right before tottering unsteadily on her high-heels along the pavement. She could see a phone box further down the street. Hopefully there would be a directory inside so she could find a number for a taxi firm. Her heart sank as she realised she had no change.

A car slowed down as it approached her and she went cold. A kerb crawler was all she needed! Gathering all her courage, Maggie stopped walking and turned, ready to give the driver a piece of her mind. As she turned, the nearside rear door opened, as if the driver expected her to get in. She nearly fainted with relief as she bent down and saw Alexander smiling at her.

'You! You left me! How could you!'

He laughed. She couldn't believe it, he actually laughed!

'Get in Maggie, let's go home.'

She settled into the black leather seats and allowed herself to be drawn into his arms. Antony changed gear and they sped away from the café and towards the Black Orchid Club.

'Did you really think we'd abandoned you?' Alexander murmured, kissing her hair.

'Yes I did! It was horrible.'

'Were you scared?'

'Yes, I was scared. Satisfied?'

He chuckled and hugged her close.

'Ah, my Maggie, you're getting to know me so well! How could I not love you?'

Maggie closed her eyes and breathed in the familiar, warm smell of him which mingled with the richness of the leather. Less than an hour ago she had hated him with a strength that had shocked her. Yet there was no doubt in her mind now that she loved him. No matter what he asked her to do, no matter how much her mind was repulsed, her traitorous body would respond. Would do anything for him.

18

Maggie awoke to find sunlight streaming through the window. She stretched luxuriously, watching the way the sunbeams cast dappled patterns across her skin as it fought its way through the lace half curtain.

On the bedside table there was a tray laid with soft rolls and honey and a covered glass of fresh orange juice. Maggie drank the juice and spread one of the rolls with sweet, sticky honey.

She felt lazy, her limbs heavy with sleep, so she put the plate aside and slipped back down under the covers, closing her eyes. There was no clock in the bedroom, but then, it didn't matter what time it was. Today, Alexander had told her last night, she was to relax and gather her strength for the night to come.

Maggie chose to turn her mind away from what the night had in store. Alex had explained everything while he bathed her when they arrived back from the café. She had lain back in the oily, scented water and allowed the regular strokes of the soapy sponge to soothe her. Alexander's voice had been soft, almost hypnotic.

'You'll be on a raised stage, softly lit. There'll be a fur-covered platform, like a bed. The audience will be in darkness, you won't be able to see anyone. But *you* will be seen. Hidden cameras will film your every shiver and transfer the image onto two large projector screens. There'll be three men. Antony, Bruno and myself. You'll accept all three of us into your body, all at the same time—'

Maggie squeezed her eyes tightly shut and burrowed deeper into the pillow. She wasn't sure whether the tense, cold feeling she had in her stomach was due to fear or excitement. Alexander had told her to rest, so she concentrated on relaxing each limb in turn until she began to drift back into sleep.

Some time later she was woken by Antony's hand on her shoulder.

'Time for your work-out,' he told her and, ignoring her sleepy scowl, he pulled back the bed covers.

'Hey! I'm still tired!'

'Have a cold shower, then. I'll squeeze some more juice for you while you dress.'

Maggie hauled herself reluctantly out of the bed and headed for the *en suite* bathroom. Her eyes were still half closed as she fumbled for the shower taps and began to run the water. As she stepped under the lukewarm spray, she realised that she had followed Antony's instructions without question.

It confused her, this gradual slipping away of her own will and sense of purpose. She had always been a fiercely independent woman, determined to make her own way in life and absolutely against any man telling her what to do. Yet here she was, caught in Alexander's thrall, willing to dance to whatever tune he, or Antony, cared to play.

She stepped out from under the shower and towelled herself vigorously. What was the point of endless self-analysis? The truth was that she would welcome the humiliation to come, even while she dreaded it.

In the gym she worked with a single mindedness which precluded all thought. Her workaday grey cotton leotard stuck damply to her back and breasts as she pumped up and down, working her stomach muscles until they began to groan. On each machine, she pushed herself to the limit, reaching out for that plateau of pain which always precluded the rush of adrenalin, the exercise 'high' for which she strove.

Under the shower again, a hot one this time, Maggie was aware of every muscle and sinew. Her skin tingled under the sharp needles of spray, each inch of her aching pleasurably.

Alexander was waiting for her in the massage room. He smiled enigmatically at her and smoothed a pristine white towel on the couch. Maggie shed her robe unselfconsciously and spread herself, face down, on the bed. She sighed at the first touch of his fingers against her heated skin.

As always, Alexander's clever hands knew just the right amount of pressure to apply. Slick with oil, they smoothed and soothed the overworked muscles in her neck, shoulders and back until they relaxed and stopped aching. Maggie had fallen into a comfortable half-sleep when he began to work his way down her arms, to her hands. Each finger joint was manipulated in turn, the backs of her hands stroked and caressed so that the skin buzzed after he had left it.

Down the backs of her legs he went, kneading and squeezing, to her feet where he massaged the soles by thumb with firm, circular strokes. Even her toes were tingling when he had finished. Maggie made to roll over, onto her back, but Alexander stopped her by placing the flat of his hand against the small of her back.

Maggie turned her head and watched him drowsily as he went over to the locked cabinet in the corner and took out a key. She had never seen inside the cabinet before. When the double doors swung back, her eyes widened in shock. It was full to capacity with row upon row of bottles and jars, but it was the top row that kept Maggie's eyes rivetted.

Dozens of dildoes, neatly placed in size order, were ranged across the top shelf. From a tiny, finger-thin instrument on the left through every shape, colour and texture imaginable to the longest, thickest vibrator Maggie had ever seen on the far right.

Alexander glanced over his shoulder at her and smiled wickedly, his hand strayed towards the monstrosity on which her eyes were fixed. Turning his attention to the contents of the cupboard, he ran his hand along to the left, as if deliberating. Finally, he selected a slim, plain white object, about five inches long with a narrow, rubber collar around its base. Picking up a tube of lubricating cream, he relocked the cupboard and returned to the couch.

Maggie's breath hurt in her chest. The lovely, soporific mood of relaxation the massage had induced in her had all but disappeared, chased away by a churning apprehension. Now her mouth felt dry, her throat parched. Yet she did not move, merely lying, acquiescent, meekly waiting for whatever humiliation he chose to impose upon her.

He didn't speak to her at all, merely easing a soft, towelling covered cushion under her stomach, so that her bottom was raised up slightly. Gently, he parted her thighs so that the pink, tight rose of her anus was presented to him. Maggie squeezed her eyes tightly closed, anticipating the violation of this, her most private of places.

So when his newly oiled palms travelled again up the length of her spine, Maggie sagged with relief. This time he concentrated on the small of her back, the effect of his fingers penetrating deeply into the muscles, relieving all her aches and pains. She sighed, stretching from her toes, up through her calves to her thighs.

Curiously, the angle at which Alexander had tilted her pelvis made the sensual impact of the massage more intense. She could feel the effects deep in her stomach, as if the movement he was creating on the surface of her skin were travelling in little ripples right through her body.

She realised, suddenly, that she was aroused. Merely by the touch of his fingers on her lower back, she had grown wet, her sex-lips swelling and parting in delicious anticipation. He must have been able to see her shorn labia protruding between her buttocks, glistening now with the evidence of her desire.

She moaned softly as he turned his attention to her raised, upturned buttocks, kneading and shaping them, spreading her cheeks further apart before pressing them together again, then repeating the process. Shamelessly, she hollowed her back and thrust her bottom higher, urging him silently to delve into her aching cleft.

The first touch of his fingers against her tender inner skin sent little shockwaves zipping down the insides of her thighs and curling round her belly. His breath was warm as he kissed the tender place behind her ear and trailed his cool lips round to the nape of her neck. She shivered as he found the sensitive spot at the base of her skull at the same time as his seeking fingers reached the hardening bud beneath its sheltering hood.

Maggie's buttocks writhed with a will of their own as he stroked the eager nub with the tip of one finger. His touch was featherlight, unbearably so, and she tried to grind herself down on him to bring about her release. He laughed softly in her ear and maintained that frustrating, ticklish pressure until she was panting softly, on the edge of orgasm.

She groaned, almost crying as he moved his attention upwards, past the slippery gateway of her womanhood, smearing her warm honey up along the crease between her buttocks. He circled the tip of his finger around her reluctant sphincter, working in her feminine juices so that she felt hot and slick with moisture.

Trying unsuccessfully to obtain release by rubbing herself against the towelling, Maggie welcomed the intrusion of his finger as he slowly slipped it inside her anus. The friction he caused as he worked it in could be felt in the deeper recesses of her vagina and Maggie found herself opening up wider, inviting him deeper into her body.

She could have wept when he suddenly withdrew, leaving her feeling curiously empty. There was a sudden, cold sensation between her buttocks and she realised he had applied a generous amount of lubricating cream to her crease. He rubbed it carefully into her skin, working it into her tight little hole, stuffing her with it. She gasped as she felt the hard, plastic tip of the dildo push against her forbidden orifice, crying out as it slipped inside her.

Alexander ignored her shocked exclamation, working it in deeper and deeper until she felt the rubber collar at its base against her heated skin. Maggie felt stretched. She bit her lip as Alexander helped her into a sitting position and the object moved inside her.

'Supposing it goes right in?' she asked in sudden panic.

'It can't,' he assured her calmly, 'don't worry. Besides, tonight it will be removed and replaced by the real thing. Would you like to see how pretty you look?'

He brought her a mirror and made her spread her legs so that her swollen, unsatisfied vulva came into view. The collar of the dildo was clearly visible between her bottom cheeks. Maggie was shocked to realise that he was right, though 'pretty' was not the word she would have used. 'Lewd' was probably more accurate.

She had a sudden, urgent desire to relieve the burning ache which had been building between her legs. She turned her eyes to him, pleadingly. He raised his eyebrows at her.

'Please . . .?' she whispered.

He smiled.

'Yes, Maggie, you may come now.'

She found her clitoris with her middle finger and pressed it firmly. Alexander held her as she rubbed it back and forth and, within seconds, she climaxed. She threw back her head and cried out as she was overcome and Alexander kissed her hair. Afterwards, he helped her dress, handling her with infinite tenderness.

A few minutes later she arrived in the apartment to find Antony about to serve lunch. He glanced approvingly at the tight jeans which moulded her buttocks and the soft curve of her pubis.

'Comfortable?' he asked as she sat down and she blushed.

Of course, he would know what had happened. Alexander told him everything. The dildo lodged in her anus was a constant reminder of the evening to come as she ate fresh tagliatelle and creamy sauce, washing it down with mineral water.

'No wine for you,' Antony told her sympathetically as he had poured a glass for himself. 'Alex wants all your faculties intact tonight. Wine would only blunt your perceptions.'

Maggie nodded dutifully, hiding a shiver. Perceptions of what? Pain? Degradation? Or merely the demonstration of the absolute power these two charismatic men now held over her?

The costume she was to wear for the night's performance was sheer kitsch, surely chosen specifically to heighten her sense of having been brought low. Maggie fingered the miniscule black leather brassiere gingerly. It was lined with the softest fur and was designed to emphasise her assets rather than cover them. Her soft, brown-tipped breasts were gathered up by it, spilling over the top in wanton abandonment.

It seemed she was to wear nothing else but a pair of thigh-high, black leather boots with impossibly high heels. As she pulled them on she noted the way the soft, supple hide caressed her shapely calves and moulded the slender length of her thighs. Her naked, shaven sex looked shockingly pink against the stark black of the leather which reached almost to the join of hip and thigh.

Turning around, Maggie saw that the deep cuffs at the top of the boots were cut to a gentle curve so that they emphasised the shape of the round, white globes of her bottom, showing it off to perfection. If she stood with her feet slightly apart, she could see the pink rim of the dildo embedded in her anus.

'Absolutely exquisite.'

She jumped as Antony's voice came from the doorway. She hadn't heard him come into the bedroom and she faced him now, her eyes widening in a mute plea.

'Hey! Come here.'

He hugged her to him, murmuring endearments against her hair. Then he gently turned her round to face the mirror again. Like her, he was dressed in leather. His black trousers clung lovingly to his long, tightly muscled thighs and emphasised the fullness at his crotch. The white silk shirt skimmed the breadth of his shoulders and glowed against his tanned skin.

Reaching round from behind her, he gathered up her breasts in their inadequate restraint and presented them to her mirror image. As she watched, her nipples swelled and he stroked his thumbs against the hard little buttons, making her shiver.

Stroking one hand down, over her softly quivering belly, he caressed her hair-free mound. Maggie leaned against him as he ran his fingers into the groove between her labia, teasing out her inner lips so that they protruded slightly between her legs. With his other hand, he caressed the crease of her bottom, twisting the collar of the dildo so that it moved inside her, sending pleasurable waves through to her erotic core.

Their eyes met in the mirror and he smiled at her. Maggie

returned the smile, tentatively, pressing her cheek against his. Antony stroked her long, dark hair away from her neck.

'I think . . . yes, that's better.'

He twisted her hair into a loose chignon and secured it at her nape with the grips she kept on a jar on the dresser. Her long, soft-skinned neck looked fragile against the heavy mass of her hair, drawing the eye down to her out-thrust breasts.

'Where . . . where will you be?' she whispered.

'On the dais, with you,' he replied, surprised.

'I know. I mean . . . which . . . you know?'

He smiled as he saw that a hot blush had risen on her cheeks, staining them pink.

'Which delectable orifice is mine for tonight?' he laughed gently as she blushed even harder. 'I think . . . yes. I think I shall have this.'

He slowly hooked two fingers into her warm, moist vagina and pressed her against him. When he withdrew, she turned in his arms and met his lips with hers. She clung to him as they kissed, loving him, until at last he put her away from him, gently.

'It's time,' he whispered.

In the auditorium the crowd had been worked into a frenzy by the live sex-shows which had started an hour before. Couples copulated wildly in dark corners as the stage was cleared and the fur-covered dais was raised.

Maggie watched impassively from the back, unnoticed in the dimly lit room. Her arms and legs felt icy cold, yet inside she was in a ferment of emotion. Her eyes flickered nervously at the two giant projection screens which had been placed either side of the stage. Her every move, every expression would be monitored, nothing would escape the attention of the crowd. Appearing in the Exhibition Hall was bad enough, but to perform here, within touching distance of all these people . . .

She shivered and Antony's arm came around her shoulder. She was glad he was with her, would be one of the men who would take her so publicly. The atmosphere was heavy, clogged with the combined scents of sex and perfume. Maggie felt dizzy as a sudden hush descended and the stage was lit. Weird, tuneless music drifted into the auditorium, New Age mood sounds curling round everyone's senses.

As she began to walk, slowly, towards the stage, Antony beside her, Maggie could smell incense, she felt the hot gaze of dozens of unseen eyes, devouring her. Looking up, she could see Alexander, sitting on the fur-covered dais, waiting for her. His blond hair shone under the spotlight, a nebula of light giving him a halo.

Suddenly, she was no longer afraid. Everyone else faded away, there was just her, and Alexander, and she knew she would do everything he asked of her, so strong was her need of him. He smiled as she reached the stage and offered her his hand. She climbed up and Antony walked past her, to the back of the dais where, she saw now, Bruno waited, his face in shadow.

She stood before Alexander and waited, patiently, for his instructions. He nodded approvingly at her and rewarded her with a long, lingering kiss. With her back to the audience, he placed his hand at the small of her back and applied enough pressure for her to guess that he wanted her to bend forward, at the waist.

The audience gasped as they saw the dildo implanted in her. Alexander stroked the soft, downy skin at the small of her back, coaxing her legs wider apart with one hand so that her shorn vulva was exposed.

Maggie felt her cheeks burn with shame as the loud exclamations of delight and admiration reached her ears and she twisted her face into her shoulder. Alexander's hand came round her cheek and lifted her face so that it could be seen by the cameras. Out of the corner of her eye, Maggie could see the projection screens. One showed her from the front, the dangling breasts spilling out of their inadequate restraint, the tremulous mouth and wide, shamed eyes. The other showed her out-thrust buttocks and the dildo lodged obscenely between them.

Thus she was able to watch as Alexander reached down and grapsed the collar of the dildo and slowly withdrew it. Her body expelled it almost regretfully and Maggie closed her eyes against the image of her wanton arsehole which relaxed forlornly in loving close up.

'Lean across the bed.'

She jumped at Alexander's curt request, teetering uncertainly on her high-heels as she hurried to obey him. Her breath caught painfully in her chest as Bruno passed a long, thin whip to Alex. She began to tremble as Antony pushed cushions beneath her stomach, raising her bottom higher.

'Ssh,' he whispered in her ear, 'it's too soon to cry.'

The first lash of the leather whip against her tender skin took her breath away. The sting seemed to spread, like liquid fire across the surface of her skin, snaking down her legs, making them shake uncontrollably. Alexander seemed to bide his time, waiting until she had felt the full impact of the lash before raising it again.

This time she moaned, to the delight of the audience who seemed to utter a collective sigh. Then there was silence save for the whistle of the lash and the sharp 'crack' as it landed on Maggie's skin. She began to cry, softly at first, huge tears rolling off her cheeks onto the fur so that soon it was sodden.

He never hit the same place twice so that within a few minutes her entire bottom seemed to have caught fire.

'Please!' she cried out. 'No more . . . I can't . . . Oh!'

The lash cut across her protest, leaving her gasping for

breath. But that, miraculously, was the last blow. She could not control her sobs as Alexander hauled her onto her knees on the platform. He watched her cry for a few minutes, his expression unreadable. Maggie tried to plead with him through her tears, but she was incoherent.

'What, Maggie? What is it you want?'

'I want . . . I . . . please! Don't hurt me any more!'

He smiled then, almost kindly at her. Then he bent forward so that his lips were against her ear and said, so that only she could hear, 'There is no feeling at all without pain. *Loving* hurts, Maggie. And now I'm going to love you – just as you have always wanted me to.'

He wiped her face with his fingers, licking the tears from her cheeks. Maggie closed her eyes as he covered her face in kisses, ran his hands over her breasts and parted her shaking thighs. She knew before he touched her that she was wet. How could she not be aroused by the whip when it was Alexander who wielded it?

She was compliant as he lay her, face down on the dais. The strange music ebbed and flowed, weaving its spell on her senses. She could feel the presence of the crowd, knew the heat around her came from the crush of their bodies as much as from the lights, yet they had become irrelevant to her.

It was Antony now who moved forward and began to kiss her, languidly at first, then with more passion as desire caught fire between them. Oblivious to everything else, they rolled together on the bed, his hands roaming over her tender flesh. At some time while she was being whipped, he had undressed. He was erect, his penis pressing into her stomach as he lay on his back and manoeuvred her so that she was astride him.

Maggie longed to impale herself on him, but he held her off, as if awaiting a signal. She felt fingers at her chin and looked up to find Bruno waiting patiently for her attention, his erect cock inches away from her face. The foreskin was pulled back, the purplish glans already shining. Sitting astride Antony, Maggie eagerly reached for Bruno's stem and caressed it, her other hand cupping his heavy, hairy balls.

She shuddered as Alexander came up behind her and began to rub a cooling fluid into her burning buttocks, working it into the exposed crease. Then came the thicker, heavier cream designed to facilitate his entry into her body.

The three men seemed to move as if in one accord once Alexander had greased her bottom. Maggie felt as if she were somewhere above them, looking down, as if it were someone else that this was about to happen to. And yet every square inch of her sensitised skin was tingling with awareness, her female moisture welling in joyous anticipation.

Antony supported her by putting two hands at her waist as she leaned forward and opened her mouth ready for Bruno. Alexander's hands held her hips steady as his slender shaft probed the entrance to her nether mouth. It was Antony who entered her first, his swollen tool sliding into her hot, wet vagina as if coming home. Maggie groaned softly and closed her lips against the bulbous head of Bruno's penis.

It was then that Alexander inched his way into her bottom, his cock sliding against Antony's through the thin membrane separating the two passages. Maggie felt Antony's ecstatic shudder as he lay underneath her and realised he was close to the edge of his climax. She was barely aware of the gasp of the crowd. She felt as if she would burst as all three men were still, content to feel themselves inside her. Then, as one, they all began to move.

The strange 'whale-song' music soared in her ears as she found herself penetrated in every available orifice. Her jaw ached as Bruno used her mouth, his hands either side of her head. Antony seemed to be lifting her hips up and down on his rigid shaft, while Alexander matched his rhythm in her back passage. Every muscle screamed with awareness, her nerve endings raw.

Antony came first, with a growl, his hot sperm shooting into her vagina, quickly followed by Bruno's swift climax into her mouth. She gulped as it hit the back of her throat, just as Alexander pumped his seed into her behind.

Maggie writhed, her own orgasm pulsing through her with an intensity which took her by surprise. And after each man had withdrawn, she rolled shamelessly onto her back and, throwing her legs open wide, she rubbed herself furiously, oblivious to the fluids which streamed from her, mixing with her own secretions.

Over and over the waves came, unstoppable, making her thrash her head from side to side like a woman possessed. From far away she heard the applause, felt Alexander's lips against her sex, Antony's at her mouth, then – nothing.

She was warm, wrapped in an all-enveloping cotton nightie in the middle of the bed. Maggie opened her eyes and frowned, trying to remember.

'She's coming round,' Antony whispered, and suddenly it all came flooding back.

'Wh-what happened?' she croaked as Alexander's arms came around her and Antony smoothed the hair tenderly off her forehead.

'Shh, it's all right. You blacked out for a few seconds and you've been drowsy ever since. Don't you remember coming to in the Jacuzzi with us?'

Vague recollections of warm, soothing water, strong hands soaping her, drying her, carrying her to the lift. Yes, she remembered. She turned her anxious eyes on Alexander and was relieved to see he was smiling at her.

'I'll go and make a warm drink for us all,' Antony announced.

Alexander pulled her further into the warm, safe circle of his arms.

'Darling Maggie – you were magnificient!'

Maggie's heart swelled with pride that he was pleased with her.

They all sat up in bed, drinking milky coffee. Every now and then, Alexander would stroke Maggie's cheek, or reach behind her to touch Antony. Maggie had never felt so happy, so loved, in her life.

'You know, Antony,' Alexander broke the companiable silence, 'I think that Maggie here might be just the person we need to run the new venture.'

'Hmm, you could be right.'

'What new venture?' Maggie asked.

'Antony is thinking of buying up a hotel – somewhere where women can go to stay for an entire weekend, out of town. Maybe we could extend it to include couples. What do you think?'

Maggie's imagination was caught, but she still regarded Alexander with dismay.

'But I don't want to live out of town – I want to stay here, with you and Antony! I want to be part of . . . of this!' she concluded inadequately.

'And you will be.' Alexander smoothed. 'If we can find somewhere close enough, so that the three of us could easily travel between the two.'

'Think of it, Maggie,' Antony continued in the same seductive tone, 'the three of us – equal partners.'

Maggie caught his eye at this last suggestion and he smiled, inviting her to share the unspoken joke that they would ever be a match for Alexander. Alex chuckled softly, indulging them.

'What do you think, Maggie?' Antony pressed.

In her mind's eye, Maggie saw the Black Orchid Club duplicated, only bigger, better, with more scope for experimentation. What more did she have to lose?

'All right,' she agreed.

'This calls for better than coffee – I'll go and break open a bottle of champagne.'

Alexander disappeared, returning with the three overflowing glasses on a tray. He lounged on top of the duvet, unashamedly naked, his body across their legs as he raised his glass.

'To the Black Orchid Hotel,' Antony proposed.

They all sipped the golden liquid and Maggie entwined her free hand with Antony's under the covers. Alexander smiled at her and raised his glass again.

'To the three of us,' he said, his voice thick with some unnamed emotion.

Antony glanced at Maggie and they both looked at Alex and nodded.

'To us three,' they chorused obediently.

Alexander unexpectedly threw back his golden head and laughed.

Visit the Black Lace website at
www.black-lace-books.com

FIND OUT THE LATEST INFORMATION AND TAKE ADVANTAGE OF OUR FANTASTIC FREE BOOK OFFER! ALSO VISIT THE SITE FOR . . .

- All Black Lace titles currently available and how to order online
- Great new offers
- Writers' guidelines
- Author interviews
- An erotica newsletter
- Features
- Cool links

BLACK LACE – THE LEADING IMPRINT OF WOMEN'S SEXY FICTION

TAKING YOUR EROTIC READING PLEASURE TO NEW HORIZONS

LOOK OUT FOR THE BLACK LACE 15TH ANNIVERSARY SPECIAL EDITIONS. COLLECT ALL 10 TITLES IN THE SERIES!

All books priced £7.99 in the UK. Please note publication dates apply to the UK only. For other territories, please contact your retailer.

Published in March 2008

CASSANDRA'S CONFLICT
Fredrica Allen
ISBN 978 0 352 34186 0

A house in Hampstead. Present-day. Behind a façade of cultured respectability lies a world of decadent indulgence and dark eroticism. Cassandra's sheltered life is transformed when she gets employed as governess to the Baron's children. He draws her into games where lust can feed on the erotic charge of submission. Games where only he knows the rules and where unusual pleasures can flourish.

Published in April 2008

GEMINI HEAT
Portia Da Costa
ISBN 978 0 352 34187 7

As the metropolis sizzles in the freak early summer temperatures, identical twin sisters Deana and Delia Ferraro are cooking up a heat wave of their own. Surrounded by an atmosphere of relentless humidity, Deanna and Delia find themselves rivals for the attentions of Jackson de Guile – an exotic, wealthy entrepreneur and master of power dynamics – who draws them both into a web of luxurious debauchery.

Their erotic encounters become increasingly bizarre as the twins vie for the rewards that pleasuring him brings them - tainted rewards which only serve to confuse their perceptions of the limits of sexual experience.

To be published in June 2008

FORBIDDEN FRUIT
Susie Raymond
ISBN 978 0 352 34189 1

The last thing sexy thirty-something Beth expected was to get involved with a much younger man. But when she finds him spying on her in the dressing room at work she embarks on an erotic journey with the straining youth, teaching him and teasing him as she leads him through myriad sensuous exercises at her stylish modern home. As their lascivious games become more and more intense, Beth soon begins to realise that she is the one being awakened to a new world of desire – and that hers is the mind quickly becoming consumed with lust.

To be published in July 2008

JULIET RISING
Cleo Cordell
ISBN 978 0 352 34192 1

Nothing is more important to Reynard than winning the favours of the bright and wilful Juliet, a pupil at Madame Nicol's exclusive but strict 18th century ladies' academy. Her captivating beauty tinged with a hint of cruelty soon has Reynard willing to do anything to win her approval. But Juliet's methods have little effect on Andreas, the real object of her lustful obsessions. Unable to bend him to her will, she is forced to watch him lavish his manly talents on her fellow pupils. That is, until she agrees to change her stuck-up, stubborn ways and become an eager erotic participant.

To be published in August 2008

ODALISQUE
Fleur Reynolds
ISBN 978 0 352 34193 8

Set against a backdrop of sophisticated elegance, a tale of family intrigue, forbidden passions and depraved secrets unfolds. Beautiful but scheming, successful designer Auralie plots to bring about the downfall of her virtuous cousin, Jeanine. Recently widowed, but still young and glamorous, Jeanine finds her passions being rekindled by Auralie's husband. But she is playing into Auralie's hands – vindictive hands that drag Jeanine into a world of erotic depravity. Why are the cousins locked into this sexual feud? And what is the purpose of Jeanine's mysterious Confessor, and his sordid underground sect?

To be published in September 2008

THE STALLION
Georgina Brown
ISBN 978 0 352 34199 0

The world of showjumping is as steamy as it is competitive. Ambitious young rider Penny Bennett enters into a wager with her oldest rival and friend, Ariadne, to win her thoroughbred stallion, guaranteed to bring Penny money and success. But first she must attain the sponsorship and very personal attention of showjumping's biggest impresario, Alister Beaumont.

Beaumont's riding school, however, is not all it seems. There's the weird relationship between Alister and his cigar-smoking sister. And the bizarre clothes they want Penny to wear. But in this atmosphere of unbridled kinkiness, Penny is determined not only to win the wager but to discover the truth about Beaumont's strange hobbies.

To be published in October 2008

THE DEVIL AND THE DEEP BLUE SEA
Cheryl Mildenhall
ISBN 978 0 352 34200 3

When Hillary and her girlfriends rent a country house for their summer vacation, it is a pleasant surprise to find that its secretive and kinky owner – Darius Harwood – seems to be the most desirable man in the locale. That is, before Hilary meets Haldane, the blond and beautifully proportioned Norwegian sailor who works nearby. Intrigued by the sexual allure of two very different men, Hillary can't resist exploring the possibilities on offer. But these opportunities for misbehaviour quickly lead her into a tricky situation for which a difficult decision has to be made.

To be published in November 2008

THE NINETY DAYS OF GENEVIEVE
Lucinda Carrington
ISBN 978 0 352 34201 0

A ninety-day sex contract wasn't exactly what Genevieve Loften had in mind when she began business negotiations with the arrogant and attractive James Sinclair. As a career move she wanted to go along with it; the pay-off was potentially huge.

However, she didn't imagine that he would make her the star performer in a series of increasingly kinky and exotic fantasies. Thrown into a world of sexual misadventure, Genevieve learns how to balance her high-pressure career with the twilight world of fetishism and debauchery.

To be published in December 2008

THE GIFT OF SHAME
Sarah Hope-Walker
ISBN 978 0 352 34202 7

Sad, sultry Helen flies between London, Paris and the Caribbean chasing whatever physical pleasures she can get to tear her mind from a deep, deep loss. Her glamorous life-style and charged sensual escapades belie a widow's grief. When she meets handsome, rich Jeffrey she is shocked and yet intrigued by his masterful, domineering behaviour. Soon, Helen is forced to confront the forbidden desires hiding within herself – and forced to undergo a startling metamorphosis from a meek and modest lady into a bristling, voracious wanton.

ALSO LOOK OUT FOR

THE NEW BLACK LACE BOOK OF WOMEN'S SEXUAL FANTASIES
Edited and compiled by Mitzi Szereto
ISBN 978 0 352 34172 3

The second anthology of detailed sexual fantasies contributed by women from all over the world. The book is a result of a year's research by an expert on erotic writing and gives a fascinating insight into the rich diversity of the female sexual imagination.

Black Lace Booklist

Information is correct at time of printing. To avoid disappointment, check
availability before ordering. Go to www.black-lace-books.com.
All books are priced £7.99 unless another price is given.

BLACK LACE BOOKS WITH A CONTEMPORARY SETTING

❑ THE ANGELS' SHARE Maya Hess	ISBN 978 0 352 34043 6	
❑ ASKING FOR TROUBLE Kristina Lloyd	ISBN 978 0 352 33362 9	
❑ BLACK LIPSTICK KISSES Monica Belle	ISBN 978 0 352 33885 3	£6.99
❑ THE BLUE GUIDE Carrie Williams	ISBN 978 0 352 34132 7	
❑ THE BOSS Monica Belle	ISBN 978 0 352 34088 7	
❑ BOUND IN BLUE Monica Belle	ISBN 978 0 352 34012 2	
❑ CAMPAIGN HEAT Gabrielle Marcola	ISBN 978 0 352 33941 6	
❑ CAT SCRATCH FEVER Sophie Mouette	ISBN 978 0 352 34021 4	
❑ CIRCUS EXCITE Nikki Magennis	ISBN 978 0 352 34033 7	
❑ CLUB CRÈME Primula Bond	ISBN 978 0 352 33907 2	£6.99
❑ CONFESSIONAL Judith Roycroft	ISBN 978 0 352 33421 3	
❑ CONTINUUM Portia Da Costa	ISBN 978 0 352 33120 5	
❑ DANGEROUS CONSEQUENCES Pamela Rochford	ISBN 978 0 352 33185 4	
❑ DARK DESIGNS Madelynne Ellis	ISBN 978 0 352 34075 7	
❑ THE DEVIL INSIDE Portia Da Costa	ISBN 978 0 352 32993 6	
❑ EQUAL OPPORTUNITIES Mathilde Madden	ISBN 978 0 352 34070 2	
❑ FIRE AND ICE Laura Hamilton	ISBN 978 0 352 33486 2	
❑ GONE WILD Maria Eppie	ISBN 978 0 352 33670 5	
❑ HOTBED Portia Da Costa	ISBN 978 0 352 33614 9	
❑ IN PURSUIT OF ANNA Natasha Rostova	ISBN 978 0 352 34060 3	
❑ IN THE FLESH Emma Holly	ISBN 978 0 352 34117 4	
❑ LEARNING TO LOVE IT Alison Tyler	ISBN 978 0 352 33535 7	
❑ MAD ABOUT THE BOY Mathilde Madden	ISBN 978 0 352 34001 6	
❑ MAKE YOU A MAN Anna Clare	ISBN 978 0 352 34006 1	
❑ MAN HUNT Cathleen Ross	ISBN 978 0 352 33583 8	
❑ THE MASTER OF SHILDEN Lucinda Carrington	ISBN 978 0 352 33140 3	
❑ MIXED DOUBLES Zoe le Verdier	ISBN 978 0 352 33312 4	£6.99
❑ MIXED SIGNALS Anna Clare	ISBN 978 0 352 33889 1	£6.99

❑ MS BEHAVIOUR Mini Lee   ISBN 978 0 352 33962 1

❑ PACKING HEAT Karina Moore   ISBN 978 0 352 33356 8   £6.99

❑ PAGAN HEAT Monica Belle   ISBN 978 0 352 33974 4

❑ PEEP SHOW Mathilde Madden   ISBN 978 0 352 33924 9

❑ THE POWER GAME Carrera Devonshire   ISBN 978 0 352 33990 4

❑ THE PRIVATE UNDOING OF A PUBLIC SERVANT   ISBN 978 0 352 34066 5
   Leonie Martel

❑ RUDE AWAKENING Pamela Kyle   ISBN 978 0 352 33036 9

❑ SAUCE FOR THE GOOSE Mary Rose Maxwell   ISBN 978 0 352 33492 3

❑ SPLIT Kristina Lloyd   ISBN 978 0 352 34154 9

❑ STELLA DOES HOLLYWOOD Stella Black   ISBN 978 0 352 33588 3

❑ THE STRANGER Portia Da Costa   ISBN 978 0 352 33211 0

❑ SUITE SEVENTEEN Portia Da Costa   ISBN 978 0 352 34109 9

❑ TONGUE IN CHEEK Tabitha Flyte   ISBN 978 0 352 33484 8

❑ THE TOP OF HER GAME Emma Holly   ISBN 978 0 352 34116 7

❑ UNNATURAL SELECTION Alaine Hood   ISBN 978 0 352 33963 8

❑ VELVET GLOVE Emma Holly   ISBN 978 0 352 34115 0

❑ VILLAGE OF SECRETS Mercedes Kelly   ISBN 978 0 352 33344 5

❑ WILD BY NATURE Monica Belle   ISBN 978 0 352 33915 7   £6.99

❑ WILD CARD Madeline Moore   ISBN 978 0 352 34038 2

❑ WING OF MADNESS Mae Nixon   ISBN 978 0 352 34099 3

BLACK LACE BOOKS WITH AN HISTORICAL SETTING

❑ THE BARBARIAN GEISHA Charlotte Royal   ISBN 978 0 352 33267 7

❑ BARBARIAN PRIZE Deanna Ashford   ISBN 978 0 352 34017 7

❑ THE CAPTIVATION Natasha Rostova   ISBN 978 0 352 33234 9

❑ DARKER THAN LOVE Kristina Lloyd   ISBN 978 0 352 33279 0

❑ WILD KINGDOM Deanna Ashford   ISBN 978 0 352 33549 4

❑ DIVINE TORMENT Janine Ashbless   ISBN 978 0 352 33719 1

❑ FRENCH MANNERS Olivia Christie   ISBN 978 0 352 33214 1

❑ LORD WRAXALL'S FANCY Anna Lieff Saxby   ISBN 978 0 352 33080 2

❑ NICOLE'S REVENGE Lisette Allen   ISBN 978 0 352 32984 4

❑ THE SENSES BEJEWELLED Cleo Cordell   ISBN 978 0 352 32904 2   £6.99

❑ THE SOCIETY OF SIN Sian Lacey Taylder   ISBN 978 0 352 34080 1

❑ TEMPLAR PRIZE Deanna Ashford   ISBN 978 0 352 34137 2

❑ UNDRESSING THE DEVIL Angel Strand   ISBN 978 0 352 33938 6

BLACK LACE BOOKS WITH A PARANORMAL THEME

❑ BRIGHT FIRE Maya Hess   ISBN 978 0 352 34104 4
❑ BURNING BRIGHT Janine Ashbless   ISBN 978 0 352 34085 6
❑ CRUEL ENCHANTMENT Janine Ashbless   ISBN 978 0 352 33483 1
❑ FLOOD Anna Clare   ISBN 978 0 352 34094 8
❑ GOTHIC BLUE Portia Da Costa   ISBN 978 0 352 33075 8
❑ THE PRIDE Edie Bingham   ISBN 978 0 352 33997 3
❑ THE SILVER COLLAR Mathilde Madden   ISBN 978 0 352 34141 9
❑ THE TEN VISIONS Olivia Knight   ISBN 978 0 352 34119 8

BLACK LACE ANTHOLOGIES

❑ BLACK LACE QUICKIES 1 Various   ISBN 978 0 352 34126 6   £2.99
❑ BLACK LACE QUICKIES 2 Various   ISBN 978 0 352 34127 3   £2.99
❑ BLACK LACE QUICKIES 3 Various   ISBN 978 0 352 34128 0   £2.99
❑ BLACK LACE QUICKIES 4 Various   ISBN 978 0 352 34129 7   £2.99
❑ BLACK LACE QUICKIES 5 Various   ISBN 978 0 352 34130 3   £2.99
❑ BLACK LACE QUICKIES 6 Various   ISBN 978 0 352 34133 4   £2.99
❑ BLACK LACE QUICKIES 7 Various   ISBN 978 0 352 34146 4   £2.99
❑ BLACK LACE QUICKIES 8 Various   ISBN 978 0 352 34147 1   £2.99
❑ BLACK LACE QUICKIES 9 Various   ISBN 978 0 352 34155 6   £2.99
❑ MORE WICKED WORDS Various   ISBN 978 0 352 33487 9   £6.99
❑ WICKED WORDS 3 Various   ISBN 978 0 352 33522 7   £6.99
❑ WICKED WORDS 4 Various   ISBN 978 0 352 33603 3   £6.99
❑ WICKED WORDS 5 Various   ISBN 978 0 352 33642 2   £6.99
❑ WICKED WORDS 6 Various   ISBN 978 0 352 33690 3   £6.99
❑ WICKED WORDS 7 Various   ISBN 978 0 352 33743 6   £6.99
❑ WICKED WORDS 8 Various   ISBN 978 0 352 33787 0   £6.99
❑ WICKED WORDS 9 Various   ISBN 978 0 352 33860 0
❑ WICKED WORDS 10 Various   ISBN 978 0 352 33893 8
❑ THE BEST OF BLACK LACE 2 Various   ISBN 978 0 352 33718 4
❑ WICKED WORDS: SEX IN THE OFFICE Various   ISBN 978 0 352 33944 7
❑ WICKED WORDS: SEX AT THE SPORTS CLUB Various   ISBN 978 0 352 33991 1
❑ WICKED WORDS: SEX ON HOLIDAY Various   ISBN 978 0 352 33961 4
❑ WICKED WORDS: SEX IN UNIFORM Various   ISBN 978 0 352 34002 3
❑ WICKED WORDS: SEX IN THE KITCHEN Various   ISBN 978 0 352 34018 4
❑ WICKED WORDS: SEX ON THE MOVE Various   ISBN 978 0 352 34034 4
❑ WICKED WORDS: SEX AND MUSIC Various   ISBN 978 0 352 34061 0

❑ WICKED WORDS: SEX AND SHOPPING Various   ISBN 978 0 352 34076 4
❑ SEX IN PUBLIC Various   ISBN 978 0 352 34089 4
❑ SEX WITH STRANGERS Various   ISBN 978 0 352 34105 1
❑ LOVE ON THE DARK SIDE Various   ISBN 978 0 352 34132 7
❑ LUST BITES Various   ISBN 978 0 352 34153 2

BLACK LACE NON-FICTION

❑ THE BLACK LACE BOOK OF WOMEN'S SEXUAL FANTASIES ISBN 978 0 352 33793 1   £6.99

Edited by Kerri Sharp

To find out the latest information about Black Lace titles, check out the website: www.black-lace-books.com or send for a booklist with complete synopses by writing to:

Black Lace Booklist, Virgin Books Ltd
Thames Wharf Studios
Rainville Road
London W6 9HA

Please include an SAE of decent size. Please note only British stamps are valid.

Our privacy policy
We will not disclose information you supply us to any other parties. We will not disclose any information which identifies you personally to any person without your express consent.

From time to time we may send out information about Black Lace books and special offers. Please tick here if you do <u>not</u> wish to receive Black Lace information. ❏

Please send me the books I have ticked above.

Name ....

Address ....

....

....

....

Post Code ....

Send to: Virgin Books Cash Sales, Thames Wharf Studios, Rainville Road, London W6 9HA.

US customers: for prices and details of how to order books for delivery by mail, call 888-330-8477.

Please enclose a cheque or postal order, made payable to Virgin Books Ltd, to the value of the books you have ordered plus postage and packing costs as follows:

UK and BFPO – £1.00 for the first book, 50p for each subsequent book.

Overseas (including Republic of Ireland) – £2.00 for the first book, £1.00 for each subsequent book.

If you would prefer to pay by VISA, ACCESS/MASTERCARD, DINERS CLUB, AMEX or SWITCH, please write your card number and expiry date here:

....

Signature ....

Please allow up to 28 days for delivery.